FIRE
IN THE
THATCH

FIRE
IN THE
THATCH

A Devon Mystery

E.C.R. Lorac

With an Introduction by
MARTIN EDWARDS

This edition published 2018 by
The British Library
96 Euston Road
London NW1 2DB

Originally published in 1946 by Collins

Cataloguing in Publication Data
A catalogue record for this publication is
available from the British Library

ISBN 978 0 7123 5260 4

Typeset by Tetragon, London
Printed and bound by CPI Group (UK) Ltd, Croydon CR0 4YY

FIRE
IN THE
THATCH

INTRODUCTION

Fire in the Thatch is an enjoyable example of E.C.R. Lorac's ability to impart a distinctive flavour to the traditional detective story. The setting is rural Devon, and Lorac's fascination with country life, and with people who "care about the land", is evident from first page to last.

Colonel St Cyres, a sympathetically portrayed landowner, is about to grant a tenancy of Little Thatch, a rather neglected property on his estate. His quarrelsome daughter-in-law June, who is staying with him because her husband is being held prisoner by the Japanese in Burma, urges him to allow her friend Tommy Gressingham to take the property. But the Colonel's daughter Anne fears that June's motives are less than honourable, and the tenancy is ultimately granted to Nicholas Vaughan, a stranger who has turned up in the area after being invalided out of the Navy. Undaunted, Gressingham moves to a house in the neighbourhood, but unlike the reclusive Vaughan, he has no interest in cultivating the land. He is an entrepreneur whose ambition is to build a country club.

The tension between the old way of life in rural England and the march of progress is sharpened by the timing of the events of the story, set as the Second World War is drawing to a close (although the book was not published until 1946). Lorac creates a vivid picture of an apprehensive society, including small social details that make the story especially interesting to a twenty-first century reader. People realise that change is in the air, but many of them fear the form that change will take.

Gressingham, however, scents the opportunities: "Farming's done well during the war, but it's not going to do so well in future... In five years' time quite a number of land-owning gentry will be glad to realise a good figure for their property." His friend Howard Brendon, a lawyer turned businessman, is more sceptical: "In five years' time the sale of land will be controlled. What you refuse to realise is that this country is going to swing to the left, and the hell of a long way, too."

We are also given an insight into the conflicting attitudes of country folk and Londoners. Some villagers resent being ordered to offer billets "which would bring bombed-out townsfolk into farms and cottages. 'We don't want them here and we can't do with them.'" But Anne St Cyres, at least, does not lack "the imagination... to realise the distresses of those who are strangers." Reading this book, and thinking of debates current at the time of writing, about immigration and the plight of homeless refugees, one is reminded that, whilst the detail of social problems keeps changing, the fundamentals of human nature—both positive and negative—are enduring.

Four chapters set the scene before we are fast-forwarded to a conversation between Commander Wilton and Chief Inspector Macdonald of Scotland Yard. Little Thatch has been gutted in a blaze, and a body has been found. It seems that the deceased is Nicholas Vaughan, and that he died as a result of an accident, but Wilton isn't satisfied. Macdonald duly takes himself down to Devon, and soon becomes convinced that there is more to the tragedy than meets the eye.

The likeable and diligent Macdonald appeared in all the books which Edith Caroline Rivett (1894–1958) published under the name E.C.R. Lorac. Macdonald made his debut in *The Murder on the*

Burrows (1931) and took a final bow in the posthumously published *Death of a Lady Killer* (1959). The Lorac novels won many admirers, including the sometimes acerbic Dorothy L. Sayers. Writing in the *Sunday Times* in 1935, Sayers heaped praise upon *The Organ Speaks*: "Mr. Lorac's story is entirely original, highly ingenious and remarkable for atmospheric writing and convincing development of character".

The next year, the renowned crime critic of the *Observer*, "Torquemada", was equally enthusiastic: "I praised the last three of Mr. Lorac's books each for a different quality, for pleasantness of style, for ingenuity, and for sound characterisation. Now I find all these qualities present in *A Pall for a Painter*. So it is safe to bet that this author will soon find himself an accepted member of that very small band which writes first-rate detective stories that are also literature." Sure enough, the following year Lorac was elected to membership of the elite Detection Club, together with the future Poet Laureate Cecil Day-Lewis (who wrote crime fiction as Nicholas Blake), Newton Gayle (a pseudonym which concealed the combined identities of Muna Lee and Maurice Guinness), and Christopher Bush.

After the Second World War, with "the Golden Age of detective fiction" effectively over, several of the genre's most distinguished practitioners, including Sayers and Anthony Berkeley, who had founded the Detection Club, ceased to write detective novels. Lorac, however, continued to write industriously. Because she produced so much, some of her books, and perhaps especially those which appeared under the pen-name Carol Carnac, were relatively routine. But she was never less than a capable craftswoman, and at her best she constructed compelling mysteries. She kept writing to the very end—at her death, a final manuscript was left incomplete. One other novel written towards the end of her life, *Two-Way Murder*, has never been published, despite the fact that it is a sound and characteristically readable piece of work. Today, her books are ripe for rediscovery, and it is a pleasure to reintroduce this under-estimated author to a new generation of readers.

MARTIN EDWARDS

www.martinedwardsbooks.com

CHAPTER ONE

I

COLONEL ST CYRES STEPPED OUT OF THE FRENCH WINDOW on to the terrace and drew in a deep breath of frosty air, conscious of the exhilaration of a glorious December morning. He always felt better out of doors. In the open air the worries and irritations of life seemed less immediate, and he felt that he lost a burden when he closed the window behind him.

The prospect before him was one to give a sense of well-being to any healthy man, and St Cyres, still in his early sixties, was vigorous enough to enjoy the keen still air and the glory of winter sunshine. Beyond the low wall of the terrace the frost-rimed meadows gleamed and sparkled, sloping down to the river a couple of hundred yards below. On the farther bank the land rose again in a series of gentle ridges, meadow land, plough land and finally wood land in the distance. Here and there a thatched roof seemed to be tucked into the comfortable folds of the rich Devon valley, and blue wood smoke coiled into the still cold air. Everything was agleam with hoar frost, scintillating in the level rays of a sun which threw shafts of intense light along the valley and made the swift-running river flash back the white beams.

Down by the river some bullocks grazed in the lush grasses which never fail in a Devon pasture. Colonel St Cyres chuckled as a couple of the lusty young beasts horned one another around the pasture—Red Devons, the famous Ruby beef cattle, snorting and blowing in their youthful vigour.

St Cyres thrust some letters into the pocket of his old tweed coat and hastened along the terrace towards the corner where a cluster of outbuildings stood against a larch coppice. In his other hand was a good crust of bread and he munched it appreciatively though with a shamefaced grin. He had done a bolt, he admitted it frankly; he had brought his breakfast to finish out of doors or in the wood-shed, and he knew just why he had done it.

"God knows why he married her, poor chap—but scent at breakfast is more than I can stomach," he said to himself.

The "poor chap" of whom the Colonel was thinking was his son, Denis, now a prisoner of war in Japanese hands. Whether the Colonel's epithet was due to Denis's plight or to the wife he had married was uncertain, but Colonel St Cyres disliked his daughter-in-law as heartily as any well-bred man allowed himself to dislike a woman. The Colonel was a countryman. He loved the country and his own ancestral acres with an unquestioning tacit devotion. He liked country clothes and country ways, the smell of dung, the rich red Devon mud, the slow slurred speech of his humble country neighbours and the inconveniences of an ancient house set miles away from trains or bus routes.

June St Cyres was a Londoner. She had been born in a flat in Mayfair, and a flat in Mayfair was her ideal of happiness. She liked fashionable clothes and shoes, French cooking, modern dance music and what she called Society. She used elaborate make-up, vivid nail varnish and Coty perfumes. When Denis had been reported as prisoner of war six months ago, Colonel St Cyres had gone up to London to see his daughter-in-law.

"Come down to us, my dear," he had said, "and bring the little chap with you. It'll be better for both of you, and we'll look after you and save you any worries and troubles we can."

Full of kindliness and sympathy, St Cyres persuaded June to give up her flat in town and to come with her small boy to live at Manor Thatch.

June had acquiesced at first. She was lonely and frightened and in debt. June St Cyres was one of those young women who can never live within their incomes, but she was shrewd enough to know that she could live at the Manor without paying anything for her upkeep. Also, she could not get a nurse for small Michael in town, or any domestic help in the flat, and she was very tired of "the damned chores" as she expressed it. At Manor Thatch there were some old servants—and Anne could help with Michael. Anne was Denis's sister, a sensible domesticated creature of thirty—though June always regarded her sister-in-law as a woman of fifty. Anne was a sober, quiet woman, who lived contentedly in the same tweed suit year after year.

June came down to the Manor, bringing five-year-old Michael and a mountain of luggage. She had been there for six months, and it was difficult to say who disliked the arrangement most—June or her father-in-law. Chivalry and a sense of duty prevented Colonel St Cyres from suggesting any other arrangement. With June, it was sheer inertia which kept her at Manor Thatch, coupled to money difficulties. She wanted to go back to London, but the rents asked for any habitation which she called "possible" appalled her. Everything was expensive, and service was unobtainable. Two or three visits to town, staying at the Dorchester, had not assisted her laudable intentions of paying her debts. Bored, grumbling and discontented, June St Cyres continued to stay at Manor Thatch. Irritated, hurt, but never complaining, her father-in-law tried to keep the peace and to put up with June's untidiness and laziness, her habit of

keeping the wireless on all day, and her total lack of consideration for anyone but herself.

2

It was Anne who uttered the warning which sent her father out
of doors before he had had his second cup of coffee.

"June is coming down to breakfast. I believe she wants to talk
to you about letting Little Thatch to those friends of hers."

Colonel St Cyres choked back his immediate exclamation of
"Good God!" and said hastily, "Er... er... later in the day will do for
that. I've got a letter from a friend of Robert Wilton's... a naval
chap, invalided out. Sounds all right... I shall be in the wood-shed
if you want me, Anne..."

The wood-shed was the Colonel's favourite refuge. He loved
wood and he loved wood fires. At the moment he had two vast
logs of ash—the split bole of an old tree—and he wanted to cut
them up in his own particular way. "Ash green or ash dry, meet
for a queen to warm her fingers by," he murmured as he rolled
the wood over to a convenient angle and considered the matter of
driving a wedge in to split it. Leisurely in all his ways, he did not
hurry. Having arranged his log and chosen his wedges, he lighted
his pipe and took his letters out of his pocket. Anne's sentence
about letting Little Thatch made Colonel St Cyres anxious to
consider the letter he had received that morning. Smoothing out
the sheet, St Cyres read:

"Sir,—I am advised to write to you by Commander Wilton,
who tells me that you have a small property to let—Little Thatch.
I have recently been invalided out of the Navy on account of damaged eyesight, and I am seeking a small holding or house with an

acre or more of good fertile land suitable for intensive cultivation. I aim at a market garden combined with an orchard and should be glad to keep a few head of stock if pasture is available. I am very fit and intend to work my own land, and I can housekeep for myself for the time being. If your property is what I am seeking, I should be willing to buy, or to take it on an assured tenancy of some years' duration so that it would be worth while putting work and capital into cultivating the land. I have the opportunity of driving over to see Little Thatch to-morrow morning at 10.30. If I do not hear from you to the contrary by 10 a.m. I shall assume that I can be allowed to view the property. My telephone number is Culverton 79. Yours faithfully, Nicholas Vaughan."

"Sounds just the sort of chap I want there. It's a fine fertile bit of land, and though it's out of cultivation now, it'll pay anyone to cultivate it," said St Cyres to himself. "I only hope he likes it…"

He replaced the letter in his pocket and picked up his mallet, aiming skilfully at the wedge he had placed to split his great gnarled log. He was only halfway through the job when the door of the wood-shed opened and a breath of Chypre wafted across the pleasant smell of wood shavings and sawdust.

3

June St Cyres stood at the door of the wood-shed, clutching her fur coat round her and surveying her father-in-law with puzzled eyes. The Colonel gave a start.

"Eh, what's that?" he asked, as he turned to face the newcomer. His jaw fell when he saw June, but he contrived a kindly "Good-morning, my dear. Deuced chilly morning for you to be out. Better get back to the fireside."

"I want to talk to you, Pops," said June, unaware of the fact that her form of address irritated St Cyres almost to frenzy. "It's about Little Thatch. I wrote and told Tommy Gressingham about it, and he wants to take it. It'd be a bit of luck for you, because Tommy's got pots of money and he'd improve it no end."

"Well, well. If your friend wants to take the place he'd better write to me in the usual way, and I'll deal with his application along with any others," replied St Cyres.

"That's not good enough," retorted June. "I won't be put off like that."

She had taken a cigarette out of her pocket and lighted it, throwing the match on the floor. St Cyres hastily stamped on the unextinguished match.

"Look here, my dear: I make a rule never to light matches or smoke cigarettes in the wood-shed. It's too risky. There's wood shavings and sawdust all over the place and if the shed catches the main thatch will catch too. It's true I smoke my pipe, but..."

"Oh, all right," she retorted, stubbing out her cigarette irritably. "About Little Thatch. I want you to let Tommy and Meriel have it. They're my friends, and it'll make all the difference in the world to me if I have somebody to talk to down here—somebody who's interested in the same things as I am. I wouldn't ask you to let them the place if there was any chance of your being done over it, but there isn't. They're well off, and he's a good business man. I do so want them to come. Promise?" she begged, drawing nearer to St Cyres and rubbing her powdered face against his coat.

Roderick St Cyres had little finesse in his nature; he prided himself on being straight and saying just what he meant, and he answered his daughter-in-law according to his nature.

"I'm sorry, my dear, but I can't make any promises of that nature. As I've told you, if Mr. Gressingham applies for a tenancy, I'll consider his application on its merits. I can't promise anything further."

"But I don't see what you mean," she argued. "I've told you he's wealthy, and he's a good business man. Anyone will tell you I'm right—his banker or lawyer. You can phone up and ask them."

"That isn't the only point, my dear. As a landlord I have a duty to the land. It's true that Little Thatch has been shamefully neglected. Poor old Timothy Yeo and his wife just let it go for years, but they were old and they'd lived in that house for quarter of a century. I couldn't turn them out. Now Yeo's dead I want to put in a tenant who will live in the house and cultivate the land."

"I've told you Tommy will look after it. He's got a lovely garden at his Surrey place."

"Then he doesn't need another garden down here. I'm sorry, June, but I don't want to let Little Thatch as a wealthy man's plaything, to be used for week-ends and kept for a toy. Little Thatch is a good house and a valuable small holding, and I want a tenant who will live in it and cultivate the land and be a responsible neighbour to me and to the farmers."

"And what about me?" she burst out. "You talk about what *you* want. You don't think about anyone else. Can't you see I'm bored and miserable to the verge of giving up? My husband's a prisoner, and God knows if I shall ever see him again. I'm poor and I can't live the life I've a right to expect—the life I was brought up to. I'm stuck down here in this ghastly place, miles from my own friends, with nothing to do and no one to care about me. I ask you for this one small thing, so that some of my own friends can be near me, and you talk a lot of hot air about cultivating—even though

I've *told* you the Gressinghams will improve the place. You're only refusing me out of obstinacy, because you hate me and hate all I stand for. It's mean and beastly and cruel."

Colonel St Cyres stood aghast. He was a reticent man and June's outburst horrified him. Something inside him told that the right way of dealing with his daughter-in-law was to administer a stern rebuke and to tell her plainly that she was a self-indulgent lazy-bones, but he was too kind-hearted to follow such a course. He protested gently:

"Come, come, my dear. You are being unreasonable. I am indeed sorry to learn your opinion of this place. We wanted you to be happy here, and we have done our best to make you comfortable and to give you a real home—to make you feel you belonged—"

"I don't belong, and I never shall. You're always criticising me and everything I want, and Anne looks down her nose at me. You don't care that I'm miserable. You all hate me. I loathe being here, and I loathe your beastly country with its mud and smells and beasts."

She was working herself up into an even fiercer temper and St Cyres felt alarmed, but his slow-working mind was beginning to resent June's unfairness. His voice was sterner as he replied:

"While I am sorry that you are unhappy with us, it is only common sense to point out that you are under no compulsion to remain here, June. I suggested your coming in the hope that you would find our home a refuge where you and Michael would be welcome to make your home—but if you are miserable here—"

"You don't care how miserable I am," she broke in. "You're just content to live like cows or cabbages, without any ideas or any society or anything that makes life worth living, and when

I tell you I'm wretched you just say clear out—as though I've
got anywhere to go. I can't bear it! I wish I were dead," and with
that she flung out of the shed running furiously over the frosty
ground—running clumsily, too, for her high-heeled slippers were
not made for frosty tussocks or cobbled yards.

Colonel St Cyres took out his handkerchief, mopped his forehead and blew his nose vigorously. "God bless my soul" was all
he could find to say, and he was still saying it when Anne came
into the wood-shed.

4

Anne St Cyres was very much like her father. She was tall and
squarely built—too solid for elegance, but built for endurance.
Her face was square, too, with a resolute jaw, low forehead and
nondescript nose. Her eyes were her best features, wide-set, grey-
blue eyes, happy and steady, and her mouth was full-lipped and
kindly, but resolute like her chin. Her hair was long, drawn back
into a plaited bun, waving prettily over her shapely ears. Anne wore
an old heather mixture tweed suit—it was a good suit, but old
enough to have lost its lines and become baggy. With her chestnut
brown hair, russet cheeks and heather mixture tweed she looked
almost part of the landscape, an appropriate sturdy figure, strong
and competent. When Colonel St Cyres saw her, he said, "Thank
God." He always did thank God for Anne.

She came straight into the wood-shed and straight to the point.
"June been having high strikes? I'm sorry for you, daddy, but it
had to happen. She's been boiling up her grievances for quite
a long time. All the same, don't let Little Thatch to her friend
Gressingham."

"I'm not going to, Anne. I don't like the sound of the fellow."

"You'd like the reality even less. I've met him. He was in the Cocktail Bar at the Courtenay Hotel in Exeter when I was there with June the other day."

Her father cut in: "Cocktail bar? That's a new port of call for you, Anne."

"Oh, I know," she replied. "I ran June in to Exeter when I had to go to see about new tyres, and nothing would please her but cocktails and an expensive lunch. I loathe wasting money like that—but I'm sometimes sorry for June. She's a fish out of water here. However, I was going to tell you about her friend, Mr. Gressingham. He's just the type you and I dislike—oozing money, very pleased with himself and inclined to be familiar on a moment's acquaintance. Oh, I *loathed* him. He's facetious and he called me Anne in the first five minutes—but I shouldn't have minded that so much—we can't all like the same people—only I wouldn't trust him an inch, least of all with June. He's got a wife, and June's got a husband—and I just couldn't bear the way he behaved with her. It made me hot all over." Anne's honest face had flushed deep rosy red, and her voice was distressed as she went on: "I hate myself for saying all this, and I shouldn't have said a word to you about it if it hadn't been that I know June is set on getting Little Thatch for Mr. Gressingham, so that she can be in and out of the place any time she likes. I just can't bear the idea of it. You and I were both sorry when Denis married her, but since they *are* married—well, I don't want any Gressinghams down here."

Colonel St Cyres nodded, but he looked very glum.

"You're quite right, Anne. I feel exactly as you do, and I want to do everything we can for Denis, poor chap—but it's going to be difficult. If June takes this attitude about hating us all and being miserable we can't very well keep her here."

"Don't take any notice of her. Leave her to me," replied Anne. "It's all very well for June to say she's going away because she can't stand us any longer—I've been hearing that for some time—but June likes her comforts, and comforts are costly these days. Let her simmer down again. Take no notice of what she's said—you'll find she'll think better of it." Anne laughed, a little bitterly. "I've no doubt she's lying on her bed at the moment, raging furiously. I shall take her up a hot-water bottle and a jug of coffee, sympathise with her over her appalling headache, draw the curtains, murmur something about chicken for lunch, and retire tactfully."

Colonel St Cyres chuckled, but he quickly sobered down, adding: "All very well to laugh, my dear, but it's deuced hard on you. You get the brunt of it."

"Don't worry about me, daddy. I've got a broad back and I can manage. Provided you and mother aren't made miserable in your own home I don't mind dealing with June. She's an idiot—according to our ideas—but I'm still sorry for her, partly because she *is* an idiot. She's never done an honest hard day's work in her life: she misses everything that seems worth while to me, and she doesn't seem to have a friend in the world who values her for herself. I love Michael, you know. He's a darling, for all that he's a spoilt little brat, and he *is* beginning to improve. He doesn't yowl nearly so much as he did, and he's healthier. Look!" She opened the door of the shed and motioned to her father.

Michael, aged five, was playing by the pump in the stable yard, throwing bits of ice about, as George, the gardener's boy, broke the crust of ice on the stone trough. Michael was very fair, with scarlet cheeks and blue eyes; muffled up in an old fair-isle scarf of Anne's, tied over his head and round his neck, he was a picture of healthy childhood, very different from the white-faced little lad of a year ago.

"That seems to make it worth while, doesn't it?" said Anne. "Denis will come back one day—I hope—and we'll show him a son to be proud of. Don't you bother about June. I'll cope with her. Now I'm going to Leighs to look at those two heifers he wants to sell. They're good stock, and we've lots of winter feed. Bye-bye, daddy. Don't worry—and get a good sound hard-working tenant for Little Thatch, and see he gets it into decent cultivation again."

And with that Anne hurried off, shutting the door of the shed behind her.

CHAPTER TWO

I

JUST AS ANNE ST CYRES SHUT THE DOOR OF THE WOOD-SHED and ran over the frosty cobbles towards Michael, a very old car drew up in the lane outside the gate of Little Thatch, and the driver got out and stood by the gate, looking at the neglected garden. He was a big fellow, over six feet tall, with such broad shoulders that his height seemed less than it was. He stood with his arms folded on the gate and stared thoughtfully at Little Thatch. The house was a long, low building—more spacious than the usual Devonshire cottage. None of its corners was a right angle, none of its walls quite vertical. The ancient cob walls seemed to crouch a little, their curves denoting strength, not weakness: the thatch over the long roof seemed like a blanket, comfortably overhanging the walls in deep eaves which cast lilac shadows on the rose and ochre of the freshly washed walls. The long, low sturdy house pleased the observer at the gate: (Anne St Cyres said later that the man resembled the house, because his heavy powerful shoulders reminded her of the thick cob walls of Little Thatch). He noted the excellent condition of the thatch, with its comely patterned ridge and plaited "dollies" at the gable ends, the tall sturdy brick chimneys bestriding the thatch, and the stonework showing through the colour wash in the squat buttress at one end. An old house but a worthy one, he meditated, thick walled, deep thatched, with good mullioned windows all facing south. To the north towards the lane, the house presented a dead wall without a window in it, an inscrutable uneven solid wall, squatting beneath its thatch, as though to snub an inquisitive observer.

When Colonel St Cyres first saw Nicholas Vaughan leaning patiently on the gate of Little Thatch, the older man said to himself, "Fine big chap: he ought to be able to dig. Shoulders like a bull..."

When Vaughan turned to face him, the Colonel had a shock of surprise, for one of Vaughan's eyes was covered by an eye-shade, and the livid unlovely line of a recently healed scar marred the left side of his face. One grey eye looked steadily at the Colonel.

"Good-morning. I hope I'm not inconveniently early. My name's Vaughan."

"Good-morning. I'm glad you took the opportunity of coming. Wilton's an old friend of mine and I value his judgment. He gave you some idea of what this property is like? Come along in."

He opened the gate and preceded Vaughan down the cobbled path, and the latter turned his back on the house and studied the garden.

"Yes," he replied. "Commander Wilton gave me a very fair idea of it. This was a small holding once, I take it? That's a shippon among the outbuildings, isn't it?"

"Shippon?" queried St Cyres. "Oh—you mean the cow shed. Our folks call that a linhey. Yes. Twenty years ago this was a flourishing small holding—twenty acres went with the house including the two orchards. Now the land's let or I farm it myself. As it stands, it's the house, garden, and orchard, with another small orchard across the road if you want it—about an acre, all told. The garden's been neglected for years."

"Yes," said the tall man, and his tone spoke volumes. There was a fork sticking in a half-dug trench in one of the weed-covered beds, and Vaughan took it and turned over a few spits of earth, bending to the job as though he loved it. "That's good soil," he said tersely. "It was well cultivated—once."

"You're right there," replied St Cyres. "Ten years ago this garden was famous in the district—and the land hereabouts is the most fertile in the county." He walked along the unkempt cobbled path the full length of the house and stopped at a small gate which gave access to the orchard. "Mostly cider apples," he said, "a few Bramleys and Coxes, some damson plums and Victorias—well worth having…"

"And some pasture… good for geese and ducks," said the other. "Now what about water?"

"None laid on. Two pumps: this well here is a deep one— forty feet. The other's a surface well, but the pump's close to the kitchen."

"I've got to make sure of the water question," said Vaughan. "If I take this place, I mean to cultivate. I can put an old petrol pump on the well if the water's there."

"It's there all right. I can give you my word you're safe over that."

"Good… I could put some glass up against that linhey or whatever you call it. I'll just look at those outbuildings."

"Like to see the house first?"

"No. The house is all right, I'll see that later. It's the land I'm thinking of. I've got my living to earn, by and large, and I'm going to earn it on the land."

St Cyres listened to him with a mixture of sympathy and amusement: an earnest young man, with a very pleasant deep voice—"a gentleman" St Cyres postulated in his old-fashioned way, but a gentleman who loved the soil, loved it enough to pick up the frosted loam and crumble it in his fingers. St Cyres let him poke round in the long row of outbuildings—pig sty, cattle shed, wood-shed, coal house, wash house, earth closet. Let him see it as it was, sturdy buildings suited to a working man's needs, no frills or comforts. Stark toil was what this place needed—but the chap had big shoulders and big capable hands.

"That's all right—the fabric's sound enough," said Vaughan placidly as he finished surveying the ancient sheds. "Look here, sir. This garden wants some muck on it before it'll be fit for much. I don't want to buy manure and I hate chemicals. What about the pasture below there, across my hedge? Is it yours?"

"It's mine all right. D'you want to keep a horse?"

"Lord, no. Not enough work to justify it. I should like to raise some bullocks or heifers—just a few. A bit of pasture and an acre or so of hay—it'd be the making of this place. I was brought up on a farm, and although it's market gardening I'm out for, I know the value of a few beasts. Can't keep up fertility without beasts."

"Something in it," agreed St Cyres. "My daughter swears by cow dung and she raises the best tomatoes in the district. I wouldn't mind letting you have some pasture and a small meadow, but think of the work involved. Labour's next to impossible to get. You might get a boy—but not a skilled one."

Nicholas Vaughan grinned. A grin which showed fine white teeth in a wide mouth, and did away with the sinister expression caused by eye-patch and scar. "Do I look the sort of bloke who can't work?" he asked. "I'm thirty: fit as a fiddle and strong as two horses. This" (pointing to his eye-shade) "isn't permanent. It's protecting a healing wound and the sight is still there. The light hurts it at present. One of our guns turned nasty on us and back-fired. Never mind that. I'm not afraid of work and I like beasts. A bunch of yearling heifers won't tire me out, I promise you."

"Good for you," said St Cyres. "Leigh, down in the valley there, has some promising beasts for sale, and I might let you have some hay. Very heavy crop this year. Come and see the house. It's a good house for all the muck it's in. I'd do it up for you, but I can't get the labour."

"We do our own walls where I come from," replied Vaughan, and St Cyres enquired,

"Yorkshireman? North Riding?"

"Pretty close. Borders of Westmorland. I say, this isn't at all bad."

St Cyres had unlocked the kitchen door, and the two men had stepped inside and turned to survey the cottage through the open kitchen door. The kitchen was at the west end of the cottage, and from a door in its eastern wall it was possible to look through the length of the building. The kitchen opened into a long, beamed sitting-room—twenty feet long at least, Vaughan estimated; beyond that came a small entrance hall with the front door, and beyond that another small square room. All the windows, which had deep window seats, faced south, with a good view across the valley of the river Mallow.

Vaughan walked into the sitting-room and studied it: the floor was of the mixture of lime and ash peculiar to the county: the cob walls bulged and curved, and were colour washed a particularly hideous shade of Pompeian red beloved by Devonians, but the proportion of the long low room was beautiful, as was the panelling of the ancient doors (now painted, like all the woodwork, a revolting chocolate colour). Three great beams crossed the ceiling transversely—their surface plastered and whitewashed.

"I say, this is a damned fine room," said Vaughan. "How came a small holding to have a great room like this?"

St Cyres came in and stood beside him. "Local history has it that this is an ancient 'house of refreshment,' to use the old term," he replied. "In short, it was the Cider House, and a bar once divided this room, with a compartment behind it for the cider barrels. The partition was taken down in my father's time. I can't tell you the exact history of the place, but I believe the kitchen end is very ancient, the further end of later date. I should say it's Tudor in origin, with Jacobean additions and Georgian improvements. Those panelled doors are Jacobean, and the stairs, too—they're oak, and as hard as iron."

"Gad, I like it… You could make a gorgeous room of this: the fireplace is decent, too." They wandered on, up the little twisting stairs, and examined four bedrooms, small sunny rooms, and Vaughan sniffed appreciatively. "It's warm in here," he said. "Surprising to find a dry house in Devon."

"This one's always dry except for surface condensation," replied St Cyres. "The fabric is sound and the thatch waterproof. The garden slopes away to the valley, as you can see and there's good drainage—the conduits are square oak pipes, probably the original ones, but they're still sound. If you listen you can hear the water running away merrily under that drain by the kitchen door. The only trouble is this: owing to the thick cob walls and heavy thatch the cottage maintains an almost even temperature inside, summer and winter. If you come inside on a scorching summer day you'll find the big room cold; now it's frosty outside and the house seems warm. The temperature is probably an even fifty degrees, but when there's a sudden change of temperature outside you'll get surface condensation on the stone floors and you'll probably think the floors are damp."

"Oh no, I shan't. I know all about condensation on stone floors. I was brought up in Westmorland," said Vaughan. "Is there another bedroom? These four don't account for all the floor space down below."

"Quite right. There's another bedroom over the kitchen, with its own stairs."

"Two stairways, by gum! Quite an establishment. That'll suit me fine. I can camp out over the kitchen while I get the rest of the house into order. I can see myself being busy for some time to come."

St Cyres hesitated, and then said: "How'll you manage about housekeeping? I've told you, it's next to impossible to get labour or domestic service."

"Domestic service be blowed! I'll manage for myself, pro tem."

"That's all very well, but a man needs a bit of comfort after a hard day on the land," said St Cyres. "Haven't you a sister, or anybody who'd housekeep for you?"

Vaughan laughed: that same merry grin which lit up his long face and contradicted its saturnine expression.

"Sister? I can see mine coming here! She's a hundred per cent intellectual. No. I shall do for myself. You needn't be afraid I shall make a mess of it. I'm a much more competent housewife than many of the womenfolk I know."

"It'll be a dull life for you," said St Cyres in his conscientious way. "There's no young society hereabouts. I've got a daughter, but she's a busy girl—she runs the house and helps on the farm, and we don't find time to entertain."

"Now look here, sir," replied Vaughan. "Let's get this straight. I'm not a sociable character. I like working on the land, I like painting doors and walls and all that, and I'm interested in books. I've got quite a number. If you want a sociable tenant to brighten country life, count me out. I'm about as sociable as a hermit crab—but I'll bring this place into cultivation again, and make the house as good as it's capable of being—which is very good. I can give you sound references, but I won't undertake to attend whist drives or play bridge, or dance or go to garden parties, or do anything in that line. What about it?"

"My dear chap, I don't want you to play bridge, or to dance— I loathe bridge and modern dancing—but a fellow of your age wants something better than a fried sausage for supper and a bed over the kitchen."

"Leave that to me. In confidence—and I mean in confidence— I'm meaning to get married some time, and when I'm colour washing walls and painting doors, I shall be doing it with an end in view."

St Cyres' face cleared. "That's a different story," he said. "I wish you all the luck in the world—but this house isn't everybody's money. No water laid on, no electricity, no indoors sanitation. Most modern young women would find it anathema. Why not bring your wife-to-be to see it? It's only fair to give her a say in the matter before you decide on it."

Again Vaughan laughed: "My wife-to-be, as you style her, isn't a modern young woman—not in your sense. The woman who marries me will know what she's in for, and that's hard work. Incidentally, I'm not such a mutt as to want to show any woman this house as it stands, with all that foul colour wash and decayed chocolate paint. You wait till I've done with it and it's gleaming cream and honey colour; when there's an engine for pumping water and a plant for electric light. I've got enough capital to make this house a good home—if you give me a square deal and an assured tenancy."

"I'll give you a square deal all right," said St Cyres, "but think it over before you decide. I tell you frankly I can't do what I should like to do—that is, get the garden clean and the orchards into order, and I can't get the house done up for the same reason—there's no labour to be had. All the builders are working under the Essential Works order, and all the farmers are short-handed. Here's my offer. I'll let you the house, garden and orchards as they stand for the same rent old Timothy Yeo paid me—that is £26 a year, and I'll rent you the pasture and meadow below the garden at current agricultural rates. I'm prepared to offer you a good tenancy and option of renewal. Think it over: if you still like it after you've considered it, ring up my lawyer in Exeter—old Bodlesham—and he'll get an agreement made out."

"That's all right," said Vaughan, "but listen to me. If I'm to get that garden fit for anything this summer, I've got to get on to it now. It's good soil, but it's foul with couch grass and gout weed and every pest under the sun—and the soil's starved. You tell your lawyer to get busy on the agreement: I won't hustle him—but give me your word I can have the place and let me go on to it straight away. I can't afford to waste a week if I'm to get a crop out of this land this year—and you know that as well as I do. I've got an option on an engine for the pump and I've got my eye on an electric plant. Let me go right ahead. Your word's as good as a lawyer's deed, I know that."

St Cyres was not a man who liked to be hustled, but seeing the eagerness on the other's face, he made up his mind then and there.

"Very well," he replied. "If you want it you can have it—but remember I've told you all the drawbacks. There's no water main nearer than three miles—and not likely to be—and the same applies to sewerage. The nearest electricity supply is two miles away. The house is ancient, and those cob walls won't stand much knocking about—but it's weather worthy, the fabric's sound and the thatch rainproof. As for the garden—it's been neglected these ten years, but it's on some of the most fertile land in the county."

"Right. It's what I want; provided the water's here and you'll allow me a free hand in cultivation—putting up some glass and a shack for my car, I'll take it—or buy it."

"No. I won't sell, but I'll give you an assured tenancy—and good luck to you."

"Thanks. I won't let you down," replied Vaughan.

2

When Colonel St Cyres went home, he left the keys of Little Thatch with his new tenant so that Vaughan could study the house at his leisure. Once alone in the place, Vaughan went carefully through the house, examining walls and windows, cupboards and floors. The more he studied it, the more he liked it. It was plain to any man who cared about old houses that this squat sturdy building could make a beautiful and comfortable home to anybody who cared for living and working in the country and who was not deterred by the lack of urban amenities. Having studied the house in detail, Vaughan went outside and put the door key in his pocket with an expression of serene content on his face. Then, taking off his old Burberry, with a grin of sheer delight, he took the fork and began to trench the ground in front of the cottage.

The night's frost was only a hoar frost—it had not penetrated the ground—and Vaughan found the soil light and workable beneath the matt of grass and weed. In the narrow beds beneath the cottage windows long-stemmed violets defied the frost, winter jasmine shone in sprays of clearest chrome yellow and aconites spread their green frills to the sun. Lighting his pipe, Vaughan began to plan out his garden: cold frames and some glass against the linhey, tomatoes on the long southward slope, potatoes and root crops in the lower beds. Some wattle fencing and fruit cages when he could get them—and all the apple trees needed pruning and spraying and banding. As he dug, he planned out his land, thought of the best way of investing his capital in it, pondering over pump and piping, electric plant and wiring, some heating for the greenhouse, and as he cogitated, his face was the face of a very contented man.

CHAPTER THREE

I

IT WAS ON NEW YEAR'S DAY THAT NICHOLAS VAUGHAN TOOK possession of Little Thatch. Just before midday he drove through the narrow Devonshire lanes in his old car, piloting a disreputable lorry which followed him round awkward corners and blind bends. The lorry belonged to the nearest coal merchant, and in it was half a ton of coal in addition to a camp-bed, some chairs and tables, a number of packing cases, garden tools and miscellaneous cooking pots. Vaughan chuckled to himself over his home-coming—never had a less impressive moving-in ceremony been performed. Transport was at a premium, so he had taken the simplest way of moving those of his belongings he wanted immediately—loaded them into the coal-lorry along with the coal. When he opened the kitchen door and went inside a surprise awaited him. There was a good fire burning in the range, the floor was scrubbed and clean, and on the wide window sill stood a big loaf of bread, a can of milk and a big pasty. As he stood staring, footsteps sounded on the cobbles and a woman's figure appeared at the door.

"Good-morning, Mr. Vaughan. I'm Anne St Cyres. I haven't come to bother you—just to say that if you want anything or if you're in a fix we're only a few hundred yards away, so please come and ask. Good luck to you in your new house."

"Thank you very much. It's very good of you—and thank you for all this—"

"Not a bit. You're miles from a shop here. The baker won't call till Wednesday and the butcher comes on Friday. You can get milk at Lane's farm in the valley. There's a barrel of cider in the larder which my father sent with his best wishes… oh, there's Timothy Yeo's cat again. It won't stay with anybody else because it's always lived here. Do you hate cats?"

"No. I like them. That's a fine chap. I'll keep him all right."

"Good. He's a grand ratter. Good-bye for now—and good luck."

She turned and walked away before Vaughan had time for another word, and he bent and stroked the big marmalade-coloured cat, muttering to himself, "Decent of them, *jolly* decent of them," as the lorry man came in at the door carrying an armful of pots.

"Want these in here, mister?" he asked, and the cat sat down sedately by the fire while Vaughan went out to lend a hand in carrying his modest goods and chattels into Little Thatch.

2

"He's a competent looking young man, daddy."

Anne St Cyres laughed a little as she spoke to her father just after lunch that day, and St Cyres nodded.

"Yes. Wilton gave him a very good character, and I like him myself. Business-like and shrewd, and ready to work hard—just the type of fellow to do well in the country, and he's used to country conditions. I hope he won't find it too lonely."

"Well, he told you he wasn't a sociable character, didn't he? You can go in and have a word with him some time, you'll soon notice if he seems hipped. I don't think he'd have taken on a place like Little Thatch if he didn't like being alone. Although I hardly exchanged a dozen words with him he gave me the impression that he knew his own mind all right. I'm glad he's moved in straight away. I only heard this morning that June's friends, the Gressinghams, have come to stay at Hinton Mallory. Mrs. Hesling's taking them as paying guests."

"Good gad! What's a wealthy stockbroker going to do to amuse himself staying in a farmhouse?"

Anne linked her arm in her father's and drew him further along the terrace.

"I suppose he's still thinking of buying a place down here—but, as we know, there's nothing on the market. I don't think he'll be successful. Anyway, I'd rather have him at Hinton Mallory than at Little Thatch."

St Cyres nodded, but he looked troubled. "Yes… I see what you mean—but I'd rather he weren't here at all. I don't like the idea of town dwellers buying up country properties and using them as playthings. I know the stockbroker type… speculators, all of them, no sense of responsibility to the land. In any case, this part of England is the last locality a man like Gressingham would choose unless he had some ulterior motive in coming here."

"His motive is obvious—he comes here because June is here. She asked him to come. You can't blame her for wanting to see something of her own friends, daddy. She's wretchedly bored—"

"Why doesn't she *do* something, then?" broke out St Cyres. "There was never a time in the world's history when there was more need for men and women of goodwill to work together to justify their existence—and justify their privileges, too."

"Yes, that's perfectly true," replied Anne, in her serene, sensible voice, "but it's not easy to find a job fitted to one's limitations when one is transplanted into a strange environment. If I were to find myself in a service flat in Mayfair, complete with central heating

and a restaurant for meals, I'm perfectly certain I should feel useless and confused, and probably I should mope and grumble—and
so would you! Imagine living in a single room flatlet like the one
June was describing last night."

"Heaven forbid!" exclaimed St Cyres. "Personally I'd rather
perish—but no one's *forced* to live in those damned rabbit hutches
in London, Anne."

"Some people adore them, daddy. It's no use expecting everyone to like the same things. They don't. The evacuee business
ought to have taught us that. We saw Londoners pitchforked into
the country, and they *loathed* it. It was only the children who liked
it, the grown women were bored and miserable, as June is bored
and miserable, and it's better to try to understand her point of
view. I'm glad for her sake that she's got someone she likes to talk
to, although I'm sorry that I don't like her friends. It seems mean
of me, somehow."

"Rubbish! She doesn't like *your* friends, does she?—or try to
be polite to them. Do you remember when old Mrs. Mansfield
came that day…?"

"Shall I ever forget it?" laughed Anne. "All the same I think
you'd better go and call on Mr. Gressingham, daddy. Just stroll
in some time and ask him if he'd care for some rough shooting.
There are lots of wild duck up the valley."

"*Me* call on Gressingham, Anne? Why on earth should I?"

"To stop people talking, dad. You know how the country gossips. If June is always running along to see the Gressinghams and
we aren't even polite to them, tongues are going to wag. It's no
use mother going—she couldn't bear them—but everyone knows
she never goes out in winter. I'll look in some time, just for manners—but you've got to do the thing properly. I may have my own

private opinion about June—I'll admit that to you—but I'm not going to have the farmers' wives gossiping about her if I can help it. It's not dignified and it's unpleasant."

"I see," said St Cyres, and his voice sounded doleful, but he went on: "but this man Gressingham's got his wife with him, hasn't he? He's not there alone?"

"She came down with him, and I gather she's to be there on and off. She has a job of sorts—something to do with ambulance driving. It sounded to me one of those comfortable jobs where you show up if you want to—and get plenty of petrol coupons to reach your job with. She's pretty frightful, daddy—from our point of view. What you'd call a hundred per cent Jezebel. She wears wine-coloured slacks and a fur coat. If you go in after tea to-day you'll miss her: she went away this morning."

"You seem to know all about them, Anne."

"Yes. I'm quite well-informed," said Anne, and for once her voice sounded edgy. "I've heard about them from everybody: June herself, then from Mrs. Hesling who came up here to talk about the ducks—or so she pretended—then from old Dickon when he was bringing the coal in, and from Tom Ridd when he brought the potatoes in, and from the post-girl. Oh, everyone's talking about them, daddy. That's why you've *got* to try to be polite."

There was a moment's silence, and then St Cyres said: "I don't like it, Anne. If June's going to import people like that here the sooner she goes back to London the better. If it's a question of money, I could…"

"It's not a question of money—not from my point of view," replied Anne. "I've always been straight with you, daddy, and I'll be straight with you now. June's bored: she married Denis because she wanted a husband to satisfy the demands of her own vitality.

She's a creature of sex, and her husband's a prisoner of war and she's left stranded. If we send June back to London to live her own life, I'm certain she'll be some man's mistress before six months are up. That's my opinion—but I've good grounds for stating it. If we keep her here we can keep her straight—or try to—and look Denis in the face when he comes home."

St Cyres was silent. Anne very seldom spoke as she was speaking now, but he trusted her judgment. At last he said: "Very well. I'll look in at Hinton Mallory after tea."

"Good," she replied. "I'm sure it's the right thing to do. Go at half-past five and I'll come and rescue you before six."

And with that she left him, and St Cyres chewed over his thoughts miserably as he sorted apples in the apple-house.

3

Hinton Mallory was one of the largest farmhouses in the district. One of Colonel St Cyres' friends who had stayed with him recently had said: "If Mallory Fitzjohn were on a bus route or near a station you'd have become a show place, Colonel. I haven't seen a finer group of houses in the county."

"Thank God we're not on a bus route then, and that our roads will never tempt the motoring week-enders," St Cyres had replied.

"The Mallorys"—as the group was described locally—consisted of three big houses with attendant cottages. Manor Thatch—the St Cyres' home—was the "great house" of the group: attached to it was Little Thatch and three small labourers' cottages. A few hundred yards from Manor Thatch was the Old Vicarage, now used as a farmhouse, with Church Cottages near by. Manor Thatch with its attendant cottages, the Church and Vicarage Farm made up Mallory Fitzjohn. Hinton Mallory was in the valley below, and Upton Mallory lay across the river.

Hinton Mallory was an unusually beautiful old house which consisted of the remains of monastic buildings coupled to a Jacobean wing. With its great stone chimneys, medieval open fireplaces and panelled walls, Hinton Mallory was finer than many a manor house. Seen from the hills, the thatched roofs and spreading stone barns made a beautiful group, embowered in the tall elms and ancient oaks which luxuriated in the rich valley soil. The approach to the farm was disillusioning to the urban mind, for the lanes, deep set between high banks and dense hedgerows, were generally thick with mud and farmyard squelch, and no view was obtainable by either driver or pedestrian, for banks and hedges shut the lanes in completely. For six months of the year it was desirable to wear Wellingtons when approaching Hinton Mallory: ordinary shoes were liable to be pulled off the feet when they adhered to the red glutinous mud; the river frequently broke its banks after rainstorms and the unwary had to paddle through the flooded stretches.

Some of these disadvantages were being expounded to Tom Gressingham by a friend who had driven over to see him at Hinton Mallory. Gressingham was a man of fifty, but he looked younger than his years. His admirers said he was a fine looking fellow, and he was, in fact, a big upstanding figure of a man, but beginning to lose in his fight against obesity. His hair was still black and plentiful, well cut, well brushed: his complexion sanguine, tending to excess of colour now, his eyes very dark but somewhat lack-lustre. When Anne St Cyres first saw Gressingham she remembered Browning's famous fines in the Pied Piper:

"Nor brighter was his eye nor moister
Than a too long opened oyster."

Gressingham's visitor, Howard Brendon, was a great contrast
to him in appearance—a long, lean, grey man, narrow headed,
narrow faced, tight-lipped and colourless: a ferret of a man, but well
groomed, well tailored, immaculately clean, and dressed in tweeds
which were not only meant for the country but looked right in the
country—which Gressingham's tweeds never did. Brendon accepted
the whisky and soda which Gressingham held out to him and said:

"I agree with you it's a fine house and an interesting house—if
you happen to value antiquities—but you'd make the mistake of a
lifetime if you bought it. However, as it's not on the market, and
not likely to be, the point's not worth debating."

Gressingham laughed, and his laugh was that of a well-satisfied
man. "I've heard that before, old chap, many times before. As you
know, I've made quite a hobby of buying old properties, spending a
bit on them and selling them again to advantage—my own advantage as well as the other fellow's. You'd be surprised the number
of times I've met with the 'won't sell at any figure' attitude, and
found that a little persuasion and a little time worked wonders.
I'm not boasting when I tell you that I've hardly ever come to a
dead-end that way."

"I'll take your word for it," replied the other, "but you might
as well face the facts this time. This place is owned by Colonel
St Cyres. He's as likely to sell his land as to commit perjury in a
Court of Law. I don't know if the analogy enlightens you, but it's
as strong as I can make it."

"Right. He won't consider selling now. He's no need to.
Farming's done well during the war, but it's not going to do so

well in future. The government's handed out a lot of soft sawder to the farmers—quite right, too—but in peace time cheap food's what's wanted, and it's cheaper to import meat and grain than to raise it in this country. In five years' time quite a number of land-owning gentry will be glad to realise a good figure for their property."

"In five years' time the sale of land will be controlled. What you refuse to realise is that this country's going to swing to the left, and the hell of a long way, too."

At that moment the door opened and Mrs. Hesling announced: "Here's Colonel St Cyres come to see you," and she ushered the latter in without further ceremony.

If Gressingham were taken aback he did not show it. Advancing with outstretched hand he said cheerfully: "Delighted to see you, sir. Very good of you to come over. May I introduce my friend, Howard Brendon? He's come over from Dulverton to look me up—a very friendly thing to do in these days of transport difficulties."

Gressingham was not an unobservant man: he was a very good amateur actor and based his performances on a habit of noting other men's foibles. St Cyres bowed to Brendon, and the bow was returned with the same reserve. "Looking at each other as though they were nasty smells—priceless," observed Gressingham to himself. Aloud he said, "A whisky and soda, sir, or gin and bitters?"

"Thanks. Not for me, Mr. Gressingham," replied St Cyres. "My daughter-in-law tells me you're enjoying staying here. I'm afraid you must find the place somewhat primitive."

"Oh, a bit of that doesn't hurt me," replied Gressingham cheerfully. "If you ask me, we tend to be over-civilised these days—mawkish—depending too much on machine products. Does a man good to get back to the earth occasionally and learn that life isn't all refinement. Nothing nice-minded about *me,* Colonel. Then there's this to it: you country folk don't understand what rationing means. In this place there's butter and cream and milk, good poultry and eggs, home cured ham and good pork. You farmers *live,* by jove! If the food they give me here is what you call primitive, give me the primitive every time!"

Gressingham's laugh rang out, cheerful and unforced, as he went and refilled his glass. "Did you smell my dinner cooking as you came in, Colonel? Smelt like privation—what? It's four years since I had a holiday, and by the lord I've earned it and I've enjoyed it."

"I'm glad you're enjoying it," replied St Cyres courteously. "I've always been told that Mrs. Hesling makes her guests very comfortable, but I shouldn't like you to run away with the idea that country folk get more than their fair share of rations. Farming is hard physical work, and it can't be done without adequate victuals."

Gressingham laughed: a noisy, cheerful laugh as he replied,

"Don't imagine I'm casting aspersions or suggesting any unfairness, Colonel. I know a bit about country life, and I agree with you that a man who is using his muscles from morning to night needs extra calories to stoke up his energy. All I meant was that I appreciate my good fortune in being here. I think the war has taught us a lot—all of us—and one thing it has taught the city worker is that the country can offer more amenities than was previously believed. Take the spate of country books issued during the war—the demand for them exceeds the supply, because the town-dweller thinks he's made a mistake in not trying to understand and enjoy the country. I'm an example: I'm London born

and bred, and yet I've an itch to get a country property and to farm
a bit on my own account."

Howard Brendon gave a dry chuckle: "Well, you've got money
to burn, and it's nobody's business how you burn it, Gressingham,
but Colonel St Cyres will bear me out when I say that a London
financier is asking for trouble if he thinks he can start farming on
nothing but a good bank balance and belief in his own capacity.
Farming is a skilled job; you need to be bred to it, to have it in
your bones, and to have generations of painfully acquired wisdom
behind you."

"You're perfectly right, Mr. Brendon," said St Cyres. "A farmer's
born, not made, and the mentality of the city man can't be adapted
to the slow judgment of the countryman. That's my opinion, at
least. Now, Mr. Gressingham, I was wondering if you cared for
shooting? We can't offer you any high-class sport, but there are
still a few partridges and wild duck—the close season doesn't start
before February—and the rabbits need keeping down."

"Very good of you, Colonel. It would give me a great deal of
pleasure. I brought a couple of guns down with me in case I got
the chance of a shot."

"Gressingham's a first-class shot," observed Brendon dryly.
"Any preserving about here, Colonel?"

"Not since the war. We don't raise any birds, and the keepers
are all otherwise employed," rejoined St Cyres, "but there has been
very little shooting since 1939, and there have been a few birds every
year. I go out occasionally and take old Tom Ridd with me—he
was a keeper in the old days and he's very knowledgeable. Hullo,
here's my daughter come to fetch me home."

Anne walked in, as serene of countenance as ever, and smiled
pleasantly at Gressingham.

"Good-evening, Mr. Gressingham. My sister-in-law tells me you've fallen in love with Hinton Mallory. It's a beautiful old house, isn't it?"

"It is, indeed. May I introduce Mr. Brendon—Miss St Cyres. Yes. I think this house is a wonderful property—and it could be improved so easily. There must be plenty of water for pumping if you dug for it, and I estimate the fall of the river by the mill would drive a fair-sized dynamo. You could get light and a small amount of power—"

"Oh, I'm quite sure you could," laughed Anne, "but have you suggested it to Mrs. Hesling?"

Gressingham laughed in return. "Of course: equally of course she said she was quite satisfied with the old ways—a hand-pump and oil lamps. Now won't you have a gin and lime, Miss Anne, or let me mix you a cocktail?"

"Not for me, thanks. I've really got to take daddy home: one of his tenants is coming in to see him about six o'clock. Have you asked Mr. Gressingham if he'd care for some shooting, daddy? and mother asked me to apologise for her because she hadn't called on Mrs. Gressingham. My mother hardly ever gets out in the winter, because of her arthritis, but she hopes your wife will waive formality and come to luncheon one day."

"Thanks very much. Very good of you," replied Gressingham. "My wife and I are most anxious to make friends in the locality, Miss Anne. We think it's a most beautiful part of the world. Of course Meriel is often away, still busy with her driving, but she hopes to be back shortly. Well, Colonel, I won't try to keep you if you want to be off, but any day you send a message I shall be delighted to come shooting. Very kind of you to suggest it: very neighbourly, as they say hereabouts."

4

"Seems a friendly sort of fellow," observed Colonel St Cyres to his daughter as they walked slowly up the field path which led from Hinton Mallory to Manor Thatch, and Anne nodded.

"Oh, yes: he's friendly enough—but I don't like him. I know it's a mistake to say you can judge people at sight, but even if I hadn't taken exception to the way he talks to June, I should still have said to myself that Mr. Thomas Gressingham was a man I shouldn't trust further than I could see him. Who is his friend, daddy?—I seem to have heard his name, somehow."

"Yes. Howard Brendon comes of an old legal family. His father was a well-known solicitor in Exeter. This man has bought a place in North Devon, near Dulverton. He's made a consider-able name as an antiquarian, and his name was in the papers a year or two back when he fought an action over a right-of-way through his property. He won his action, but at the cost of alienating himself from all his neighbours. I believe he's very much disliked, but he's a wealthy man and of some consequence amongst the archaeologists of the county. Probably Gressingham is his broker."

"Wait a minute—didn't Mr. Brendon get married a year or so back—he married a young wife, rather a lovely girl. Now I remember. I saw the pictures of the wedding in the papers. I don't remember who she was—not a Devonshire girl, anyway."

"Maybe. You've a better memory than I have, Anne. Somehow I didn't like the combination of Gressingham and Brendon together down here: suggested to my mind that they're up to something. Gressingham's got this idea of acquiring a country property—and Brendon must have known all about the folk in

these parts at one time. His father would have acted for many
of them."

"Anyway, Mr. Brendon doesn't seem to be encouraging his
friend's idea of a city man turning farmer."

"Quite true," agreed the Colonel, "but you were talking just
now of judging people at sight, Anne. Admittedly I don't care for
Gressingham—he's not in my line of country at all, and between
you and me I've only one name for him—a bounder—but I liked
Brendon even less. I wouldn't trust that man a yard. He's like…
by gad, Anne, he's like a ferret. He'd bite you if he got the chance.
Never saw a harder face in my life—a grim face without any
humanity in it—though he looks a gentleman and speaks like one."

"I didn't mind him so much," replied Anne. "I felt I knew
where I was with him. He's as hard as nails and made no attempt
to pretend he liked us. Quite obviously he didn't—but never mind
that. However, it doesn't matter about him, he's not likely to come
over here very often. When you see June, daddy, just say something pleasant about Mr. Gressingham and tell her you've asked
him to shoot. I'm doing my best to get her to be more friendly:
if I can only make friends with her a bit things will be easier. I
admit I don't like her, but I'm sorry for her—and I do think a lot
about Denis."

"I can't think why the poor chap ever married a girl like that,"
said St Cyres, and Anne retorted:

"It's no use going back to that each time, daddy. He did marry
her, and he's had the rottenest luck in getting taken prisoner. I
want to do what I can for Denis, and so do you, and that's why
we've got to go on trying with June."

"Quite right, my dear," said Colonel St Cyres humbly, "but I'm
sorry she has to have friends like Mr. Gressingham down here."

5

When Anne and her father had left, Tom Gressingham walked back to the fire and observed to Howard Brendon, "I wonder why the old chap turned so civil all of a sudden: seems a bit fishy to me."

"I suppose his daughter-in-law asked him to call," replied Brendon. "It'd be a bit awkward all round if her in-laws wouldn't countenance her friends in a place like this, especially if she's going to run in and out while you're here. Country folk gossip, Gressingham, for all they seem so dumb."

"Oh, let 'em gossip," replied Tom indifferently. "All the same, I wish I knew what had induced the old man to do the polite. It certainly wasn't June. She'd had a bit of a dust with him already on my account. St Cyres has a lovely old cottage—a derelict mess of a place but it'd pay for reconditioning—and June asked him to let me take it and improve it. Nothing doing. He wouldn't hear of it."

"Of course he wouldn't. What did I tell you? St Cyres won't let any townsfolk develop his properties. A cottage can be condemned and only fit for cattle to live in, but he wouldn't have it altered, let alone sell it. I suppose he'd put some farm labourers in it rather than let it to you at a good rent."

"I can't quite make it out. The cottage—Little Thatch—is let. There's a big tough there, working in the garden. I've no idea who the chap is, but Mrs. Hesling says he's living there all by himself, pigging it in the kitchen. I can't make it out. He's not a farm labourer, that's certain. I spoke to him over the gate when I passed, and although he wouldn't bother to be civil, from the dozen or so words he spoke it was clear enough he's an educated man, though I'd hazard a guess he's a north-country man—dour, hard sort of chap. He was digging in the garden, up to his knees in mud and muck like a labourer."

"Perhaps Miss Anne St Cyres has taken a leaf out of her sister-in-law's book and got daddy to let the cottage to a boy friend of her own," replied Brendon, and Gressingham sniggered.

"Think so? I don't—and I shouldn't admire her taste if she had. The bloke's got a patch over his eye and a scar right down one cheek—a proper tough. The funny part of it is that I'm convinced I've seen his face somewhere. I couldn't get a good look at him, because he turned away almost at once: then to-day, when I walked past again, he'd fixed up a wattle which screens the garden, so I didn't get another look at him."

"He sounds a shy bird," commented Brendon. "Well, I'd better be off—I shan't get to Exeter before seven as it is. If I do hear of any properties likely to come into the market, I'll let you know, though if you take my advice you'll go back to the Home Counties. This part of the world's no good to a man like you, Gressingham. The landowners are a sticky lot, they'll never welcome a Londoner, and you're not the man to be satisfied with your own company for long. Give up the idea and buy a decent modern house in Berkshire or Surrey—you're far more likely to get value for money there."

"Thanks for the advice, old man. All the same, I don't give up easily, any more than you do. My experience in life has been that you can get what you want if you want it enough."

"If you're willing to pay for it, in short. They say money talks, but the man who said that had never been in Devon."

CHAPTER FOUR

I

AS THE DAYS LENGTHENED, NICHOLAS VAUGHAN WORKED steadily over his ground at Little Thatch. Colonel St Cyres, who looked in on his new tenant occasionally with a fatherly eye, was impressed with the amount of work Vaughan accomplished. The garden was dug through before January was out, and then Vaughan fitted up a lean-to greenhouse against the wall of the linhey. A petrol pump was fitted to the farther well, and a second-hand electric plant was assembled by Vaughan in the outbuildings and insulated piping laid to connect it with the house and greenhouse. By Lady Day he had the greenhouse well stocked with seedlings and he had bought four sturdy young bullocks to graze in the pasture below Little Thatch. During the past month he had persuaded old Reuben Dickon—brother to the gardener at Manor Thatch—to come and work for him, and Colonel St Cyres was amused and interested to see the old man and the young one digging side by side in tacit understanding. Dickon was a bent, gnarled old peasant, as sturdy as the gnarled and ancient hawthorn trees which grew in the hedge banks, and the old man still dug with the slow, practised skill which achieved so much more than seemed possible from the slow action. Dickon was very deaf, and on the rare occasions he spoke it was in a husky roar which could be heard right along the valley.

"Thiccy weeds, dang 'un!" he would shout, as he triumphantly routed out an intractable root stock of sow thistle or dandelion, or yards of leathery runners of couch grass or gout weeds. "That's got he, the barstard!" he would roar in occasional triumph.

It was at Easter that Anne St Cyres was asked by Vaughan to come to inspect his house. She had met him in the lane as she returned from church on Good Friday, and had stopped to talk to him.

"My father waxes eloquent about all you've done in your garden," she said. "I believe he's a bit jealous: he says your ground's better tilled than ours is now."

"Oh, the garden won't look like anything this year," he had answered. "I shall get some decent crops off it, given reasonable luck, because the ground's good, but you can't make a garden in a year. House painting's much quicker work. Won't you come in and inspect some time? I'd value your opinion."

"Thanks very much, I should love to come," she replied. "I've always been fond of Little Thatch. I've often said that when I'm old I shall live there myself. It's such a friendly house."

"It is that," he replied with that sudden smile of his. "I believe I talk to it! Often when I've been painting or distempering the walls on these long evenings I've found myself having a chat with the house. Will you come in and have tea one day next week and tell me what you think about it?"

"Thanks very much. Will Tuesday do—about five o'clock—and may I bring you some seedlings, or are you one of those haughty people who despise all plants save those you've raised yourself?"

"Indeed I'm not—especially during my first year at Little Thatch. Tuesday at five—that'll be fine."

Anne was a correct young woman. When she arrived at Little Thatch on Tuesday she went to the front door and knocked, instead of going to the kitchen door, which always stood open.

Nicholas Vaughan opened the door with a smiling face. "Come in," he said. "You're my first visitor—"

He broke off as Anne cried out in sheer delight. "Oh, but it's lovely! I wouldn't have believed you could have done it all so quickly."

She stood in the little hall and saw the long, sunlit sitting-room agleam in the mellow light. The walls were now pale honey colour, the paint work shining cream, and the great beams were stripped and stained, almost black against the cream ceiling. A fire burned merrily in the old grate, and the floor was stained dark like the beams. Against the long wall opposite the windows book cases had been fitted into position, their shelves filled with books, and one comfortable grandfather chair stood by the fire.

"The furniture will arrive by degrees," said Vaughan. "I'm buying things as I see them. Come and see the kitchen—I hope you don't mind having tea in the kitchen, but I thought it'd be more comfortable. The parlour's not ready for company yet."

The kitchen compared very favourably with the "parlour," for it was as clean and comely. The table was scrubbed to whiteness, and the china neatly set out, with loaf and butter, oatcakes and honey, and a big fruit cake. The kettle was boiling on the small range, and Nicholas Vaughan made tea with the neatness of a man well accustomed to managing for himself.

"Will you pour out?" he enquired, after he had held Anne's chair in place for her. "I made that cake. I had to tell you. I'm just bursting with excitement over it. It's only sheer will-power which prevented me cutting it before you came, because I'm all agog to see if it's cooked properly."

Anne laughed back at him, noting how much his face had changed since she first saw him. He had discarded his eye-shade,

and though the scars on his face were still obvious they were no
longer disfiguring. He looked happy, and his weather-tanned face
was fresh and healthy.

"It looks a jolly good cake," she said, "and I'm sure it's well
baked—it's risen so nicely. Where did you learn to cook?"

"I was always keen on sailing, and I had to cook in the cuddy—
you learn to be neat on a small sailing boat. It took a bit of time to
get on terms with the range here—I hadn't seen one of that type
before. It's peculiar to the county, isn't it? but I've got it tamed,
even though I had to take it half to pieces. The chimney was partly
blocked with birds' nests, and it smoked like Hades. I'd say your old
Timothy Yeo didn't do much cooking, and as for smoke, he must
have loved it. Do have some honey. I got that from young Hesling
down in the valley. I'm going to get a few hives of my own soon."

"You like plenty to do, don't you?" laughed Anne. "What with
the house and the garden and the ducks and the geese and bullocks
you can't find any time left to be bored."

"No, rather not. I find the days go all too fast, there's such a lot
I want to do," he replied. "It's all a great lark. I've always wanted
a bit of land of my own, and I'm enjoying it."

As Anne ate her tea—and being a healthy creature she enjoyed
a good tea—she observed the neat kitchen in which they sat.
Vaughan obviously used this room as his living-room, and he had
a small table with a bookshelf above it on one side of the chimney
piece. There was a typewriter on the table, and the books appeared
to be reference books. Vaughan caught the direction of her glance,
and observed, "I've found the typewriter useful while my eyes
have been out of action. I couldn't see at all for the first month or
two after I was knocked out, and I was glad I'd learnt to type. I'm
able to read again now, though only for a short while at a time.

You can guess how useful all the gardening and house-painting were—kept me from moping. Now what about this cake?—oh, who the dickens is that?"

He got up as Anne cut the cake and opened the kitchen door in answer to the knock. Anne did not look round, but she heard the visitor's voice—it was Tom Gressingham.

"I hope you don't mind me looking you up, Mr. Vaughan," said the deep, complacent voice. "I was wondering if you'd care for a game of bridge. I'm staying down at Hinton Mallory and I've got a couple of cronies staying with me. We'd be delighted if you'd look in for a drink and a game of bridge one evening."

"Thanks, I don't play bridge," replied Vaughan stolidly, and Gressingham replied:

"No? What a pity. This is a very nice little property you've got, Mr. Vaughan. Just the sort of thing I fancy myself."

"I'm afraid it's not to let, and neither is it for sale," replied Vaughan, and his voice was not encouraging.

Gressingham replied: "Oh, I wasn't suggesting anything of that kind, but I hope you won't mind if I just glance round your garden. I'm interested in gardens."

"So am I, and when mine's ready for inspection I'll put up a notice to that effect," replied Vaughan. "Until then, it's private property, like anybody else's garden. Good day to you."

He closed the door and came into the kitchen again. "I hope I haven't been being offensive to a friend of yours, Miss St Cyres," he said, "but that fellow gets my goat. He's always snooping round, and if there's one country habit which I respect it's that of not prying on your neighbours."

"So do I," said Anne firmly. "That, as you probably know, is Mr. Gressingham. He retains rooms at Hinton Mallory and comes

down here frequently. He is a friend of my sister-in-law's, so I try
to be civil to him out of politeness to her, though I admit I don't
like him—and I wasn't a bit sorry to hear you speak to him as
you did. I think it's insufferable for a stranger to come and poke
his nose in and expect to be made free of other people's gardens.
I congratulate you on your cake, Mr. Vaughan. It's a jolly good
cake."

Vaughan cut himself another large slice with a happy grin.
"Seems all right to me," he said, "but I'm not exactly a connoisseur.
Steak and kidney pudding's my long suit, though I often wonder
where all the kidneys go to these days. They're as rare as new-laid
eggs in the Navy."

After they had finished tea Vaughan took Anne round the
empty house, showing the freshly painted bedrooms with the
pride of a schoolboy. He was evidently very clever with his
hands as well as something of a mechanic and electrician. He
had got some of the rooms wired for lighting, but his great pride
was "water laid on." He had contrived a frame to hold a water
cistern at one end of the house and the pipes were already in
place to feed the kitchen sink. Later he intended to fit a bath
in, and told Anne how he overcame the difficulties of boring
holes in the ancient cob walls. She found him an entertaining
person, and entered into all his plans with enthusiasm coupled
to a helpful knowledge of old buildings and the peculiarities
of their fabrics. When she stood at the door to bid him good-
bye and thank him for his courtesy Anne added: "You'll have
to give a party when you've got the house finished—a real
house-warming."

"Rather—I shall—and I hope you and your father will come,"
he replied.

2

When Anne left Little Thatch and turned along the lane to her own home—it was only a few hundred yards away—she saw with some annoyance that Tom Gressingham was just walking towards her in company with June. The latter laughed when she saw Anne.

"So that's where you've been, my dear, hobnobbing with the hermit. I hope you enjoyed yourself."

Anne realised with discomfort that her own face had flushed—a thing which seldom happened. June's voice and manner irritated her, but she replied sedately: "Yes, I enjoyed myself very much, thank you. Mr. Vaughan was showing me how much nicer the house looks now it's all clean and repainted."

"But how nice!" exclaimed Gressingham. "You are privileged, Miss Anne. I thought no one was permitted to view the hermit's property—but you are the exception to prove the rule."

"Walk down to Hinton Mallory with us, Anne," said June. "Tom's got a new radio, and he's also got a new cocktail."

"Come and sample both, and meet my guests, too, Miss Anne," added Gressingham.

"Thanks very much, but I must be getting back," said Anne. "Dickon has a day off, and I've got to see about the hens and ducks."

"Oh, you'll turn into a hen yourself one day," retorted June, and Gressingham put in:

"Not a hen, my child, a duck—it sounds so much prettier."

Anne was conscious of a desire to box his ears, but she replied placidly, "It's all very well for you two to laugh about hens and ducks, but you both love eggs and poultry. If somebody didn't see the birds were fed regularly and safely shut up at night you'd get neither eggs nor roast chick."

"How true," said Gressingham. "Robbing the hen-roost, or the dirge of the duck. I can't tell you how much I admire your constancy, sweet Anne of Manor Thatch."

The two strolled on laughing, and Anne moved on her way, walking parallel with Vaughan's garden. To her surprise she saw him standing by the gate of his pasture.

"I say, if you'd ever like that chap to have the hiding he richly deserves, you've only got to say so," he said. "He's my own idea of a very dirty dog."

"Thanks for saying it, but please don't have any brawls here," replied Anne. "It would make things a lot worse, and I find it hard enough to keep my temper as it is."

Gressingham and June walked together down the sloping meadow path towards Hinton Mallory. It had been one of those rare spring days when the sun was hot enough to make the daffodils hang their heads, and every hedgerow was gay with budding foliage, with blackthorn in drifts of snow whiteness, with willow trees asmother with pollened flowers and primroses shining in enamelled bosses among the fresh green on the banks. June cared nothing for wild flowers, for budding trees or singing birds: lambs could caper and calves leap—she was quite indifferent—but she was aware that her own vitality responded to the rising temperature, to the radiance of the sun and the sense of wellbeing imparted by the gay spring day. She hummed a song as she walked through the meadow, and Gressingham pinched her arm.

"Feeling the old world's not such a bad place after all, honey?—a place to be happy in."

"Oh, the world'd be all right, especially if the damned war was over and I was walking down Piccadilly in decent clothes with some money in my pocket," she replied.

"Why not?" murmured Gressingham, and then added: "I can't make that man out—Vaughan, as he calls himself."

"Why not?" mocked June. "It's his name, isn't it?"

"Maybe, though I should hate to put any money on it," responded Gressingham. "The more I think about him the more I'm convinced there's something fishy about him. Why does a chap like that hide himself down here—because hide he does. He never so much as shows his face outside his own garden, and he's put those wattle screens across every gap in his fences."

"Perhaps he doesn't like people looking into his garden every time they pass by," replied June.

"Does Miss St Cyres go there often?" enquired Gressingham, and she laughed.

"Scenting a scandal, Tom? Don't you believe it! Anne's as virtuous as she's dull, and I can't give her a more complete testimonial. She approves of the Vaughan man, and so does Pops, so he must be a creature after their own hearts, a man who loves mud and dung and farmyard smells, and never expects to enjoy anything. Don't go harping on about him, he bores me, Tom. Tell me about these men you've got staying with you. Anyone amusing?"

"There's Bill Potter—he's been a film actor and he's a very good dancer, also a very good bridge player. He's about thirty years of age and has done most of the things he shouldn't if that's any recommendation. Then there's Rummy Radcliffe—I believe his real front name is Raymond but he's always known as Rummy. He made a pot of money before the war, speculating. He's one of those uncanny birds who can always smell the way the market's going. It's a sort of extra sense, I've never known him slip up—and there aren't many speculators you can say that for."

"Perhaps he'd like to speculate with some of my pennies and make a bean or two for me," said June, but Gressingham laughed.

"Not during the war, sweet—that sort of game can't be played these days. If you want money, June, you can have it. I've told you so."

"Oh, what's the use of saying that—we've argued it all out before," she retorted. "I'm the wife of Denis St Cyres, and the daughter-in-law of that old ramrod, and sister-in-law to that virtuous suet pudding, and here I'm stuck. Damn everything! How do you persuade your friends to come down to this hole, Tom? You must be very attractive to get your men-friends to put up with Hinton Mallory."

"Oh, but I am very attractive—hadn't you noticed it?" he laughed back. "You're very shrewd, June—it's quite true that my visitors have a reason for coming which isn't always connected with roast chicken for dinner and ham and eggs for breakfast. I've got a few ideas, you know, and some of these fellows like to cash in on ideas. Now I don't believe you'd find this part of the world nearly so boring if there was a first-class hotel near at hand—one of the country club variety, with a cocktail bar and a dance floor and all the trimmings."

"Goodness, is that the idea? I thought you told Pops you wanted to farm."

"So I do, until I've acquired some land, honey—then: well, we shall just see."

"Shall we?" she asked speculatively. "You won't get any land here, Tom, and I can't see why you should choose this neighbourhood. It's not the sort of place for a hotel."

"No? Well, you think things out, angel. There's a lot to be said for seclusion—and, believe me, the hotel industry is going to boom in a year or so. Ah, there's Rummy. Don't be put off by appearances, June. I know he's fat—but he's amusing."

They had reached the gate of Hinton Mallory: a pleasant garden lay in front of the old house, and the grass plot had just been scythed—for the benefit of Gressingham and his friends. A very stout man in a checked tweed suit was practising putting on the so-called lawn, and Gressingham called to him.

"Come and be introduced, Rummy. This is Mrs. St Cyres. May I introduce Rummy Radcliffe, June?"

"Charmed," said the stout man. He had a deep booming voice and his round face was almost ludicrous, for he had a tiny pursed up mouth and globular eyes behind exaggerated horn-rimmed glasses.

"He's just like a fish... one of these things in the Zoo Aquarium," thought June to herself. Rummy's hands were fat, podgy and clammy.

"I take it that you come from the Manor," boomed Rummy, "a very fascinating old property, I'd say, but in need of modernising. It's shocking what people put up with. I've been having a nose round, Tom. I should love to be able to develop this property. It'd be the easiest job in the world to make a private road across those fields. No object at all in meandering for miles before you get here. Did you ever see such a crazy business as the road-system hereabouts, Mrs. St Cyres—and as for blind corners, God bless my soul, it's criminal! I was frightened out of my wits before I got here."

"So you may have been," said June, "but the people hereabouts would be delighted to hear you say so. They don't encourage other people's cars in this part of the world, and they're quite happy to drive their own at an average of ten miles an hour."

"You don't say so!" boomed Rummy, and Tom Gressingham put in,

"Come inside and have a quick one, June. Ah, here's Bill."

Bill Potter was tall and lanky—a good contrast to the rotund Rummy, and the four of them strolled into Gressingham's sitting-room, where a new cocktail cabinet had been fitted into a corner and a big portable radio was crooning noisily.

"Did you find a fourth for bridge, Tom?" enquired Potter, but Gressingham shook his head.

"Sorry, I'm afraid I haven't. I'd counted on Howard Brendon, but he couldn't come. Tiresome of him. He's been coming over twice a week for some time past, and he's a damned good bridge player."

"Brendon? Is it true his wife's left him?" asked Rummy, who had been manipulating the cocktail shaker, and Gressingham replied,

"God knows, I don't. I've never seen the lady. I did my best to get a fourth for you, Bill. I went and asked the bloke at Little Thatch."

"Good heavens!" exclaimed June, "you must be mad! Did you really imagine the hermit could play bridge? You're an optimist—and if he did, he'd come in corduroys and reek of cow dung, and lick his fingers every time he played a card. Why, the creature's simply uncouth!"

"Why? Been trying to do the glamour girl at Little Thatch?" enquired Gressingham, and Radcliffe put in:

"Little Thatch? That's the hovel up the hill, isn't it? In the layout I was planning I should make that cottage the lodge—I can see it all."

"Who's the creature you're talking about?" enquired Potter, and Tom Gressingham replied:

"He's the tenant of Little Thatch. He's uncouth to look at, I grant you, but he's an educated man, and he's been in the Navy—and some of those naval blokes are very hot bridge players."

"You make me tired!" laughed June. "He couldn't have been anything but a common rating."

"No matter. Takes all sorts to make a world," said Rummy amiably. "I should like to have had a word with him. If we get things going according to plan, an ex-naval man at the lodge might be useful."

"Useful as chucker-out?" enquired June. "Look here, Tom. It's time you left off leading your friends up the garden path. You *know* you can't get any land round here. It all belongs to my father-in-law, and he'd die rather than sell you any land."

"Keep cool, darling. Your pops isn't the only landowner in the county. Rummy's a bit premature in his plans, but he's always like that. I can't tell you how many properties I've seen him reorganise—on paper. It's a hobby of his, and believe me, some of his ideas come off."

"Don't *you* play bridge, Mrs. St Cyres?" enquired Potter, but June answered, "I do—but my bridge isn't out of the top drawer, and I'm not going to play with you three. I'm too lazy to concentrate. I'd rather play vingt-et-un or roulette."

"That's O.K. by me," said Rummy amiably, and Gressingham put in:

"Toddle home and put on a pretty frock, darling, and come and dine with us. Safety in numbers, and we'll see you home."

"A lovely idea!" said June. "Put on a long frock and pretty slippers and splash through the mud or walk down the field to get here, and then remember Manor Thatch is locked up at ten o'clock. If I stay out after that Anne will sit up until I come in, and offer me hot cocoa when I arrive. No thanks. I said I was lazy, and I am. It's too much bother to argue with them. I've tried it and I'm beaten."

"Darling, don't say that," expostulated Gressingham. "We shall have to get you out of this. Can't have your spirit broken."

"I shall be all right when I live in a civilised place again," said June. "I'm not intending to stay here indefinitely."

She took a few steps in tune to the radio, which was producing dance music, and Bill Potter slipped an arm round her and they slithered in and out between the heavy furniture.

Rummy filled his glass again and addressed Gressingham, "Who is that chap at Little Thatch? I saw him back his car in when I passed. Big hulking brute, what? Think I might go and have a word with him. You never know. That cottage of his might come in very useful."

"You can try to have a word with him if you like, Rummy, but I tell you it's no go. The chap's bats—or else he's a ticket-of-leave man. The one thing he's quite determined about is that he's going to steer clear of everybody. If you go and see him he'll only be offensive."

"That so? Well, a ticket-of-leave man might have his uses. When I'm on to a scheme I'm always out to employ local talent, and, if a fellow's got something to hide, in my opinion it's policy to find out what that something is."

Gressingham shrugged his shoulders and called across the room to June,

"Have another one, honey—just a little one!"

CHAPTER FIVE

I

"COLONEL WRAGLEY SUGGESTED I SHOULD COME AND HAVE a talk with you, Chief Inspector. My name's Wilton, and Nick Vaughan was a friend of mine. I gather you are going to take over that case at the Mallorys."

"How do you do, Commander. I'm very glad to see you, though I didn't know—officially—that I was going to take over in the case you mention."

Chief Inspector Macdonald, C.I.D., stood up to greet his visitor, and the two men took stock of one another. Wilton was a short, squarely built, grizzled fellow, with blue eyes and weather-beaten face: Macdonald was nearly six inches the taller and considerably slimmer, dark haired, grey eyed, with a lean face which had acquired tired lines on it of recent months. According to Macdonald's own comment to one of his colleagues, "chasing criminals all day and dodging buzz-bombs all night is bound to affect a man's temper eventually"; the colleague's reply was worth relating: "If you'd said chasing buzz-bombs all night you'd have been nearer the mark. Never known such an enthusiast for sticky jobs, Jock: rescue squad jobs seem to draw you like a magnet."

In spite of those same tired lines, Macdonald's face looked about ten years younger than Wilton's—they were both close on fifty—so it might be assumed that life on a destroyer detailed for Russian convoys was an even more wearing experience than the London blitz.

Wilton shook hands and added, "Well, I'm not letting any cats out of bags when I tell you that you'll be proceeding to Devon before many hours are over—and about time too."

"The delay hasn't been of my making," said Macdonald. "The trouble is that the County men haven't been able to make up their minds if they've got a case or not."

Wilton growled something inarticulate as he lowered himself into his chair, and then asked, "You've had a report on the business?"

"Yes," replied Macdonald, "though not a very full one. I know that Nicholas Vaughan's body was found in the burnt-out débris of his cottage on May 1st. The cottage was a thatched one and was completely burnt out, the walls collapsing as well as the roof. The local men incline to attribute the outbreak of fire to faulty electric wiring, and the fierceness of the fire to the fact that deceased had a considerable store of paraffin, petrol and paint on the premises."

"Quite correct, and the first assumption was that Nick was asleep and was overcome by smoke and never woke up, and that his skull was cracked by a falling beam. I don't believe that assumption. That's why I'm here," said Wilton, and Macdonald nodded.

"Quite—and that's why I shall be going to Devon. Now I always believe in first-hand evidence. You were not at Little Thatch when the fire occurred, but you know Nicholas Vaughan, so say if you tell me all you can about him. Nobody knows anything much about him at Mallory Fitzjohn."

"Right. Now stop me if I wander on too much, but I'd like to give you a clear picture. I first met Nick Vaughan ten years ago. He was a keen sailor, and we met while we were both sailing our own boats up round the Summer Isles. I liked him, though he was only a youngster. He was only twenty then, and he'd the qualities which make a good sailor—endurance, common sense, manual dexterity, and imagination. I add that because it does something to explain why a man chooses the discomforts and hazards of cruising in a small boat entirely by himself for a holiday."

Macdonald nodded, and held out his tobacco pouch. "I get you," he said, and Wilton took the pouch and filled his pipe as he continued:

"Nick was born in 1914. His father was the son of a small land-owner on the borders of Westmorland and Lancashire—Kirkby Lonsdale way—know it?"

"Aye," said Macdonald.

"Nick's father was killed on the Somme, and his mother died in 1918. Nick was brought up by his uncle and aunt in Lannerdale, on their farm. He went to a north-country grammar school and later to Glasgow University, where he read engineering—marine engineering. He was an able fellow and got a first in his finals. I tell you all this to explain the two qualities in him—he cared for two very dissimilar occupations, seafaring and agriculture. He never saw a garden without wanting to dig in it, and he never saw a seafaring craft without wanting to tinker with it. He could scythe and plough and milk and tend beasts, and he loved doing it. In 1939 he was 25: he'd done his engineering course and he had a job on Clydeside, and a year later he volunteered to take small craft over to Dunkirk. You'll know that story?"

"Aye," said Macdonald. "It's my chief grouse this war that I wasn't on one of those small craft."

"Oh well—can't do everything," said Wilton. "It was a story, though, gad, it was a story!" Wilton puffed away at his pipe and then went on: "Nick made himself useful in that racket: he volunteered as a rating afterwards, and soon found himself in one of those damned-queer shore establishments we improvised to train naval officers. He wrote to me from there, and later he joined my ship. He was one of the most useful chaps I've ever had. He got laid out eventually through trouble with one of our own guns. It was the only turret which could still fire—and then it jammed. It was nearly red hot anyway, and the engineers worked like hell to get it going again—we were under fire the whole time. Then something happened—most of the gun crew got their ticket and I thought Nick had got his, but he lived, and the surgeon wallahs saved his eyes. He was invalided out—for months he was blind, and it was unlikely his eyes'd ever be very useful again. I went and saw him while he was in hospital, and he told me he'd made up his mind to get a small holding and go on the land. I happened to know Colonel St Cyres—he's a distant relative of mine—and I got news of Little Thatch from him, and that was that. Nick loved it at sight, and I reckon he had four happy months there. Now some blackguard has done him in, and it's up to you to find out who."

"Right," said Macdonald. "I haven't had enough opportunity to examine the evidence to tell you whether I shall agree with your assumption eventually, but let's use it as a working hypothesis. You believe Vaughan was murdered. Can you tell me your grounds for that assumption?"

"Take the police theory and examine it," replied Wilton. "They suggest the fire started from faulty wiring. If Nick did that wiring you can take it from me it wasn't faulty. He was not only a skilful mechanic, he was a scrupulously careful one. He wouldn't have run any risk in that cottage of his: if the fire was caused by the wiring, then somebody tampered with the wiring. Then the next bit is about the petrol and paraffin and paint stored in the cottage. I tell you it's all wrong. Nick never kept quantities of petrol and paraffin in any place where he had a kitchen range going. He had an allowance of petrol for his pump and plant, I grant you, but he'd have stored it in the outbuildings. If there was petrol to help the cottage burn—well, it was planted there without Nick's knowledge. Finally, he didn't wake up when the fire started and was asphyxiated in his sleep. Kindly remember that Nick was a sailor—he had the knack we all get of waking up when anything happens. If he had been a farm labourer and nothing else, I'd have believed he might have slept while his roof burnt over his head, but for a sailor to do that, a man who has been trained to an alertness which *smells* danger before it occurs—tell me that man stayed asleep to be burnt in his bed—rubbish! He stayed asleep because his skull was cracked *before* the fire got going, not afterwards."

"Yes, I can see all the points you've made, and they're good points," admitted Macdonald. "I could put up a counter-argument if I wanted to, but I'm not out to argue with you at the moment. I'm out to collect information. You say Vaughan was murdered. If so, by whom and for what reason? In other words, do you know if he had any enemies, or was there anybody who had a reason to murder him?"

"Frankly, I don't know. If I knew of anybody who was out for his blood I should have told you so."

"Was Vaughan a quarrelsome man?"

"No, certainly not—not in the sense of picking quarrels, but he was a damned difficult beggar if he got a down on anybody. If Nick believed a man was a wrong'un he'd watch out and pin him down somehow—and I've never known him mistaken in his judgment. It's difficult to tell you much about him because he was one of those reserved fellows—never talked about himself or his own affairs. I told you I've known him for ten years and been shipmate with him for three, but I know precious little about him. I know he was straight, and he was a man I could rely on, utterly. He was incapable of letting you down."

"Did he write to you at all? I take it's some months since you saw him?"

"I saw him last December, when I had a week's leave. It was then I told him about Little Thatch, and I damn well wish I hadn't."

"Where did you meet?"

"At my cousin's place at Culverton, Okehampton way. I knew Nick was out of hospital and due for discharge, so I got George to ask him along—I'm a bachelor myself. Nick had written telling me that he was looking out for a place in South Devon."

"Have you any idea why he wanted to live in Devon?"

"No, I don't think I have. I never questioned it. Seemed a good choice to me—Devon's my own county. It's fertile, good climate and that, wonderful pasture, and you're not too far away from the sea. There's good sailing around Salcombe, and you can get across to Falmouth and the Cornish ports."

"Did he mention sailing when he talked about settling in Devon?"

"No, but it wouldn't have been far from his thoughts. Why do you ask?"

"Only this. You're a Devonian. I'm of Highland extraction. I like Devon for a holiday, but I could never settle there. Too warm and lush, with those deep sunken lanes and dense vegetation. I happen to know the country where Vaughan was reared—just to the west of the Pennines. It's grand hill country, where you can see for miles with the limestone hills clear against the skyline. A clean, clear, cold, untrimmed country. I can't understand anybody reared in sight of Ingleborough going to live in Devon."

"Then your judgment's at fault, because Nick did so choose. It wasn't I who suggested Devon, it was he who asked me about it."

"Right. Next, did you have any letters from him while he was at Little Thatch?"

"Yes. I had a couple of long screeds—both typewritten. I'll show them to you sometime. The first was all about his property and the work he was doing. The second mentioned some of the folk at the Mallorys—and there's a point worth noting in it. He mentioned a chap staying at Hinton Mallory and called him a proper chiser—that for Nick was equivalent to saying a bad lot. He may have spotted some queer goings-on. You'll be looking round the place yourself, so you can see if there's anything in it. No names mentioned in his letters."

"I'll certainly look around. Now think over this next question carefully. You say Vaughan was a fine engineer, and that he got a first. You also say he had imagination. Do you think it was likely that he was doing any original work which might have been valuable?"

"Designs, patents and that? No, I don't. To begin with, you need equipment—workshop, lathe, materials: you work on models. Paper work doesn't get you far. It's the model which tells you the snags. Then there's his eyesight to remember. It was still weak— that's why he typed in preference to writing. And you've got to remember the amount of work he put in on the house and land. He worked in the garden till dusk: then he got busy house painting. In addition to all that he cooked his own meals, tended his stock, fetched all the goods he needed in that Heath Robinson car of his, and he'd fitted an old petrol engine to the pump, put up a greenhouse and assembled an electric plant. No. He'd have had no time for anything else."

Macdonald sat and meditated, then he said: "It comes to this: a peaceful, law-abiding agriculturist is suddenly murdered for no reason that anybody can provide. Before you can convince any jury that the man was murdered you've got to provide a reason—a motive—for murdering him. That will be my first job—to look out for a motive. Meantime, since you're the man who is shouting murder, it's up to you to give every possible detail to help the enquiry. So far as is known at present, Vaughan hadn't got anything of value in his cottage. It's known he kept no cash on the premises—his banker can assure us of that. There were no portable valuables, silver or plate, and the cottage wasn't really furnished. His bedroom and kitchen had only the minimum of equipment. So far as it's possible to ascertain, robbery is ruled out. Any comment to make on that?"

"No. Nick had a limited amount of capital—"

"Yes. It's still intact, barring what he'd spent on equipment for the cottage. He was a methodical soul and his bank statement covers every item of expenditure. His living expenses cost him a pound a week. Other cheques drawn covered his petrol pump, electric plant, and greenhouse—all bought second-hand. He paid cash down for his stock and feed."

"Gad, you seem to have made a few enquiries," said Wilton, and his naive expression caused Macdonald to laugh a little.

"Yes, just a few. The Royal Navy isn't the only competent service on His Majesty's pay-roll. I'm not being offensive when I say this: I am about as competent to query the manner in which you command your craft as you are competent to criticise police-work. We don't make a song about it, but the amount of honest conscientious enquiry carried out by every country bumpkin of a police constable is a thing of which I have a right to be proud."

Wilton's jaw had dropped a little, and then he laughed too, as he stretched out his hand.

"Shake hands, Chief Inspector. I like that. I'm damned proud of my own ratings. Now, see here. It looks to you as though I've made a tidy-sized bloody fool of myself. I sail in and make fast alongside and proceed to teach you your business—a job of which I know nothing. I apologise, but I *don't* withdraw. I believe Nick Vaughan was murdered."

"And you're perfectly right to say so and to stick to it, and I respect you for it," said Macdonald. "Now let's get down to it. At first glance it seems reasonable to dismiss robbery as a motive: no valuable plans or strategic secrets, no portable valuables: no show of wealth—rather the reverse. Vaughan lived like a working man: he paid market rates to anybody he employed, but he didn't chuck his money about—I recognise his type, a straight, hard-dealing north countryman. He didn't drink: he looked in at the nearest local occasionally and chatted with the farmers, but he made one pint of cider last a long time. Next, what about his dealings with women? Anything to contribute along those lines?"

Wilton shook his head. "Nix. Never known him to run after a skirt. You know what it's like when a ship gets to port after a long cruise—the lads are out after the women. I've never known Nick bother his head about a woman. You said he was canny over money—not mean, but careful. That's true: he hadn't got it in him to rip or play ducks and drakes. He was often ragged about it in the ward-room. He wasn't exactly what's called an ascetic—he enjoyed good living—but he was what I should call selective—critical, and tending to be remote from men who took their pleasures lightly. I suppose what I'm telling you is that Nick was an idealist. He wouldn't have liked the word, because he hated the high-falutin', but just as he kept his capital intact, so he kept his emotions intact. Didn't hold with spreading himself or loose living. I hope I'm not giving you a wrong impression. Nick wasn't one of those censorious Puritans who're always blaming other people: he was popular with his fellow-officers and popular with the men, but he just didn't go out after women. As for getting drunk, I've seen him lower enough liquor to lay most men out, and he never batted an eyelid. Told me afterwards it was a damn' poor way of spending your money."

"Yes. I know the type: it's all of a piece with his upbringing," said Macdonald, "but see here. Nicholas Vaughan was making that cottage into a home any woman might have been happy to live in. Do you believe all that paint and polish was for himself—electric points here and there, negotiations for an electric boiler, a valuable second-hand carpet for the sitting-room and carpet on the stairs. Does that sound like continued bachelorhood to you?"

"Well, no," agreed Wilton. "The further you go into this the more I realise I'm out of my depth. I'd never have thought about carpets—but how do *you* know about them, anyway? The place was properly burnt out—I've seen it."

"Yes, you've seen it. I haven't seen it yet, but I've got the report of the County men—despise them if you like. Some large-footed constable went into a lot of shops and slowly and painstakingly found out just what Nicholas Vaughan had got for the cheques he'd paid out. He paid £7 1os. at one sale for a tea-set—I'm told it'd have fetched £20 in London."

"Tea-set?" queried Wilton helplessly. "£7 1os. for a tea-set?"

"Yes, Commander, and Nicholas Vaughan was no spendthrift. Any comments?"

"Well I'm damned!" said Wilton. "It looks as though you're right, doesn't it? He must have been meaning to get married, but he never told me anything about it."

"Does that strike you as odd? You'd been good friends, you say."

"Yes, confound you, nothing phoney there. Nick was my friend and I was his, and it's on that account that I'm here, no matter what sort of fool I look."

"You don't look any sort of fool to me, Commander," said Macdonald. "I tell you frankly that I'm as likely to waste time over fools in my department as you are in yours. You're a man with a hunch. You've looked into this business of Vaughan's death and you believe it was caused by foul play. That belief is strong enough to make you put up with a certain amount of plain speech from me without resenting it. But if anybody walked on to your bridge and told you that some knave was monkeying with the navigation, I take it you'd ask for evidence. This is my bridge, in a manner of speaking."

"Yes. All right," growled Wilton. "I'm doing my best, you know."

Macdonald chuckled. "Right. Let's try again. You admit that the evidence goes a long way to show that Vaughan intended to get married, but he never mentioned it to you, though you were good friends, and it was due to your good offices that Vaughan got that cottage. Think again: hadn't the subject of matrimony ever been mentioned between you?"

"Yes, in a manner of speaking. One or two of our ship's company had got spliced, and in the usual way we gave 'em a wedding present and drank their healths, and the remaining bachelors made a few ribald remarks concerning their own immunity from trouble."

"In which remarks Vaughan joined?"

"Not particularly. He just sat tight. Nick never told bawdy stories, but neither did he complain when the others did. He had a gift for taciturnity."

"When you told him about Little Thatch, wasn't the subject of housekeeping mentioned between you?"

"Yes. Now I come to think of it I did say he'd have to look out for a housekeeper—unless he intended to get married."

"And he made no comment?"

"Just so. He made no comment."

"You may think I'm labouring this issue unduly, Commander, but I think the point which emerges is important. Here was a man planning his house with an eye to matrimony, and he's so secretive about it that he doesn't give his best friend an inkling of his intentions. It seems odd to me."

Commander Wilton rubbed his short-cut grey hair, with a puzzled look on his face. "I don't know about that," he growled. "You've no proof Nick *did* mean to marry. A man can have carpets on the stairs and buy tea-sets for himself."

"Admittedly. I've taken a circuitous route over this for reasons of my own, because I wanted to be quite certain that Vaughan had never mentioned the subject of marriage to you—but he *was* going to get married. He told Colonel St Cyres so in confidence when he first negotiated the property, and St Cyres, being punctilious about confidences, had not mentioned the matter to anybody. He told the Superintendent about it when the matter of Vaughan's next-of-kin was raised after his death."

"All right. I expect Nick had his reasons for not talking about it," rejoined Wilton testily. "Who's the lady, anyway?"

"I don't know, Commander. Neither does anybody else. You see, all his papers and letters were destroyed in the fire, and the lady has not put in an appearance. Now you probably know some of Vaughan's friends. I think you might try to find out something about his 'intended,' as folks used to say."

"I don't fancy myself in that rôle," growled Wilton. "It's bad enough for the girl to lose her man without being badgered by enquiries."

Macdonald sat silent for a while. Then he said:

"You're convinced that a friend of yours has been murdered. You're so certain of it that you go over the heads of very competent and conscientious police officers to impress your point of view on an old friend—my Assistant Commissioner, Colonel Wragley. It so happens that the Commissioner's Office had already been consulted, but that is not the point. You've put before the authorities your own belief that Vaughan was murdered. In all honesty, you have got to implement that belief to the best of your ability. It's no use having compunction about badgering people—now. It's no use saying chivalrously, 'Leave the women out of it'—now. It won't do. You've come to me, and you have helped to convince me that further enquiry is desirable. The things you don't know have done as much to convince me as the things you do know. There it is. You've urged the necessity for an enquiry. Don't blame anybody else if the course of the enquiry isn't palatable."

There was a moment's silence again, then Wilton said: "Yes. I suppose I asked for all that. I'll say this: if I were a murderer I shouldn't care to have you on my track. I'll do what I can, and if I get any information you shall have it."

"Right. Meantime I had better find out from the authorities just where I stand in the matter."

"You'll be going down to Mallory Fitzjohn?"

"Presumably—if I'm given the case to investigate."

"Then may I come down and tell you anything I find out?"

"That's as you wish, Commander. I can promise you no privileges beyond those shared by the general public, but I do want your co-operation."

"Right. You'll see me there before long. I'm not much of a hand at writing reports. I'd rather report in person."

"As you wish. Good-day to you."

Commander Wilton left Scotland Yard rather less critical of police procedure than he had been when he arrived. In fact as he left Cannon Row he took out his handkerchief and mopped his forehead. "The hell of a fellow," he said to himself. It was quite a long time since Commander Wilton had been firmly dealt with by a mere civilian.

2

When Wilton had left, Macdonald went down to see Colonel Wragley, and the Chief Inspector knew from long experience what the Assistant Commissioner's gambit would be. Wragley's "Well, what do you make of it?" was a familiar query in the C.I.D.

"It's an interesting story, sir. I feel disposed to think further investigation is indicated—though that is in no sense a criticism of the County men. They have done their part of the job well. While I'm by no means prepared to say that I believe Vaughan was murdered, I think there are a few gaps in the evidence which ought to be filled in."

"Hm... cautious as ever, Macdonald," said Wragley. "I look forward to the day when you'll commit yourself to a really rash whole-hog and certain opinion—which I shall have the pleasure of disproving later. Carry on, fill in the gaps and don't be in too much hurry. I doubt if you've had a full night's sleep since you were up in Lunesdale last September. Go and browse in Devon and good luck to you. We shall survive without you for a week or two."

Macdonald chuckled: he was accustomed to Wragley's rather ponderous humour, and he was very fond of his old chief, despite the number of occasions they had been at cross-purposes.

"Thank you, sir," he replied. "I feel that your attitude is an exposition of practical Christianity, whether to me, or to the Department, or to the Royal Navy, I'm not quite sure."

"Call it all three, you hair-splitting Presbyterian," chuckled Wragley. Then he sobered down and added: "This Nicholas Vaughan seems to have been a damn' fine sailor. We owe it to a chap like that to do all we can to... er... honour his memory."

"Yes, sir," agreed Macdonald. "Battle honours from the C.I.D. I'll do my best to see that nothing's left undone which should have been done."

CHAPTER SIX

I

MACDONALD DECIDED TO TRAVEL DOWN TO DEVONSHIRE by the night train. He calculated that it would be less crowded than the morning trains, and he would probably get a chance to sleep for a few hours instead of standing in the corridor. He was fortunate, for having taken a first-class ticket without any conviction that its possession would ensure him a first-class seat, he came across an old guard who knew and liked him: this worthy led Macdonald to a compartment where three naval officers occupied three corners, and the C.I.D. man gratefully took the fourth and asked no questions as the guard locked the door.

During the first hour of his journey Macdonald studied the report sent in by Superintendent Bolton, and memorised the salient facts. Nicholas Vaughan, for four months tenant of Little Thatch, had last been seen alive on the evening of April 30th. Vaughan had gone out in his car at 6 o'clock in the evening—several witnesses vouched for this fact—and Vaughan had returned, according to old Reuben Dickon, at 9 o'clock. The road to Mallory Fitzjohn was a lonely one: on the two miles between the main Exeter road and Little Thatch there were only two houses built direct on to the road: one was Ridd's farm, a mile and a half away from Little Thatch, one was Corner Cottage, inhabited by Reuben Dickon. Corner Cottage was well-named, for it stood just above one of those difficult blind corners hated by all motorists. Every driver had to change gear to crawl round the corner and to negotiate the steep gradient beyond, and every driver also sounded a horn and waited for a response before turning that corner. To meet another vehicle head-on on a steep gradient in a lane which was just wide enough for one car was an experience to be avoided. Reuben Dickon lived at the cottage with his wife and a boy of ten years named Alf. Alf had been billeted on the Dickons during the 1940 blitz, and there Alf had stayed. His parents, who had lived in Shoreditch, had both been killed. Mrs. Dickon had got fond of the small Cockney and found him increasingly useful as he grew larger and stronger. The Billeting Officer looked into the matter occasionally, but saw no reason to interfere with an arrangement which gave mutual satisfaction. Alf had almost forgotten his parents and he had no wish to return to Shoreditch: he had grown to like cows and calves and fields and farms. Life with the Dickons was "Oke." The village school was "Oke." The Billeting Officer wisely let well alone. Alf was a not unimportant witness in the matter of Nicholas Vaughan's death. Dickon had attested that Vaughan had passed his cottage on the return journey to Little Thatch at 9 p.m. on April 30th. The interrogating sergeant had asked, "How can you be certain?" Dickon was very deaf, and his eyesight none of the best. For reply, Dickon had roared, "Alf! Come 'ere."

Alf had come, an alert, comic-looking urchin in a cut-down pair of corduroy trousers which were hitched up to his arm-pits. Alf claimed—and demonstrated later that he could substantiate his claim—to be able to recognise the sound of every car and vehicle which passed Corner Cottage. He knew the sound of Colonel St Cyres' big Austin and of Anne St Cyres' small Morris: he could tell Mr. Gressingham's Daimler and Mr. Hesling's Ford, he could even tell whether the tractor which passed the cottage was the tractor from Hinton Mallory or that from Ridd's Farm. Furthermore, Alf

was an expert on Klaxons, horns and hooters. He could hear any
motor horn sounded at the road-bend half a mile away, and Alf,
like many small boys, had a precocious memory for subjects which
interested him. He gave the Superintendent a full and correct list
of every vehicle which had passed Corner Cottage on Saturday,
April 30th, plus the approximate time such vehicle had passed. The
time of Vaughan's journeyings were fixed very easily. Mrs. Dickon
had an old wireless set (given to her by Anne St Cyres) and the
old lady tuned in to the news at 6 and 9 o'clock regularly—she
had grandsons on most of the battle fronts and liked to hear the
news from France and Italy, Burma and the Pacific. Alf bore out
old Dickon in saying that Mr. Vaughan's car had passed Corner
Cottage at six, driving in the direction of the Exeter road, and that
Vaughan had waved his hand, as he always did when he passed.
Dickon and Alf had been working in their own garden at six. At
nine Dickon was smoking his pipe at the gate and Alf was chew-
ing a crust of bread and jam at his bedroom window. They both
saw the car return and again Vaughan had waved to them. Some
time later—about half-past ten, Alf thought—Mr. Gressingham's
car had passed, travelling in the direction of the main road, away
from Hinton Mallory. Alf was in bed then, but he was as sure of
the car and its direction as if he had seen it.

Sometime in the middle of the night Alf had woken up, and as
he turned over he saw that his small window was aglow with light.
For the first time for years an old fear had assailed the Cockney-
bred boy. He had seen a light like that before and his reaction was
"air-raid." He had tumbled out of bed and gone to the window
and realised there was a big fire burning somewhere. As his sleep-
bemused mind cleared, he knew from the direction of the flare
that it must be Little Thatch which was burning. Alf's bedroom

was a tiny slip of a room opening out of the main bedroom where old Dickon and his wife snored peacefully. The boy had gone into them and at length awoken them, yelling, "Mr. Vaughan's 'ouse is afire. It's burning like blazes."

The old couple refused to believe him, or to get up and go to the window. Alf was fond of Nicholas Vaughan: the ex-sailor had been kind to Dickon's "vaccy" and the small boy hero-worshipped Vaughan after his kind. Alf had put on his boots and coat and run down the lane to Little Thatch, and it was Alf whose shrill cries had roused the household at Manor Thatch at 3 o'clock on May morning.

2

Day was dawning as Macdonald's train ran along the Exe valley. The C.I.D. man stretched himself contentedly, not to say luxuriously. He had slept well in his corner seat: even the train stop at Taunton had only caused him a vaguely pleasant awareness, "Taunton... I needn't wake up yet." Now he looked out on lush green meadows where the first buttercups were shining, and saw the swift running river wending its devious way through the water meadows, fringed with willows in the glory of May time foliage. "A good world... and what a mess we do make of it," meditated Macdonald. His three naval companions still slept peacefully, and continued to sleep as Macdonald alighted from the fuggy compartment and stepped in to the chill freshness of early morning as the station announcer gave out: "Exeter, St Davids. This is Exeter, St Davids. Change here for the Southern Railway."

Suitcase in hand, Macdonald went to the barrier to ask about a train for Mallowton, and saw a tall fellow in uniform.

"Chief Inspector Macdonald? I drove in to meet you. There isn't a Mallowton train for nearly two hours, and it's poor work waiting on a platform at this hour."

"Jolly good of you," said Macdonald as he shook hands. "Superintendent Bolton, is it?"

"That's right, Chief. I've got a thermos of tea in the car. I expect you can do with it."

"By jove I can!" said Macdonald. "This is a real Devonshire welcome."

"We do our best, but the county's shorn of its glories in wartime," laughed the other. "Still, my missis will have a good breakfast waiting for you. The time-honoured ham and eggs, though the cream is missing."

"Sounds like a dream to me," said Macdonald. "My monthly egg was laid by a bantam—a long time ago."

Bolton turned his car along the road parallel with the railway after Macdonald had put down the steaming cup of tea.

"Reckon you don't want to see our ruins like most visitors do," said Bolton. "Blitzed cities can't be any new sight to you."

"My God, no," said Macdonald fervently. "Don't mention bombs to me—but, by gad, I like your meadows and the river. That must be a bonny fishing river in the upper reaches."

"You've said it. There's a reach I'd like to show you between Bickleigh and Tiverton—and it looks as though I might have the pleasure. I didn't want to put you off coming—only too glad to see you—but I can't see there's any room for a criminal in this Little Thatch business. That poor chap didn't realise the danger from fire in these old thatched cottages. The same thing's happened again and again when strangers have taken over old properties in this county. However, I don't want to spoil your breakfast by talking shop at this hour. This village we're coming to is Newton St Giles; pretty place—used to be much prettier when all the cottages were whitewashed. Someone said the white village made too good a target by moonlight, so they painted it mud-colour."

Macdonald studied the layout of the village as they drove up the curving street between ancient thatched cottages, whose eaves seemed to huddle together as for company. How old were these cottages? Centuries old, he guessed—and they hadn't caught fire...

Beyond Newton St Giles the road rose to an eminence which gave them their first wide view of the countryside, and Macdonald was almost dazzled by the vividness of its colour in the sunrise. Emerald green of river meadows, rose red of banks and soil, pink and white of fruit blossoms—the brief panorama glowed with an intensity of colour which could not be rivalled in England. It had a jewelled aspect, but Macdonald's Scottish mind was not wholly given to admiration. Was it too vivid, too luxuriant, too flamboyant?—but at least it wasn't battle-scarred: serene, peaceful, complacent perhaps, Devon glowed in the May sunshine.

The Superintendent drove his visitor to a pleasant little modern house on the outskirts of Mallowton: brick and tiles, Macdonald noted, with steel-framed windows.

"You don't favour thatch and cob walls yourself, then?" queried Macdonald, and Bolton laughed.

"Not for me, thanks. You can have your picturesqueness—like Newton St Giles—but give me upright walls which don't collapse when you put a book-shelf up, and a decent damp-course, and taps that run. If you'd like a wash you'll find the water's nice and hot in the bathroom."

It was: and the bathroom, like the whole house, was immaculate—modern, hygienic, labour-saving. "How glad his wife must be that he doesn't hanker for the county picturesqueness," said the Chief Inspector to himself. "Yet this house might be anywhere—Eastbourne, Gorlestone or Hampstead Garden City: still, constant hot water *is* a pleasant asset."

Mrs. Bolton gave Macdonald a very excellent breakfast, introduced him to her two charming round-faced infants, and saw to it that no "shop" was talked at her breakfast table. When Macdonald had eaten his fill she said firmly to her husband, "Take the Chief Inspector to your study, Frank. The room's been done and no one will disturb you."

Mrs. Bolton was undoubtedly a jewel of a wife.

The Superintendent led Macdonald to a sunny little room redolent of furniture polish, and said:

"I think I put everything germane to the case in my report. Now if there are any questions you'd like to ask?"

"Actually there are very few," replied Macdonald. "Your report was admirable, and I congratulate you on the work you and your men put into it. I said all this to Commander Wilton—and he wasn't quite so sceptical about the ability of the police to paddle their own canoe when I'd finished saying my bit."

"Thank you for that, Chief. I admit he got my goat a bit, but I look at it this way, as I said to my missis. He's certain his friend was murdered: he just feels that way. I feel the opposite, and each of us tends to read the evidence in a way which will support our own ideas."

"Very fairly put," said Macdonald. "Now tell me, if you can, why you feel that foul play is ruled out."

Bolton sat and formulated his thoughts, and then he said: "This man Vaughan was a stranger to these parts. When he came nobody knew anything about him. The tendency was, as it always is in the country, to view him with some misgivings—criticise him and wait for him to make mistakes and come a cropper. Well, that didn't happen. Folks liked him. The farmers liked him. They found he was unassuming and that he talked sense and was anxious to learn a bit about farming methods in vogue down here. He admitted to his own ignorance of the strains of cattle we raise in Devon, and to our methods of treating them. He wasn't used to seeing dairy cattle out at pasture all the year round, and he admitted he tended to underrate the amazing fertility of the soil. But the farmers judged that he was a pretty shrewd and hard-working fellow. 'Him was making a do of it,' one old chap said to me, 'and him's a good judge of cattle.' To put it shortly, he was generally liked, and folk were pleased that he *was* making a do of it in a modest way. It seems he was liked in the Navy, too. I went and talked to a young chap in hospital near Plymouth. Been on Vaughan's ship—Destroyer, wasn't it? He was popular with his men, too. They liked him and trusted him. Now why on earth should a nice chap like that get himself murdered? It doesn't make any sort of sense to me. He was quiet and modest—didn't put people's backs up by being pretentious: he was straight and steady-going, didn't drink or carry on. It wasn't a matter of robbery, I'm pretty certain of that. I just can't see any sense in suggesting he was murdered."

Macdonald nodded. "Yes. I see your point of view. You have looked into his affairs to some extent and found that he was a business-like fellow, everything straight and in order. You know he was liked and respected in the district, and you can learn nothing of any enmities or disputes."

"That's so. I can't find a soul who's got a grudge against him. Vaughan achieved a difficult thing: he came to a district as hide-bound in tradition as any in England, and in four months he'd earned the respect of his neighbours."

"Duly noted. Now about this wiring for his house. I take it it wasn't inspected by anybody since it was a private plant?"

"That's so. He bought the plant second-hand and a lot of the wiring and insulating pipe second-hand. The plant came from old Lord Bodley's house: the rest of the stuff was bought from a builder and electrician who is retiring from business. Now I ask you—isn't there a good chance of a short circuit when you buy wiring that isn't new?"

Macdonald nodded. "Admitted, but I think Wilton made a point when he urged that Vaughan was a very competent engineer as well as a very careful chap. A man like that would have tested every bit of his wiring and seen to it his fuses did the job they were meant to do. However, to look at another aspect of it: did Vaughan have anybody in to help him with the job?"

"He had only two people working for him at any time. One was old Dickon, who helped in the garden and lent a hand occasionally in lifting stuff which was awkward for one man to lift: the other was Mrs. Warren, who did Vaughan's laundry—the straightest old dame who ever 'obliged' a lonely bachelor. No, if there was a fault, Vaughan was the man responsible for it."

"Did he have any neighbours in to show them the place?"

"It's difficult to say he had any neighbours—barring the St Cyres at the big house. I do know this: Vaughan wasn't the sort of man to encourage passers-by to come in and have a look-see. He believed in the adage about the Englishman's house being his castle, and the country folk respected him for it." Bolton paused for a while and then added: "See here. That cottage—Little Thatch—hadn't been overhauled for goodness knows how long.

Miss St Cyres told me that Vaughan had been up his kitchen chimney and found some bricks out of place, which made the fire smoke. Doubtless he removed the bricks, and how do we know he didn't bare a beam, which smouldered for days, maybe? I tell you it's not safe for any man, naval engineer or otherwise, to monkey with chimneys in thatched cottages in Devon. Those old buildings require specialist attention from builders who've known such fabrics all their lives."

Macdonald laughed. "I'm beginning to feel I've got a trip on false pretences: you haven't left me much to do. Now what about this suggestion concerning petrol and paraffin."

"Yes, Chief. The arson-raiser's delight. We had the Fire Service wallahs on to it. The fire started at the west end of the cottage, in the kitchen. The room Vaughan slept in was over the kitchen and his camp bed stood by the chimney wall. The stairs from kitchen to bedroom were comparatively modern—about seventy years old, not made of old oak like the main staircase. Vaughan kept a four-gallon drum of paraffin in a cupboard under the kitchen stairs. We know that, because the man from the stores which supplied his paraffin told us so. His store of petrol was in drums outside, *but* he had had a gallon tin of petrol in the kitchen some time. Here is the most probable explanation of what happened. A beam in the chimney smouldered and eventually the smoke seeped through the upper part of the chimney into Vaughan's room while he was asleep. Then the floor caught: that floor was a light wood floor put in when the kitchen stairs were built. Then some wooden packing cases caught fire, then the wood round the window, then the thatch. After that it was all UP. The bedroom floor crashed down fairly early on, the paraffin drum burst, and the petrol can, and thereafter the thing was a raging inferno. It was three o'clock when young Alf woke up the Manor Thatch people—probably five hours since Vaughan had gone to bed. The thatch was burning from end to end like merry hell then. What could they do? The farm men came up with ladders from Hinton Mallory, hoping to tear the thatch down, but the kitchen ceiling had fallen in and the bedroom floor, and the paraffin was ablaze. The sparks got on to the linhey and part of the outbuildings blazed up. My God, when that Naval Commander came and told me that houses don't burn unless someone sets fire to them, I asked him what he knew about old thatched cottages, after a month's drought, if you'll believe it. We had no rain in April—a thing unknown hereabouts. There had been a dry east wind blowing for three weeks and a hot sun shining the last few days as well."

"Yes," said Macdonald. "It was just the moment for a thatch to burn. Now I've got two questions to ask—not connected with the fire. First, have you been able to learn anything of the woman Vaughan was to have married?"

"No. Nothing. Personally I don't believe he meant what Colonel St Cyres thought he meant. You ask him—he's a very exact old chap. Vaughan did *not* say he was engaged. He only said he hoped—or meant—to get married."

"Right. The second question is this: where did he go that last evening of his life, when he was away for three hours on a fine light evening at a season of the year when most gardeners toil till dusk?"

"Yes," admitted Bolton. "There you have me. I don't know, and nobody has offered to tell me. We've tried to trace his car and failed."

"Well, I'm glad you've left me some pretext for earning my keep. Now I think I'll go out and view the ruins—not a cheerful job."

"You've said it. I hate fires. Gave me the pip to see that place… Would you like a car?"

"No, but I'd like a push-bike. It's only three miles."

"Good for you! I'll lend you mine—but you can have a car if you'd like it."

"No need. I haven't had any decent exercise for months. Thank your wife again for my good breakfast and say I'll be seeing her before I go back to London town."

"Don't be in too much hurry—there's a nice bit of fishing for you up Bickleigh way…"

3

Having studied his map, Macdonald mounted his borrowed bike and pedalled off along the Tiverton road on his way to Mallory Fitzjohn. It was a glorious morning and the Devonshire orchards were at their gayest: Macdonald's only grouse was that he couldn't see over the hedges, the road was too deep set between its banks. When he reached the signpost which pointed to Mallory Fitzjohn, Hinton Mallory and Upton Mallory, he turned left as directed, and found himself in the Devonshire lane proper, a narrow, twisting roadway deep sunk between hawthorn hedges: the effect of the snowy blossom and the prolific cow parsley which brushed his handle bars was bridal in its gaiety, though the Scots inspector found the heavy fragrance and balmy air made him sleepy. He would have liked to take his coat off and roll up his shirt sleeves, but decorum forbade such indulgence. He soon passed Corner Cottage, and noted the old man working in the garden: that would be Reuben Dickon, but, remembering that the old man was very deaf, Macdonald decided to leave any conversation with him until some future occasion. After negotiating the corner he saw the tower of Mallory Fitzjohn Church rising above the hedgerows, but

with characteristic Devonshire complexity the road turned away
from its destination and wandered leisurely round the borders of
several eccentric fields before it made another bid for its objective.
A steep hill and a couple more turns brought him into a straight
stretch of lane and to the charred ruins of Little Thatch.

Macdonald was inured to charred ruins—he had worked in
many since 1940, seeking the remains of not one human being but
many, yet the pathos of this ruin caught at his throat. The house
was but a heap of shapeless cob walls, with a stone buttress and
open chimney at one end. The rest had fallen in, but apple blossom
swayed within a few yards of the ruin and thrushes called in the
garden. The garden seemed the saddest sight of all: close to the
house the neatly dug beds were trampled to mud: farther down,
towards the hedges, every bed clearly defined and neatly edged.
Cottage tulips still bloomed in the borders, Arabis and Aubretia
spread gay carpets of colour: wallflowers scented the air. Young
Brassicas grew bravely in orderly rows, potatoes were well forward,
broad beans and carrots. Looking from ruined house to trampled
garden, Macdonald found himself saying, "Damnation... It's not
fair. That chap must have worked so hard." It was as though the
ghost of Nicholas Vaughan haunted the garden, and Macdonald
visualised him as a big broad-shouldered chap happily putting in
pea-sticks and planting those neat rows of young lettuces. "A sorry
sight": the futile words echoed in his mind, and their rejoinder,
"A foolish thought to say a sorry sight," while a big marmalade
cat came and rubbed hopefully round his ankles. "Well, Nicholas
Vaughan, if there was any dirty work here I'll damn well see that
somebody gets what he deserves," said Macdonald to himself, and
bent to caress the optimistic cat.

CHAPTER SEVEN

I

JUST AS HE WAS TURNING TO LEAVE LITTLE THATCH, Macdonald came face to face with an elderly gentleman clad in pleasant, comfortable-looking tweeds of faded greyish blue. So sure was Macdonald of the gentleman's identity that he said, "Colonel St Cyres?" without much of a question in his voice.

"Yes. You have business here?"

"Yes, sir. My name is Macdonald, and I am an officer of the Criminal Investigation Department. I am here on duty, concerning the enquiry into the death of Nicholas Vaughan. He was your tenant, I understand."

"Yes, Chief Inspector. I don't know if there is any way in which I can assist you, but if you want to make any enquiries of me, will you come to my house—it is quite close at hand. Frankly, I find all this"—and he waved his hand in the direction of the desolation which had been Little Thatch—"intolerably distressing."

"I have every sympathy with you, sir," responded Macdonald. "I thought I was hardened to the sight of burnt-out ruins, we have had too many such experiences in London, but the sight of this place is enough to depress anybody. I should be glad to talk the case over with you when you can spare the time."

"Come now—I'm at liberty any time you wish," said St Cyres, turning away from the gate. "I can't tell you how wretched we have felt over it. Vaughan was a man after my own heart, and though I had only known him for a few months I was much attached to him."

He led Macdonald along the lane behind the cottage, and they continued for about a hundred yards until the gates of the Manor came into view. As St Cyres opened the big gates he said: "You can see for yourself that although the two houses are only a short distance apart, they are so placed that they have no view of each other. We can't see Little Thatch from any of the windows—and vice versa."

He walked on, after closing the gates, along a short stretch of drive edged with irises and flowering shrubs. Lilacs of many colours, laburnums, cherry blossom, crab apples, magnolias, and many another tree made a mass of colour along the drive, and a great wistaria grew along the house covered in cascades of blossom. The short drive widened to a terrace in front of the house, and the borders were gay with Darwin tulips and wallflowers. At the further end of the terrace a *chaise longue* was stretched in the sunshine, protected by a gay umbrella, and Macdonald's long-sighted eyes perceived a young woman resting there who did not look at all like a country girl: her dress and hair and make-up were all of the ultra-sophisticated variety. A little sturdy boy came rushing up to Colonel St Cyres. "Grandy, grandy, my tadpoles have comed, they've comed in the night."

"That's right, Michael, you run and watch them and tell me if they have legs before lunch," replied St Cyres, and motioned Macdonald into the house by a garden door. "This is my study, we shall be quiet in here," said St Cyres. "My daughter-in-law and her small boy are living here with us... Sit down, Chief Inspector. Now what can I do to help?"

Macdonald studied the kindly, troubled face of his *vis-à-vis*, and guessed quite a lot from his brief observation of the Colonel: of his house, and of his daughter-in-law. The C.I.D. man replied with a courteous diffidence which set St Cyres at his ease immediately. "Well, sir, I've been given a pretty full report by the County men: they have done their work well, and they do not agree with Commander Wilton's convictions. Won't you tell me just what you think yourself? Did any misgiving cross your own mind?"

"Not at first. None at all. It just seemed the most unhappy tragedy—one of those accidents which do occur," replied St Cyres. "When Wilton came down here and told me his suspicions I was almost angry with him. It seemed just a taradiddle, but I couldn't get it out of my mind. I talked to the chief constable about it. You see, Wilton is right in this—Vaughan *was* a careful fellow. He was conscientious in everything he did, and a very good workman. I warned him about the danger of fire and he didn't pooh-pooh it, as so many young men of to-day would do. He said he was fully aware of it—he'd seen a thatched house burning—and he said he'd take precautions to test every bit of his wiring."

"You liked Vaughan very much, I gather?" enquired Macdonald, and St Cyres nodded:

"Yes, very much. I respected him, too. He was an honest hardworking fellow who felt towards the land as I feel towards it myself. He was responsible—I felt that when I first let him the place. I've always had a deep affection for that property, and I was particular about whom I let it to."

Macdonald caught at an implication here: "Was there much competition to get the place, sir? I know houses in the country are at a premium these days."

"Not exactly competition," said St Cyres rather unhappily. He broke off and studied Macdonald a moment before he went on, "Look here, Chief Inspector, can I talk to you in confidence? I know you're on duty and you've got to collect evidence, but I do feel about you as I did when I first talked to Vaughan—you understand the word responsibility too, or I'm much mistaken. Now I don't want to voice foolish suspicions, and above all I don't want to cast slurs on my neighbours."

"I quite follow that, sir, and I know what is implied by the word neighbourliness in the country," responded Macdonald. "I think you can talk to me without reserve. I shall give weight to all you say, but if it's irrelevant it will go no further."

"Very good. About this matter of letting Little Thatch. I had four applications. One can be dismissed—it was a worthy lady from Mallowton who wanted to keep a cat's home. One was from a young fellow named Benworthy: he's a farm labourer at Ridd's farm and wants to get married, but I didn't fancy him as a tenant—comes of a slovenly family, always in a mess over something. The next applicant was Vaughan, with Wilton's recommendation behind him. Finally, I was approached indirectly on behalf of a man named Gressingham, a wealthy London business man. I didn't want this gentleman as tenant, because I don't like to see country properties treated as playthings by wealthy men who have their real interests elsewhere. Now this man Gressingham... Perhaps you'd care to see him yourself. He has taken rooms, more or less permanently, down at Hinton Mallory, and he tells me he's still hoping to buy property hereabouts."

"I'll certainly make a point of seeing him," said Macdonald. "Have you any idea why he is anxious to settle in this particular part of the country? It's very little known to Londoners. I have been in Devon a good deal, but I have never heard of the Mallorys before this case was put before me."

"Quite so, quite so. We're not in the public eye, thank God," said St Cyres, getting rather red in the face. "Gressingham heard about Little Thatch from my daughter-in-law. She was very anxious to have friends of her own down here. Her husband—my boy Denis—was taken prisoner in Burma: very hard on his wife. I suggested she should come and live here: very glad to have her, and the little chap, too, but she finds the country dull, you know."

"I quite understand that," replied Macdonald. "Once a Londoner always a Londoner is a well-known saying. If I may say so, I see your difficulty and sympathise with it, sir. You can rest assured I shall be very circumspect in approaching Mr. Gressingham."

"You'll find him pleasant enough—a very friendly person in his own way. Not quite our way, y'know, but we're very conservative folk down here. I don't want to give you a false impression. I've nothing against Gressingham. Nothing at all."

"Have you any idea if he got on to terms with Vaughan—went to see him or called at the house?"

Again St Cyres grew rather red in the face. "You might care to talk to my daughter Anne about that—sensible girl and very reliable. I gather from her that Gressingham did... er... make approaches, but wasn't exactly encouraged. The fact is, town-bred people aren't used to country ways and think they can... well, make free with land that isn't their own. I don't know if you've ever lived in the country, Chief Inspector?"

Macdonald smiled. "I've lived mainly in London, sir, but my forebears were Highland Scots and I spent my holidays as a boy on a Highland croft, and there I had some country manners instilled into me. I think I can claim enough acquaintance with country life to respect rural customs as well as to like them. I have a very deep respect for the traditional ways which ensure good relations between those who live on and by the land."

"Very well put, Chief Inspector. If that's your outlook you'll be able to understand some aspects of this business. Now I should like to put certain points before you—and if it's a repetition of what you've heard before, you can stop me. I last saw Vaughan on the Saturday afternoon before his death. I went over to Little Thatch to talk about cutting his meadow. Of course, it's weeks before hay time, but I like to make my plans in advance. That meadow I let him is generally one of the earliest to be fit for cutting—it's a southward slope, very well watered and gets all the sun. I suggested that he might borrow the cutter and get Dickon and one of my men to help him cart and stack, or I'd get the job done for him on a business-like basis."

"And if my notion of Nicholas Vaughan is anywhere near right, he told you he wanted to cut it himself," put in Macdonald, and St Cyres nodded.

"Quite right, quite right. He was grateful for the offer of my gear, but he was used to haysel and he was just longing to cut his own meadow and build his own stack. I sympathised, of course. I'd have felt the same myself. I told him I'd look in again in the evening after I'd had a talk with Ridd—he's my foreman—and there we left it. I shall always remember Vaughan that afternoon: he came with me to look at the grasses in the meadow—marvellously well on it was, despite the drought. He was a real land lover—said he'd never seen grass like it up in his own country. Happy as a sandboy, he was, poor chap."

"And he did not tell you he was expecting to be out that evening?"

"No, he didn't—but then I didn't mention a time. Maybe he thought I meant after dusk, as indeed I did, being a busy man myself. As it happened I didn't go across until half-past nine.

When I saw his door was shut and the house locked up I came away. Thought he'd gone to bed early, as we tend to in the country when we're up betimes. I can't tell you how much I've regretted the fact that I didn't knock him up. If I had, this tragic business might never have happened."

"It was getting on for dusk at half-past nine?" queried Macdonald. "It'd be dark in London, but you get an extra twenty minutes of daylight in the evenings in the west country, don't you?"

"Yes, and correspondingly later mornings, of course. It was dusk when I went over to Little Thatch, but there was light enough to see one's way. I walked along the front of the house—there are gates at either end of the garden—and I looked at Vaughan's motor shed. He only locks it at night, before he turns in. When I saw it was padlocked I knew he was in the house, and as there were no lights showing I didn't knock."

"Did he keep any ducks or hens?"

Colonel St Cyres looked surprised. "Yes. He kept ducks. Khaki Campbells."

"Did you notice if the ducks had been shut up? I suppose they were shut up at night?"

"Of course, or the foxes'd have the lot. Vaughan would have seen they were in the duck-house before he turned in himself."

"You found the ducks in the duck-house next morning?"

St Cyres shook his head. He looked worried and puzzled.

"No, no. One of the things we did that night was to open the linhey and duck-house. It was probable they'd catch fire from the sparks. Vaughan had bought a calf a few days back, and he put her inside at night—we always remember the beasts if there's a fire on farm premises."

"Yes. I know that," said Macdonald patiently. "I'd better make my point quite clear, sir. I want to ascertain that Vaughan was perfectly normal—well and sober, if you like—when he got back to Little Thatch about 9.5 that Saturday evening. If he left home before six o'clock—which is four o'clock G.M.T., isn't it probable he didn't shut the ducks up before he went out?"

"Quite probable. He'd have left them to forage in the orchard and shut them up when he came back."

"Exactly—so it's worth finding out who opened the duck-house during the fire. If the ducks were not in their house, it points to one deviation from the normal, as we say."

St Cyres rubbed his white head with his square, stubby fingers. "I see. You want to know who came to Little Thatch on Saturday night. The lad from Dickon's woke us up, just after three. I've no men sleeping in the house, and I told the boy to run down to Hinton Mallory as fast as he could—he's a good little lad. Before he got back, the constable who had been patrolling across the valley reached here—silly fellow! He thought it was a rick burning, and came over to see instead of ringing up the Fire Service. My phone had gone dead—the wire goes over Little Thatch and the flames from the thatch got it. I was there, the constable, and my daughter. A few minutes later Hesling brought up a couple of men from Hinton Mallory. I think the Dickons' boy—Alf—opened the duck-house. Hesling got the linhey open, then that caught fire, too." St Cyres' voice broke, and he looked a very old man as he went on, "I'm sorry, Chief Inspector. I can't bear to think about it. There we were, and it was so hopeless. Hesling's two men, Fordham and Nympton, got a length of sapling which had been felled, and battered the kitchen door in—perfectly useless, the place was a sheet of flame. Then they tried at the other end of the cottage, and Fordham got inside the dining-room, and we had a job to get him out alive. The place was a furnace, for the beams and floor boards were burning."

"Yes, sir. I don't want to distress you by asking you to tell me about the fire, but I do want to know who was there."

"Very good. Myself and my daughter, the constable, Hesling, Fordham and Nympton, and the boy Alf. The Mallowton Fire Brigade arrived soon after four o'clock, and that man Gressingham and a friend of his named Radcliffe came along shortly after Hesling. They tried to get some of the thatch down—it's very thick—but it was a useless risk."

St Cyres paused a moment and then went on: "You asked just now if Vaughan were normal—well and sober, was the way you put it—that evening. I'm certain he was well; I saw him at four o'clock in the best of health, and as for being sober, I'd give you my word he was that. Apart from an occasional glass of cider Vaughan didn't drink. He was as abstemious as I am myself. Then there's this to it. He drove his car home safely and backed it into that narrow shack he'd built for it—no easy job. If he hadn't been sober he'd have had the whole thing down. A tipsy man can't back a car into a doorway which only gives a couple of inches grace on either side."

"Yes, sir. That's quite a point. Now when you went over to Little Thatch that evening did you see anybody about?"

"No, Chief Inspector, not at the cottage. I walked on to the post-box—there's a collection from that box at midday on Sunday: it's at the junction of the Mallory Fitzjohn and Hinton Mallory turnings. When I reached it I saw Mr. Gressingham in front of me—doubtless he was also posting letters."

"Did you speak to him?"

"No. Perhaps it's not quite accurate to say I saw him, it was too dark to recognise anybody. I saw the dark blur of a man's back and then the white of his collar, and I also smelt the cigarette he was smoking—a Balkan Sobranie. They're Turkish cigarettes, very expensive, and the aroma is quite distinctive. Gressingham's the only man who smokes expensive Turkish cigarettes about here."

"Yes," said Macdonald. "I know those cigarettes." He paused, then added, "Now, sir, if I'm not greatly mistaken there's something else you could add to what you have already said, but you don't feel happy about putting it into words. Isn't that true?"

"Perfectly true, Chief Inspector. It's not evidence of a tangible kind, and it's not evidence of which you can get any corroboration. There's only my own word for it, and I don't feel at all happy about producing it. You said just now that you knew the smell of Balkan Sobranie cigarettes. I smelt the smoke of one of those cigarettes when I walked the length of Little Thatch at nine-thirty that evening—just before I went to the post."

"You didn't mention this fact to the Superintendent, sir?"

"No. How could I? A smell… the aroma of a Turkish cigarette—it seemed an absurd thing to mention—and there's something unworthy about casting suspicion when you have no evidence to support it."

"Did you mention any of this to Mr. Gressingham?"

"I asked him if he'd seen anything of Vaughan that evening, mentioning that I'd seen him—Gressingham—at the post-box. He said no, of course. He told me that he had been for a stroll with my daughter-in-law, had seen her back to this house at twenty minutes past nine, and had then walked through the spinney and by a field-path to the post-box. By that route he would not have gone near Little Thatch."

"He was quite sure about the time—twenty minutes past nine?"

Colonel St Cyres grew very red in the face. "The time was vouched for by my daughter-in-law, June. I asked her if she noticed what time it was she came in, and she told me she glanced at her watch and complained to Gressingham that she had missed the nine o'clock news."

Macdonald was silent for a moment. Then he said, "I realise this is all very difficult for you, sir, and I assure you that I won't make further difficulties without good reason, but I think you ought to answer this question quite frankly. What degree of enmity existed between these two men—Vaughan and Gressingham?"

"It's difficult for me to say. Vaughan never mentioned Gressingham to me—Gressingham spoke disparagingly of Vaughan once or twice, and inferred that he was secretive and had something to hide. I gather Vaughan was short with Gressingham when he called at the cottage—but it all seems so preposterous, making mountains out of molehills! If Gressingham did bear a grudge because Vaughan was in possession of a property which the other coveted, is it reasonable to suppose that he would have gone to criminal lengths to express that grudge?"

"I don't know, sir. Arson has not infrequently been committed to pay off a grudge, and arson may lead to deadly results. Don't imagine I shall jump to any conclusions on account of what you have told me. All I can say is that it is my duty to investigate all contacts made by deceased. As you can see for yourself, there is no proof at all at present that there was any foul play: accident can explain the whole tragedy, and I think it's worth while remembering that your local police, who are a most efficient and conscientious body of men, were satisfied with the explanation of accident, as was the Coroner and his jury."

"Yes," agreed St Cyres sadly. "If it hadn't been for Wilton and his insistence, I don't think any doubt would have arisen in my own mind, but"—he paused and looked at Macdonald—"now you are here, Chief Inspector. I know Wilton is connected with your Assistant Commissioner, but I don't believe it's only on that account that an officer of your standing was sent down here to investigate."

"That's quite true, sir. I was sent because your acting Chief Constable, having consulted with his own men, was not fully convinced that the Coroner's verdict was substantiated. Very few members of the public are aware of the full extent of police enquiries in this country. Very often no further evidence is published, and none will be published in this case unless I find very good reason to disagree with the verdict of accident. Now there are a few practical points on which you can help me. It's important to bear in mind that the verdict of accident rests on two possible explanations—a fault in the electric wiring, or a structural defect in the kitchen chimney. The latter has collapsed too far to show what might have happened. Can you tell me when repairs were last done to that chimney, and who did the repairs?"

"That chimney hasn't been repaired since I left the army in 1924," replied St Cyres. "My father died in 1922, and I resigned my commission and came back here to live in 1924. I made a point of seeing all my tenants and enquiring about repairs. Timothy Yeo had no complaints beyond a leaky roof, and the cottage was rethatched in 1926—a very good job it was, too, a beautiful piece of work. As for the chimney—it probably hadn't been touched since the kitchen range was put in when Timothy Yeo got married in 1904."

"And who put the range in?" enquired Macdonald, and St Cyres held up his hands in despair.

"How should I know? I was at Sandhurst in 1904. Probably old Potts and Bulham of Mallowton did it. They did most of the work for my father's property. Are you hoping to get evidence of work done forty years ago, Chief Inspector?"

"In the absence of any younger evidence, yes," replied Macdonald cheerfully. "If the man who worked in that chimney in 1904 is alive now I'm going to try to find him. From my experience of rural builders, you generally get one old man who has the experience, plus one young man who has the muscles. Perhaps I shall find the young man of 1904 who would have been sent up to examine the inside of that chimney—he won't be much over sixty, and country folk have long memories."

"And what on earth can he tell you that would be useful in 1944?" asked St Cyres helplessly.

"This, sir. You say there have been no structural alterations at Little Thatch since 1904. If I can get evidence from a reliable workman that no beam impinged on that chimney in 1904, there couldn't have been a beam to smoulder in 1944. From my knowledge of old buildings—a layman's knowledge, admittedly—I don't believe a beam did run through or rest on that chimney. The chimney was a stone one: it was built by itself and big cross beams wouldn't have gone near it, and the roof tree was independent of it. Obviously I can't get architect's plans of Little Thatch—but I can get more information than has been adduced thus far. My function is to worry people, and to that end I am given more leisure than the County men."

Colonel St Cyres sighed—an old man's sigh: "Well, Chief Inspector, I respect your zeal. For my part, I will disinter any of the old estate papers I can find. We keep old bills in the country, despite the salvage drive. I've often said that some of the most interesting local histories have been made from old account books."

"I quite agree, sir. Now, if it's not inconvenient, may I see your daughter, Miss Anne?"

"By all means. I think she's about somewhere, I'll find her. Meantime, a glass of cider or a cup of coffee, Chief Inspector?"

"Thanks very much, sir. A glass of cider. I hope it's a local brew."

"It is, and the best in the county in my opinion," replied St Cyres.

2

Anne St Cyres was exactly what Macdonald had anticipated. Neat, self-contained and reliable looking, moreover "a bonnie lassie," with a fresh skin, pretty hair and her father's blue eyes. Macdonald had never admired cosmetics, and he always tended to like a rosy-cheeked young woman who had the courage to ignore the temptations of perming and beauty-parlour experts—but Macdonald was growing into a real old stick in the eyes of those born since he first entered the Metropolitan Police in 1920.

"You know what my job is, Miss St Cyres," said the C.I.D. man, "and since I've arrived on the scene rather late in the day, I shall need all the help I can get. Your father suggested that Mr. Vaughan didn't see eye to eye with Mr. Gressingham on the matter of private property."

Anne flushed, and looked rather distressed. "Yes, that's true in a way," she rejoined. "Mr. Vaughan asked me to go over and see Little Thatch after he had finished painting the house—at

Easter—and I was there when Mr. Gressingham called. He was quite friendly and asked Mr. Vaughan to make up a four at bridge. Mr. Vaughan said he didn't play bridge, and then Mr. Gressingham made a few rather condescendingly polite remarks about Little Thatch and said he'd like to walk round the garden. Mr. Vaughan said it wasn't open for exhibition—but it was all quite trivial. Of course they didn't like one another, but there was nothing in that. I don't like Mr. Gressingham myself: he's much too sure of himself and too disposed to be familiar at short notice—but all this was trivial, as I just said. It never occurred to me to magnify it into anything serious."

"Would you be willing to state that to the best of your knowledge and belief there was no enmity between the two men?"

Again she flushed, and a frown deepened the lines on her forehead.

"I have said that in my judgment they disliked each other, and I think I could add that they despised each other, but it was a surface matter. Mr. Vaughan didn't brood over it or get irritable because Mr. Gressingham tried to be superior, and I don't think Mr. Gressingham had any other feeling than a slight contempt for a man he described as an oaf or a tough."

"That's very fairly put," said Macdonald. "Now I wonder if you can tell me a bit more about the house and the work Vaughan had done on it. I ask you, because it seems that you had seen more of Little Thatch than anyone else. I know your father went over there fairly frequently, but he was more interested in the garden and land than in the house."

"Yes. He was delighted at the way the place was looked after—the garden cultivated and the orchards pruned and put into order."

"Quite—every man to his own job. Now about the wiring. It had been connected up with the plant?"

"Oh, yes. He got that done nearly a month ago, and I went in and we turned all the lights on, it was great fun, but I believe he wasn't satisfied with the way the engine was working. Some of the lights flickered, and he said he was going to disconnect it and examine the engine again. He said if he could only get at some-body's lathe to make a new connection it would be a hundred per cent more efficient."

"I see. Do you know if he had turned the current on again?"

"Yes, I passed the cottage fairly late one evening—after sunset, I mean—and the lights in the windows certainly weren't lamplight."

"Next, can you tell me just how far the place was furnished?"

"Not exactly, because I haven't been over it since Easter, but I know he'd bought a good many things in the past month and a lot of wood and old panelling, too—that came from Hartsworthy House. He was building cupboards and putting up book shelves. He had an enormous number of books—well, it seemed enormous to me—crates and crates of them. I expect you mean, was there anything to burn? There was—a whole lot."

"Now wasn't it to you that Mr. Vaughan said he'd found some loose bricks in the kitchen chimney?"

"Yes, I asked about that particularly, because if the chimney was faulty it was the landlord's business to put it right. He said it was perfectly sound: there's a ledge halfway down the chimney—you often find them in old houses—and there was a jackdaw's nest on the ledge, and two bricks had fallen in from the chimney stack, which has a brick coping. I did try to explain all this to the Superintendent, but he would keep on saying 'Yes, yes,' as though I were a child. That chimney is a stone one, Mr. Macdonald, it's not built of brick at all, and if Nicholas Vaughan took two bricks out of it, it was because he knew where they'd come from—the coping of the stack. He even put a ladder up and found where the coping had been repaired. He was a thoroughly sensible person, and I won't agree with anybody who says the fire was due to his own carelessness or stupidity."

Macdonald nearly said, "Well, well"—he felt he had learnt quite a lot from Anne's long speech: instead, he said, "That's very important evidence, Miss St Cyres. You agree with Commander Wilton then in being sure that the fire was *not* caused by accident due to the work done by Mr. Vaughan."

"Oh dear." She uttered the two words wearily, and then made another effort to talk quietly. "I agree with Commander Wilton this far: that Mr. Vaughan knew what he was about, and that he was careful to the verge of caution. I do *not* agree with him that Mr. Vaughan was murdered. I think it's a horrible suggestion and there's nothing to support it. Accidents *do* happen. Isn't there some advertisement on the hoardings about fires often being caused by careful people? However careful you are, accidents happen sometimes. You must have known lots of fires which happened quite accidentally."

"Of course I have," replied Macdonald. He did not add that he had investigated quite a number of fires whose origin had only appeared to be accidental. "All the same, I wish you would tell me if anything about this accident struck you as suspicious?"

"At the time, nothing," she said. "Since Commander Wilton came, and there has been all this gossip and enquiry, I admit I caught the suspicion bug for a little while—but I don't believe it. I think the Superintendent was perfectly right in his argument: why should anybody have wanted to murder Mr. Vaughan? Nearly everybody liked him and respected him, too. He was buried here, you know, in our churchyard, and the farmers came from miles round to his funeral. That may not mean much to you, but in the country people don't go to funerals out of curiosity. They go because they have respected the man who died, and although Nicholas Vaughan had lived here only a short time, they all respected him, and he'd got to be friends with them, too—and that takes a bit of doing in these parts."

"I think Vaughan would have been very contented to see the farmers at his funeral," said Macdonald, and his voice was gentle. "He would have valued their regard."

Anne flicked away some tears from her eyes impatiently.

"I just can't help feeling wretched over it," she said. "He was such a whole-hearted, hard-working, decent-minded fellow, and it was such rotten luck, because, whatever people say, it was *not* his fault. I'm certain of it."

CHAPTER EIGHT

I

"WHAT I WANT TO KNOW IS THIS, CHIEF INSPECTOR." It was Thomas Gressingham who spoke. He had answered a number of questions which Macdonald had put to him, and answered, apparently, without reserve or resentment. Now Gressingham considered it was time he asked a few questions himself, and Macdonald had said, "By all means. Ask anything you want to."

Thomas Gressingham pointed a rather podgy, well-manicured finger to emphasise his query, "What proof have you got that the remains found in the embers of Little Thatch were the remains of Nicholas Vaughan?"

A sound of exasperation came from the third man in the room—this was Howard Brendon, who had been with Gressingham when Macdonald first called. Rather to the C.I.D. man's interest, Gressingham had asked Brendon to remain and witness the conversation, and Brendon, to Macdonald's eye, had something of a legal cut about him. He had sat in silence throughout the interview until now, when he gave an exclamation of disgust.

"My dear Gressingham, you've been reading an excess of detective fiction," he said. "Your question savours too much of the cheaply sensational."

Macdonald replied next, "Obviously, Mr. Gressingham, I have no proof. A man's body is found in the burnt-out remains of a cottage. The first supposition is that the remains are those of the man who lived in the cottage. While the remains were not identifiable in the usual way, there were certain observations to be made—approximate age, height, build—all these tallied with the expected. Since you have raised the point, do you care to state if you have any reasons for believing that the remains were *not* those of Nicholas Vaughan?"

"Obviously, Chief Inspector, to follow your gambit, I have no evidence to offer. I never saw the remains, and it's probable I shouldn't have been any wiser had I done so, but that doesn't debar me from using my reasoning powers."

"Nor debar you from making a fool of yourself," said Brendon acidly. "If you think you can teach the police their job, Gressingham, you are in process of making a very tidy-sized fool of yourself."

"But I should be very much interested to hear Mr. Gressingham's theories on the matter," said Macdonald, and Gressingham needed no further encouragement to talk.

"Look here, Chief Inspector, I've told you my views. From the little I saw of Vaughan I judged him to be a man who was intent on avoiding observation. When I first saw him in his garden and called a perfectly polite 'good morning,' he replied by turning his back on me. Country people don't do that—they always pass the time of day cheerfully. I put him down as a town lout—an artisan. Fellows of the factory-worker type are too above themselves to have any manners these days. When I finally came face to face with him and spoke to him I realised he wasn't an artisan type, he was an educated man, but a man who had something to hide. One of the first things he did in that precious garden of his was to put up wattle screens inside the fences."

"Got any hedges round your Surrey garden, Gressingham, or any walls? or are your lawns and borders open to the public eye?

Have you got notice boards up, 'Come and look chaps! My flowers are for your pleasure'?"

Mr. Brendon's sardonic tones pleased Macdonald. The thin man went on in his incisive voice, "The reason that Vaughan *did* put wattle screens was that you and your friends persisted in stopping and staring into his garden, Gressingham. Country people don't do that, to quote your own words. This Nicholas Vaughan sounds a man of common sense to me. I'm only sorry I never met him."

"I'm sorry too, Howard. I told you the chap reminded me vaguely of someone I'd once seen somewhere—but that eye-shade of his was good camouflage. Difficult to recognise a man with an eye-shade on—but he took it off when he was at home, so to speak. For public circulation only."

Howard Brendon got to his feet. "It appears that the Chief Inspector has the patience to listen to you, Gressingham. Frankly, I have not. As I see it, there has been a case of very deplorable accident resulting in the death of a hard-working, decent-minded fellow. I'd like to remind you that this Nicholas Vaughan once protected your prosperity by sailing in Arctic convoys. Now he's dead he has no protection against libel or slander—"

"But *is* he dead?" shouted Gressingham. "Prove to me he *is* dead! Somebody's dead, but is it Vaughan?"

Brendon turned to Macdonald. "You need patience in your trade, Chief Inspector."

Macdonald laughed. "In the words of a forgotten novelist, sir, I have the patience of innumerable asses. Not that I need to exercise it now. I am genuinely interested in Mr. Gressingham's theories."

Brendon snorted. "You can hand that sort of blarney to those who're dense enough to take it at its face value," he said. "I recognise the good old technique—get a man talking and let him make a fool of himself. Fortunately Gressingham is too palpably foolish on this occasion to be taken seriously—but I underline my protest. Vaughan's death shouldn't be used as material for sensational balderdash."

"All right, old chap," replied Gressingham, quite unnettled. "You come over again in a month or two, and we shall see what we shall see."

Howard Brendon nodded to Macdonald, and with a curt, "Good day to you," to Gressingham, he left the room.

"Vitriolic customer," said Gressingham placidly, "but I never mind a bit of vituperation. Amuses me in fact. Brendon's a very astute fellow and a very good judge of landed property. He often gets mad with me, but he soon gets over it. I watch his interests on the market and he finds it worth while. Where were we? I know. I'd been making the point that Vaughan behaved as though he had something to hide."

"A very interesting point, Mr. Gressingham," said Macdonald, "but do you think you can substantiate it? You say that Vaughan avoided you, but he didn't avoid everybody. The St Cyres knew him pretty well. The farmers around met him at market, and he certainly did not avoid them. He went out of his way to talk to them and to discuss the farming methods in vogue hereabouts."

"Admitted, but how far afield do any of these farmers go? They go to their market town, certainly, but no farther. Similarly with Colonel St Cyres and his daughter, they live here and here they stay. When it came to myself, and my own friends, fellows who get around, Vaughan avoided us like poison. It was the same with young Mrs. St Cyres—June—if he saw her coming he edged off."

"So you suggest that Vaughan had something to hide, Mr. Gressingham? I take it you didn't risk making that suggestion to Commander Wilton, who was Vaughan's friend?"

"Of course I didn't. I should never have raised the point at all if it hadn't been for the fact of your own appearance on the scene, Chief Inspector. If the Coroner's jury were satisfied with the verdict of accidental death, it wasn't up to me to cast aspersions. But—and it's a pretty large but—since Scotland Yard has put in an appearance it's plain there's stinking fish somewhere. If there weren't more in it than meets the eye you would not be here. Isn't that a fair assumption?"

"It's rather an over-statement of the case," replied Macdonald. "I am not here because any new evidence has emerged, nor yet because there is any official disagreement with the verdict of the Coroner's court. I am here to reaffirm that verdict if possible."

"So you may say," replied Gressingham, "but if there weren't some sound reason for querying the verdict the Yard wouldn't have sent a big gun down here to investigate things."

Macdonald paused a moment and then said, "Your friend, Mr. Brendon, saw the point more clearly than yourself, I think. Nicholas Vaughan was a very gallant seaman, and when his senior officer demanded a more detailed enquiry into his death, the Commissioner's Office was glad to do its best, if only to honour the Royal Navy."

"Sez you," replied Gressingham imperturbably. "I see all that—and very nice too—but I see a bit further."

"And what exactly do you see?" persisted Macdonald.

"This. I see that there has been an opportunity of fraud and crime," replied Gressingham. "Mark you, I say opportunity. I should like to make three points. In the first place, is there any proof that the man who took Little Thatch *was* the Nicholas Vaughan who earned such a reputation on the Arctic convoys? A man came here and examined the property, hustled old St Cyres into letting him have the tenancy and came into residence living entirely by himself and keeping aloof from observation. No friends of Vaughan's ever turned up. The lawyer who acted for him down here had never seen him before, nor had the banker at Mallowton, where his account was moved to. Mark you, I'm not making rash statements: I'm not even making allegations, but you'll find my observations are reliable."

"Would you like to state exactly why you made the enquiries you evidently made?" asked Macdonald, and Gressingham nodded.

"Certainly. I'm an easy-going chap by and large, not irritable or quick-tempered, but I do admit I was a bit nettled over the letting of Little Thatch. I wrote to Colonel St Cyres, and I made him a very generous offer for the tenancy, or for purchase—very generous. He replied with a curt announcement that the property was not on the market. When I came down here, I found that big tough already in possession, and I tell you I was a bit mad. I did make some enquiries—why not? No one knew the chap and he looked a queer guy to me. I did no more about it—obviously there was nothing I *could* do, but I've always believed there was more to it than met the eye."

Again Macdonald sat and pondered. It was all very well for Howard Brendon to deride Gressingham's ideas, but Macdonald did not believe that Gressingham was any sort of fool. He was much more astute than Colonel St Cyres, for instance. Thoughts flashed through Macdonald's mind very swiftly: Vaughan had typed all his letters… he had had no friends to visit him… his relatives were not sufficiently interested in him to come to his funeral…

"Well, Chief Inspector?" asked Gressingham, and Macdonald replied:

"I note your point, Mr. Gressingham: you postulate both fraud and crime. The man who lived at Little Thatch was not Nicholas Vaughan at all—so presumably the latter had been disposed of at an earlier date. Is that it?"

"I don't know. All I'm doing is to ask questions in return for some of those you asked me. Can you tell me this? When was the last date that Nicholas Vaughan was seen by someone who really knew him?"

Macdonald was very wary: he needed to consider his answer, because it was quite probable that Gressingham knew the right answer.

"I think I require notice of that question, Mr. Gressingham, but, broadly speaking, the answer is in December last."

"December, eh? I don't expect you study the West of England newspapers, do you? No reason why you should. I like local papers myself, they're well worth reading. There's a cutting I kept from the *North Devon Observer,* of January 20th last. I'll show it you later. It describes the coroner's inquest on the body of a man washed up from the sea on the Devon-Cornwall borders. The police surgeon gave it as his opinion that the body had been in the sea for at least three weeks—quite unrecognisable, of course, and not a shred of clothing left on it: the corpse was that of a big man, probable age between thirty and forty. Well, there it was. Nothing to be made of it. Corpses *are* washed up these days, nothing to be surprised at in that. An order for burial was given and the poor chap interred. An open verdict, of course. See?"

"Yes. I see," replied Macdonald. "You've quite a feeling for correlating events, Mr. Gressingham."

"If that's a polite way of saying I'm fond of making up stories I don't resent the imputation, Chief Inspector, but bear the old saying in mind: 'Truth is stranger than fiction.'"

"I'm well qualified to know that," rejoined Macdonald. "I have been interested in your ideas, Mr. Gressingham—they will be looked into. Now, have you any more suggestions?"

"Lashings of 'em," replied Gressingham cheerfully, "but I'm thirsty. Will you join me in a drink? Listening, like talking, is much easier when you've got a glass in your hand."

"Not for me, thanks," replied Macdonald. "I'm on duty, you know, and you could report me for drinking on duty."

Gressingham grinned. "That's a really nasty back-hander, Chief Inspector. I don't deserve that one. I'm a good-natured chap, taking me all round. Better natured than our Colonel Ramrod up yonder." He was pouring himself out a good generous whisky, and he turned and waved it gaily at Macdonald. "Here's how! If I were asked to lay a bet on the reason why you have a tendency to believe I'm a liar, I wouldn't mind risking a fiver on the guess that somebody in the Manorial Thatching gave their opinion that one Thomas Gressingham is a very dirty dog. I don't expect you to affirm or deny that; I'll save you the trouble, but, believe me, I'm not a liar, nor yet a hundred per cent fool. I've a great respect for intelligence, and you are an intelligent man. The—er—corollary is obvious! Good word that."

2

Macdonald was in no hurry to get Mr. Gressingham back to the main subject of their conversation: he was too much interested in the man himself. Obviously Tommy Gressingham was not the type of man to inspire Colonel St Cyres with anything but repugnance: he was too complacent, too impudent, too blatantly well-off, but Macdonald had met many men of the same type before. The manner which St Cyres would have described as "bounding" was in one sense a camouflage. It served to conceal the speaker's thoughts. No one could have guessed the thoughts behind that persistently amiable countenance. Nevertheless, Macdonald knew enough about such men to know that it was a mistake to assume that they were either dishonest or ill-natured *au fond*—they simply left you guessing, they might be anything.

"I wish you'd answer a purely personal question, Mr. Gressingham," said Macdonald, and the other said:

"Ask away. 'There's nothing I have done yet, o' my conscience deserves a corner.' Can *you* place that one, Chief Inspector?"

"Shakespeare. Henry VIII," replied Macdonald. "You won't misunderstand me when I say I never accept that statement at its face value."

Gressingham laughed—a cheerful roar: "A pity you won't have a drink, old man. The more I see of you the better I like you. What's your question? Double or quits I can guess." He tossed half-a-crown on the table. "What made you so anxious to come to live in these remote parts, Mr. Gressingham?"

Macdonald allowed himself to laugh that time. The mimicry of Colonel St Cyres was so excellent, even to the little nervous cough which punctuated so many of his sentences.

"Yes, you have won, but I didn't take the bet," said Macdonald. "What's the answer?"

Mr. Gressingham sighed, and then put down the larger part of his drink. "Haven't you all got one-way minds?" he asked. "Here am I, Tommy Gressingham, a Londoner, born and bred there, brought up on stock markets and tape machines, sucking in sophistication with my mother's milk. If I want to live in the country, there's Surrey and Berks and Bucks and Herts—nice and snug and suburban, eh? I tell you there's no snob in the world like your country snob. To him, the City man's a nasty smell, something the cat brought in. It's all wrong, you know. Whatever I've bought it's always been genuine and good of its kind. My Surrey place is good of its kind—hundred per cent gent's suburban resort plus a little larch wood, a garden designed by a Chelsea snob landscape wallah, and central heating throughout. Now what's to prevent me wanting a real country property, primitive and robust, redolent of farmyard stinks, no refinery nonsense about it? Why not? I like experience: I believe in doing everything once, even to spreading muck in a sou'westerly gale. But I like to see a friend or two about. I've known that pretty little girl, June St Cyres, since she was fifteen—and a damn' pretty fifteen, too. She wrote and said she was lonely and bored, Why not come down here? So I came. She was glad to see me, and believe me she looks a hundred per cent happier since I came and imported a spot of life into the place."

He finished his drink and took up his story again: "One more bit of the confidential, old boy, and I'm through. Then I'll get on with the shorter catechism again. Why wouldn't old Colonel Ramrod let me have Little Thatch? I'll tell you for why. Because he's got a very nice-minded daughter. God defend me from nice-minded women with Puritanism in their blood. They've got really nasty minds. That one—Sweet Anne of Manor Thatch—decided I wasn't a nice person to know. Familiar, y'know. A born seducer of young wives. God save the King! Did I need to come down here to seduce young wives? Queues of 'em in London if I'd been that way disposed. I tell you it was Anne put a spoke in my wheel. Do

I bear a grudge? Not I! She just makes me laugh. Well, that's that. On with the dance, let joy be unconfined! I'm not drunk, y'know. Not on one whisky."

"No. I'm quite sure you're not," said Macdonald. "I put down the effervescence to what Bergson called the élan vital."

"I say—you're not getting intellectual, are you? Take my advice and don't. Intellectuality leaves me stone-cold. Well, I've given you Solution No.1—the chap who got the lease of Little Thatch was *not* Nicholas Vaughan at all."

"Duly noted—but who was the corpse?" enquired Macdonald.

"You can pay your money and take your choice. If you care to disregard the shipwrecked mariner washed ashore at Morwinstow, you can make a good case for the corpse being Vaughan himself. It was probably conveyed in one of those crates which arrived on the coal lorry or in farm carts at regular intervals."

"I see—but while admitting the ingenuity of the idea, I am not convinced. You see, the man who took Little Thatch knew that Commander Wilton, for instance, might arrive to look him up any time, and then the band would have played."

"Oh, rather," said Gressingham, "but don't you think it's probable these Naval wallahs have a very good idea about how long their cruise will last? Wilton probably said, 'So long, dear old boy. See you again on May Day,' or words to that effect, and by May Day the balloons had gone up. However, I have an open mind. Take your own idea on the subject, and postulate that Vaughan *was* the tenant of Little Thatch. I still maintain he had reasons for secrecy. He did *not* want to be observed by anyone outside the Mallorys. Very good. We return to my original question: 'How do you know the corpse found at Little Thatch *was* the corpse of Nicholas Vaughan?'"

"And I have admitted that I have no irrefutable proof," rejoined Macdonald.

"Then you've got to admit that the possibility exists that Vaughan took a comparatively simple way of paying off an old score," persisted Gressingham. "He left a corpse in the ashes which he could bet would be taken for his own, and off he goes to some other nice little tenancy elsewhere. I bet he never foresaw the snag that his dear old pal, Wilton, would mess the whole show up by demanding a further police enquiry. That's what I call a bit hard."

3

At this stage in Gressingham's narrative, another person strolled into the room. Macdonald had observed him hovering about in the garden for some minutes past—a preposterously fat man, one of those men who seem fated to look ridiculous.

"I say, forgive me if I'm butting in," he said. "Hate to interfere, but could I possibly get to the phone. I want to book a long-distance call."

"Come in and get on with it, Rummy. Sorry we've kept you out. This is Chief Inspector Macdonald—Raymond Radcliffe."

Radcliffe surveyed the C.I.D. man through the enormous lenses of his glasses, and Macdonald found himself thinking, "This one isn't stupid either, he only looks stupid."

"I'm honoured, Chief Inspector. I've always wanted to meet one of you big noises at the Yard. I hope you haven't been taking Tommy too seriously. He's got imagination, I'll say that for him—but he overdoes it. By the way, Tommy, did you tell the Chief Inspector about Vaughan's telephone code? I think he'd be interested."

"I certainly should," said Macdonald. "What's the story?"

"Well, it's my story, really," said Radcliffe. "You see, if Vaughan wanted to have a telephone message left for him, he got Mrs. Hesling to take down the message and send one of the farm boys up with it. I answered the phone one day and a lady asked for Mrs. Hesling. I said she was out, could I take the message, and she said, 'Will you ask her to be kind enough to send a message to Mr. Vaughan at Little Thatch and say that Mrs. Jones would be glad if he could leave the ducks' eggs at six to-morrow.' I asked where he was to leave them and she said, 'Oh, he knows the address,' and rang off. Well, that seemed all plain and above board and I thought no more about it until a fortnight later I answered the phone again, and the same voice said that Mrs. Jones wanted her eggs left at half-past seven that day. Well—I ask you—nice neat bit of code work. Neat and not noticeable. You ask Mrs. Hesling if she often got messages from Mrs. Jones."

The fat man lighted a cigarette (it was a Churchman, Macdonald noted) and added, "Mind if I use that phone? it's in the cupboard there. Rum place to have a phone, but there it is."

Macdonald got up to go. He felt he had had his money's worth. Gressingham walked to the door with him and said, "Come in again some time. Always glad to see you. Don't play bridge by any chance?"

"Not by any chance," said Macdonald firmly.

CHAPTER NINE

I

M ACDONALD WALKED OUT OF HINTON MALLORY BY WAY OF the farmyard, passing the open kitchen door as he did so. Mrs. Hesling did not seem to be about, and the C.I.D. man crossed the farmyard where ducks and hens waddled and clucked, cats preened themselves in the sunshine and a very ancient sheep-dog thumped its tail in response to a greeting. It was getting on for milking time and the milking cows had assembled at the gate of their pasture and were telling the world that they needed attention: they lowed at Macdonald as he emerged from the fold-yard, and he wished—as he had wished on other occasions—that farming had been his lot.

As he shut the gate he was startled by the sound of an engine just behind him—a good full-throated roar as somebody "revved" the engine up, and on turning he saw Howard Brendon bending over the open bonnet of his big Sunbeam.

"Still here, Mr. Brendon," said Macdonald, and the other replied:

"Yes. Choke in the feed. This Pool petrol's death to any decent engine. Taken me all this time to clear it. Can I give you a lift anywhere? You don't know the meaning of the word mud if you haven't traversed this road."

"Thanks very much, if I'm not taking you out of your way," rejoined Macdonald. "I only want to go up to Little Thatch to recover my bike."

"I'll take you up there with pleasure. Get in."

Macdonald got in, and Brendon fastened the bonnet and wiped his hands on a duster before he got into the driver's seat, and the car moved forward cautiously over the slimy road.

Macdonald risked an enquiry: "What do *you* make of it all, Mr. Brendon? You must have heard the matter discussed in all its bearings."

"I've heard a bit too much for my patience," replied Brendon. "I'm afraid my opinion isn't worth having, Chief Inspector, because I don't know the facts at first hand, and I wasn't acquainted with deceased. I do know he had a good reputation among the farmers, and as far as I can gather he was a shrewd, steady-going fellow—not at all the sort of customer to stage a melodrama. Doubtless the police have good reasons for continuing the enquiry, but I regret that it has to continue. The amount of tommy-rot which is being talked makes me sick." He paused, bending forward as he negotiated a particularly bad patch of road, then he went on, "It's not my business to volunteer opinions, but I should like to say this: Gressingham isn't a fool by any means. He's a very astute man of business, and he's an honest one, or I should have no dealings with him. The trouble is that he fancies himself in the rôle of detective, and along those lines he just makes a thundering fool of himself."

"I'm not so sure," said Macdonald. "He's a man who could be useful to a detective. He's shrewd, as you say, he's observant, and he correlates his facts. I found him interesting, as I said. Take that point about identity of deceased. It's got to be considered—until we can find definite proof that the remains are the remains of Nicholas Vaughan."

"Yes, I see that," answered Brendon. "You want to silence the rumour-mongers, and every decent-minded man is with you in that. It shouldn't be too difficult. Vaughan was in hospital, wasn't he? I should think one of the surgeons or physicians could put the thing beyond doubt. Nearly every human being has some deviation from the normal in their bone structure I'm told. Of course, it ought to have been done before. That's the one criticism I'd make of the conduct of the case—it was assumed too easily that deceased was Nicholas Vaughan. I'm quite certain myself that such was the fact—but one has to forestall rumour and sensation-mongers."

He pulled up the car saying, "The cottage is only a hundred yards away—to the right there."

"Thanks very much," replied Macdonald. "Shall I be seeing you again in these parts? Certain questions are bound to arise, concerning the character and bona fides of witnesses, for example. You are a Devonian, I am not. Your judgment might be very valuable to me."

"I shall be over again within the week. If you are professionally interested in my allowance of petrol I should like to put your mind at rest. I am consulted by the Probate Office on certain valuations, particularly on antiques—furniture, domestic fittings, etc. It is an expert job. I am willing to act if transport facilities be allowed."

"An excellent arrangement for both parties to the transaction," said Macdonald. "Good-day, and many thanks for the lift."

He walked back to the entrance of Little Thatch, noting the wattle screens which had so much annoyed Gressingham. Macdonald wanted to make a fair estimate of all the characters he had encountered in the case so far. He put on one side Gressingham's theory that the tenant of Little Thatch had not been Nicholas Vaughan. Although a case could be argued along these lines Macdonald did not believe in it. Such a case involved the assumption that Vaughan had been murdered and that his murderer then came and impersonated him at Mallory Fitzjohn.

It seemed absurd to imagine that anybody could impersonate Vaughan; the latter had been an expert gardener, experienced with beasts, a good practical engineer and a man of considerable ability in a dozen different ways. Macdonald went and sat on the orchard bank and chewed over his case. Gressingham had insisted that Vaughan had something to hide; the insistence seemed almost naive to Macdonald, for it was obvious that Gressingham was the very type whom Vaughan would have detested. That being so, was it possible that a much stronger enmity existed between the two men than had been observed by anybody else? Anne St Cyres had insisted that their aversion for one another was trivial—but she might not have had an opportunity of observing the real state of affairs. The question which really emerged was this: was there any way in which Vaughan was a danger to Gressingham, or in which the one man menaced the other's plans or security? Was there anything which Vaughan could have known that would bring such discredit on Gressingham that it was worth the latter's while to take the risk of murdering him?

His mind busy with the problem, Macdonald examined all that was left of Little Thatch. The outhouses, apart from their thatch, were still standing. Here was the damaged remains of the electric plant, there was also the petrol engine which worked the pump by the orchard gate, and the broken greenhouse against the linhey—pathetic testimony to a man's industry and mechanical skill. The house had gone: books, papers, furniture, clothes, everything that might have given information about the man who lived there—it was all gone, mingled with the ashes of floors and beams and rafters. There was nothing but the carefully tended garden and orchard to tell of the man who had lived in Little Thatch, those and the remains of his ill-fated electric installation and the neatly boxed-in petrol engine which worked the pump.

2

Alf got home to Corner Cottage in time for tea, and Mrs. Dickon gave him a good tea. He had his midday meal at school, but Alf always counted tea as his best meal. The Dickons kept hens, and hens meant eggs: there was also a beehive, and Alf liked honey. Old Mrs. Dickon was one of those women who suspected that all meals cooked in institutions were "rubbidge"—schools, British Restaurants, canteens and cafés all came under her stigma of "rubbidge" and she saw to it that Alf got at least one good meal a day, and that meal was tea.

When Macdonald got off his bike at Corner Cottage Alf had just come out into the garden in a state of comfortable repletion, and he gazed at Macdonald with the acute appraising stare of the Cockney boy, so different from the ruminating stare of the country children.

"Good-evening; you're Alf, aren't you?" asked Macdonald.

"Yus," replied the imp.

Macdonald knew quite well that it was no use trying to conceal his business and identity from this sharp-eyed urchin. Alf would guess who he was in two-twos, so the C.I.D. man went on, "You were born in London, weren't you? Ever heard of Scotland Yard?"

"Cripes! Yus! You a 'tec?"

"Yes. I'm a 'tec. I want you to answer a few questions. O.K.?"

"O.K. cap'n. Come inside. There's a seat 'ere-along."

Macdonald accepted the invitation, much interested in this product of Shoreditch. Alf's Cockney origin still sounded in his speech, despite the slurring burr which association with Devonshire children had developed, but the great difference between Alf and his country schoolmates was the quickness of the Cockney's reactions. He was still as sharp as a needle.

Sitting on a bench in the garden, Macdonald said, "Now I want you to tell me all you can about that night when Little Thatch was burnt, Alf. I know you've told it before, but never mind that. I want to hear about it from you, direct. Now, did you ever go to help Mr. Vaughan in the garden?"

"Yus. I cleaned them cobbles: 'e put weed-killer on 'em, but 'tweren't much good. Them weeds always came up agen. Mr. Vaughan, 'e paid me sixpence a week if them cobbles was clean, not so much as a blade o' grass showing. If they wasn't clean, well, I got nix. See?"

"Yes—a very good idea, too. Payment by results. Any other jobs?"

"Yus. Sticking. Sixpence a crate for kindling, dry and properly broken and stacked. If it weren't dry—nix. No spots on 'im."

"I'd say that didn't pay you quite as well as the cobbles," said Macdonald, and Alf grinned.

"Nope. Took a long time to collect thiccy sticks and dry 'em, but I got an armful every day, coming back from school, and I stacked 'em Saturdays. He often giv me a toffee, too."

"Any more jobs? Did you ever clean out the duck-house?"

"Yus, but it weren't done quite to's liking. Fussy like, 'e was, very partic'ler."

"Did you go along to Little Thatch on the Saturday of the fire at all?"

"Yus. Took them sticks and 'is piper. Always took the piper Saturday morning. Lent 'im an 'and with the wire for 'is fruit

cages, too. It was all O.K. Saturday morning, guv'ner. Cheerful
'e was. Whistling."

"Did you ever go inside the house?"

"Nope. Only to the door. 'Ated mud on the kitchen floor, 'e did."

"Think this out, Alf. Did you go to the kitchen door with his
paper?"

"Yus."

"Was the kitchen fire alight?"

"Lummy! I dunno…"

"Think again. Was there any way you could tell, apart from
seeing the fire was alight?"

"Lummy! You're a one. I never thought o' that there," said Alf,
and sat with his chin on his grubby hands, deep in thought. "'E
didn't always light 'is fire first thing, not these warm days. 'E'd got
a Primus wot 'e boiled 'is kettle on, and sometimes 'e didn't light
the fire till tea-time, but 'e always did the range—ashes and that,
and laid 'is fire ready to put a match to it. Then 'e swep' the kitchen
and left it all O.K. 'E put the ashes on a path 'e was making—ashes
and concrete, see? 'E burnt coal in the range and coal ashes ain't
no good for the soil."

"Quite true, Alf. Did Mr. Dickon go and work at Little Thatch
that day?"

"Yus. Scything nettles 'e was, in the orchard, and putting 'em
all on compost 'eap in t'corner there."

"When he worked in the morning, did Mr. Vaughan give him
a cup of tea at any time?"

"Yus. Tea at eleven. Cider with 'is dinner, which 'e eat in the
linhey. Cripes, guv'ner, you've got it! 'E made tea middle morning,
and 'e lighted that there Primus. I remember now, I was doing
them cobbles and I 'eard 'im pumping it—you know."

"I know," said Macdonald. "Now how can you be sure? I want you to be quite certain."

"Yus. I know 'twas Saturday, 'cos that's the only morning I go doing cobbles. I did the path front o' kitchen door. I always watched 'im light Primus if I could: 'e said Primus was a bitch to light sometimes along 'o the paraffin and meth bein' all mucky these days. I didn't know 'e was goin' to light it, 'cos I'd have axed for a drink o' water or summat so's I could watch, but I 'eard 'im pump and I 'eard the flame singing like. That's true, guv'ner, honest it is—and if 'e lighted Primus, 'e 'adn't got fire alight or kettle'd've been 'ot, see?"

"That's it, Alf—but he may have lighted the range at tea-time, when you say he generally lit it."

"Not 'im. Not if 'e was goin' out all evening. 'E was careful like. Always on at me if I wasted anything; even them weeds 'ad to go on compost heap. 'Wot you tike out of a garden, you've got to put back on it,' 'e said. Always saying that, 'e was."

That one, pondered Macdonald, was certainly straight from the horse's mouth—the wisdom of a gardener being handed on by an evacuee urchin from Shoreditch.

"You want to know if 'e lit 'is fire tea-time," went on Alf. "I'll bet 'e didn't, but I'll ask t'others. We played up 'ere Saturday afternoon—on the bank there, and you can see Little Thatch chimneys up there. 'E lighted 'is fire with kindling and billets to get it going, and 'e banked it up with coal later. Wood smoke's blue, see? If 'e'd lighted 'is fire tea-time one on us'd've seen it for a cert. I'll ask t'others—but if I didn't notice, them wouldn't 'ave, neither—unless it were Tommy Briggs. Comes from the Isle o' Dogs, 'e does, and 'e notices things."

Macdonald chuckled. He liked this evidence of London Pride.

"Well, let's get on to Saturday evening, Alf. You saw Mr. Vaughan pass in his car?"

"Iss." The affirmative was pure Devonshire this time. "Saw 'im and saw 'is car. Hadn't got trailer on it, nor big baskets inside, neither. I could see right in, 'cause the garden 'ere's higher than the road. Waved, 'e did, like this, same's usual."

"Had he got a hat on?"

"Yus. Always wore an 'at, even in garden, 'cause of 'is eyes. I'd know that 'at anywhere. Some 'at. Said 'e pinched it off a Jew in Lime'ouse—but that was only 'is joke."

"Oh, he'd got his old hat on, had he. Not dressed in his best, so to speak. Had he a coat on?"

"Yus. Old brown coat: patch on the elbows wot 'e did 'imself. 'E'd got the windows of the car down and 'is elbow was outside, like this, see?"

"And you saw him again when he came back at nine?"

"Iss. I'd gone up to bed, but I 'eard 'is car, 'ooting at Ridd's cross, three 'oots 'e always gave. I watched at me window, just to see 'im go by."

"But you couldn't see so much from up there?"

"No, but I saw 'im wave, and I saw 'is elbow. Always drove like that, as though 'e were too big to get all of 's self inside. Elbow sticking out, see?"

Macdonald nodded. "You couldn't see inside the car, not to see if there was a passenger?"

"There wasn't. I saw through the back window as 'e turned, and Uncle Roob, 'e saw t'car, and 'e knew there wasn't nobody else in it."

"Right. Now we'll get on to what happened later. You ran to Manor Thatch and woke them up?"

"Yus. Chucked stones at t'windows and yelled. Colonel, 'e told me to run to 'Inton Mallory—phone was dead, 'e said, and I ran down t'big pasture. All thiccy beasts, cows and that, looked that big. Moonlight 't'was. I wasn't 'alf rattled, tell yer straight, and that cottage burning... cripes... I blubbed, I was that..."

"I'm sure you did, and I think you did jolly well to keep your head, Alf. You woke up Mr. Hesling and then you ran back?"

"Iss, but they caught me up before I got to cottage. I was blown, my legs wouldn't run no more."

"When you got back to the cottage what happened? Did they tell you to run off home?"

"Iss. Not me. I stayed. Mr. 'Esling 'e shouted something about the beasts, and Ted got the linhey open. I thought of they ducks. I ran round and climbed t'hedge into orchard—'twas too fierce along by the fire, so I went by the pasture—but someone'd got there first. They ducks were all in a 'uddle bottom of orchard, far away as they could get. I druv 'em into pasture."

"Well, you did all you could, Alf. I'd have been proud if I'd done as much when I was ten."

"But 'twasn't no use, see? I woke up too late," said Alf forlornly.

3

It was well on in the evening before Macdonald returned the Superintendent's bike, and Bolton said:

"You've had a day of it, and no mistake. You'll be glad of supper and bed, seeing you were in the train all last night."

"I've had some supper and bed can wait a bit," rejoined Macdonald. "I've got some extra items to add to the evidence if you'd like to hear them now."

"I certainly should," said Bolton, looking keenly at the other. Macdonald's voice did not give the impression that his "items" were negligible. The two men sat down in the well-polished room where they had consulted that morning, and Macdonald began speaking:

"On the assumption that the fire was due to accident you suggested two probable causes: one was faulty wiring leading to a fuse: one was the uncovering of a beam in the kitchen chimney. I think it's certain that a fused wire had nothing to do with it. I got an electrician out this evening, and the batteries in the electric plant were not charged. They had been charged, or partially charged, some time, because Vaughan had had all his lights on, but it seems probable he located a fault in the batteries. Be that as it may, the electric fittings could not have been responsible, because there could have been no current on."

Bolton's face flushed uncomfortably: "I ought to have thought about that," he said. "I hadn't even realised that there were storage batteries... I don't know a thing about such jobs. I ought to have got a man out before, but I only thought of the wiring inside the house—and that had gone west in the fire. Well, that's one point settled. What about the chimney?"

"I haven't got any conclusive evidence about that yet, but one point is worth considering. Vaughan said he got two bricks out of the chimney—Miss St Cyres is willing to swear that he said bricks. That chimney is built of stone: it's only the upper part of the stack that is brick. It seems probable to me that at some time the brick coping was damaged in a gale, and a couple of bricks fell in and got lodged in the bird's nest Vaughan found on the ledge in the upper part of it. When the stack was repaired the builder didn't bother about the whereabouts of the fallen bricks. If this idea is right it doesn't look as though the removal of the bricks should have bared a beam—but I'm hoping to get clearer evidence about this later."

"Then, taking the balance, you're disposed to believe that Commander Wilton is right?"

"I don't know, Bolton. If this case is not what it appeared to be—pure accident—then it may prove to be the devil of a complex business. Wilton may have been right in some of his reasoning, but quite wrong in his conclusion. However, listen to a few more of the items I corkscrewed out during a very garrulous day. About those ducks."

"Good lord, what about 'em?"

"Young Alf—who struck me as a very sharp, sensible laddie—says that when he got to the duck-house that Saturday night to let the quackers out, the door was wide open and the ducks were at the bottom of the orchard—but nobody else had let them out. Another of Alf's items, corroborated by Dickon, was that Vaughan didn't light his kitchen fire at all that Saturday. He used his Primus."

"Where are you leading to, Chief?"

"It looks like foul play somewhere, Super, but by whom there's no evidence. Have you talked to one Thomas Gressingham?"

"I had a few words with him, but he had no direct evidence to offer."

"No, he hasn't much direct evidence now, but he's got the deuce of a lot to say. So far as I can gather, if the verdict of accident had gone unchallenged, Mr. Gressingham would have been happy to let well alone. Now that he realises a further investigation is being made he's very forthcoming, with a spate of queries and sugges-tions—proper red herrings. Mr. Gressingham wants to know what proof we have got that the remains found in the ashes are in truth the remains of Nicholas Vaughan."

The Superintendent swore, softly but vigorously, and Macdonald nodded. "I quite agree—but the gentleman has what counsel would call a nice point. If we don't tidy this case up, it looks like being a *cause célèbre*: Commander Wilton suggests that Nicholas Vaughan met his end by foul play. I think Mr. Gressingham is going to suggest that some other chap met his death by foul play at the hands of Nicholas Vaughan."

"I just don't believe it!" spluttered Bolton, and Macdonald replied:

"I don't either, but what we believe is going to butter no parsnips. When the identity of a victim is in doubt we generally have nice tidy methods for determining the facts—finger-prints, Bertillon measurements, old operation scars, dentistry. Even the latter will fail us, because, if old Dickon tells the truth, Vaughan told him that he had never had toothache and never been to the dentist. Now while it's unusual for a man of thirty to have no stopped teeth, it's not quite phenomenal. It does happen. When I was thirty I was in that happy state myself."

"Good God!" groaned Bolton, and his exclamation—or groan—was in no way concerned with Macdonald's teeth. The Superintendent was just beginning to realise some of the complexities which Macdonald had perceived to be potential in the case when he first studied it. Bolton was no defeatist, however. He sat up, squared his shoulders and spoke firmly.

"I've no doubt you're right in describing it as a 'nice point,' but I damn' well don't believe it, and the fact that Gressingham put the idea forward simply makes me ask what he has got to gain by confusing the issue. Now look here. You have had more experience of these sticky cases than I have. What can we do to kill that particular rumour?"

"At the moment all I propose to do is to get a report from the hospital authorities, and also to ask Wilton if he can make any helpful contribution."

"Good. It's up to him—he barged in with cries of Wolf. I wonder how he'll like this development."

Macdonald chuckled. "Admittedly I sympathise with your line of thought, but it looks like plenty of work ahead of us. Now leaving the fertile Mr. Gressingham for the moment, just concentrate on those ducks. It seems to me that if the ducks were not shut up in their house on Saturday night, the probability is that Nicholas Vaughan did not get back to Little Thatch. A careful chap like that would never have forgotten to shut the ducks up, would he? You ought to know more about ducks than I do, Super. Wouldn't you say it's true that poultry keepers do certain things by routine—that is, they do not go to bed leaving their birds on the loose?"

"Quite true," said Bolton, "but say, if this is the explanation, for once in his life Vaughan got drunk: that would explain everything. He forgot the ducks, and he knocked over his paraffin lamp as he staggered into bed."

"Yes, that would explain quite a lot, but you've got to remember that he drove his car home along a very awkward road: he remembered to wave in his usual way when he passed Corner Cottage, and he backed his car into a very narrow gateway in a manner which denotes sobriety of mind."

"Yes. All right. Since everybody else is guessing in this case, I'm going to guess too. When Vaughan got back to Little Thatch, he found somebody—or something—waiting for him which quite put his usual routine out of his mind. How's that for a start?"

"That's all right. I'm pretty sure Commander Wilton would agree with that for a beginning."

"Damn you, I didn't mean that," protested Bolton, and Macdonald replied:

"No. I know you didn't—but we've got to foresee other people's suggestions in this case. However, take your idea for what it's worth. What evidence have we about Little Thatch between the time Nicholas Vaughan would have got home and the time the fire was observed? We know that one person at least went into Vaughan's garden. That was Colonel St Cyres. He admits this himself: further, he told me that when he was in the garden he smelt the smoke of a Balkan Sobranie cigarette, and the only person known to smoke those cigarettes hereabouts is Mr. Thomas Gressingham."

"But here, steady on! Why didn't the Colonel tell me that to begin with? It's the first I've heard of it."

"Yes. Apparently he was ashamed to put forward a piece of evidence for which he could offer no proof. I think that for once, although he would not have admitted it, Colonel St Cyres was of the same mind as Mr. Gressingham: accept the verdict of accident and leave bad alone. It wasn't until I came on the scene that Colonel St Cyres, *and* Mr. Gressingham, began to think."

"But, heavens above, Chief! St Cyres is above suspicion. He's…"

"To my mind, nobody is above suspicion," said Macdonald. "Detection involves a sceptical attitude towards one's neighbours. Give me one clear, obvious motive to kill Vaughan—any really sound reason for killing him—and I'll suspect anybody. Lots of people may have had the chance of killing Vaughan. An unsuspecting man is not difficult to kill. Any fool can do it with a coal hammer."

"Oh my God!" groaned Bolton. "If you go on like this I shall suspect that chap Wilton killed him."

"Suspect by all means, but bear in mind that what you want is a motive—and remember this, too. If a motive for killing anybody can be ascribed to Nicholas Vaughan there will be plenty of people to point out how easy it was for him to have killed an enemy and to have left the body in the burning cottage."

And Bolton had no choice but to agree.

CHAPTER TEN

I

T HE MATTER OF THE FIRE AT LITTLE THATCH AND NICHOLAS Vaughan's tragic death had inevitably provided food for discussion and debate throughout the locality. It has been said by many townsfolk—especially by Londoners—that countryfolk who have not suffered from bombing or the major tragedies of war are callous in their disregard of other people's sufferings. The Billeting authorities and the W.V.S. had frequently to argue with recalcitrant housewives who wished to refuse to accept billeting orders which would bring bombed-out townsfolk into farms and cottages. "We don't want them here and we can't do with them." Anne St Cyres had often countered this objection by saying: "Can't you imagine what it feels like to have had your home destroyed, to be left standing in a bombed street with nothing but the clothes you've got on, and then to hear people who have lost nothing at all saying 'We don't want you. You're only a nuisance'?"

The fact was, of course, that imagination—particularly the slowly moving imagination of folk in a safe and remote countryside—fails to realise the distresses of those who are strangers. London, Bristol and Hull might be showered with incendiaries and thousands might be homeless, but this fact did not impress the rural mind as did the burning of one thatched cottage and the death of one man who was coming to be regarded as a neighbour.

"That's a bad business: oughtn't never to've happened, and him a careful, sensible fellow. Can't see how't came about. 'Tisn't natural." So said the farmers and their wives, who had lived in thatched houses for generations. "'Twasn't as if he went meddling with t'place, putting in new fireplaces and that," argued old Amos Coddling in the bar of the Blue Boar, but Joe Hosgood replied: "'Twas all along o' they wires he put in. Better've left well alone and used lamps like all of we."

The Coroner's verdict had been accepted on the whole, though a few dissentient voices argued darkly that if all were known that ought to be known, 'twould have been other than accident the Coroner would have found. Macdonald's appearance on the scene reanimated the discussion.

"Iss, what did I tell mun? 'Twas no accident at all," cried many, and theorists aired their views in field and kitchen and bar regardless of the law of slander. One of the suspects named by many was Tom Benworthy, the farm labourer who had applied for a tenancy of Little Thatch prior to Nicholas Vaughan and had been refused it. "Mun did it for spite," declared his neighbours—for Benworthy and his slatternly young wife were unpopular and generally distrusted. "No, not Tom. Him'd never have dared," argued old Amos Coddling. "More like 'twas that London gent to Hinton Mallory: hated Mr. Vaughan proper, mun did—and goings on there such as shouldn't be with that brass-faced young madam the Colonel's so good to."

"Now, now, none o' that, Tom," expostulated Joe Hosgood. "Her's wed to young Mr. Denis, and I won't hear nought like that. If you asks me, 'twas that tu'rble fat chat along o' he. Him's a praper bad un, after the maids of an evening."

All this conversation was carried on in the bar of the Blue Boar, and came to the ears of Mr. William Holsworthy, who was having a glass of cider in the private saloon bar. Mr. Holsworthy was a small landowner and a very prosperous farmer whose land adjoined Colonel St Cyres. Holsworthy was a man of seventy, but still hale and hearty and quick of hearing. He made his way into the bar and spoke his mind.

"Listen to me, all of you," he commanded. "It's lucky for you it was I who heard you chattering. I know you all and I won't misjudge you. You, Amos Coddling—you're an honest man and the finest thatcher in the county, but you're a damned old fool, chattering like a jackdaw. If your words were reported to the police you could be put in the dock for slander, and don't you forget it! And you, too, Joe Hosgood—you're old enough to know better. Now you hearken to me. If any of you have got any evidence in this matter, it's your duty to report it: if you haven't got any evidence, don't go slandering other folks. I've warned you, and I shan't warn you again. I won't have slander circulated. Amos Coddling—what evidence have you got that Mr. Gressingham had ought to do with the fire at Little Thatch?"

Old Coddling looked foolish and fiddled with his glass, but a younger man spoke.

"Mun told Mr. Hesling he went to bed just after ten o'clock that night—but his car was out later than that. Young Alf 'eard it pass. Ridd, he saw it heading for t'main road. Benworthy saw it just past Ridd's cross. If mun's honest, why do he tell lies about bein' in bed?"

"What's his car got to do with the fire at Little Thatch?" demanded Holsworthy, and Joe Hosgood plucked up his courage.

"If mun's telling lies, mun's got summat t' hide," he declared, "and 'twas Mr. Gressingham keeps on saying that the Colonel, he was the last man inside Little Thatch, and us won't have nought said against Colonel."

"Quite right, too," agreed old Holsworthy. "If I hear Mr. Gressingham say that, I'll warn him as I've warned you—but think a bit, all of you. Has any one of you got any evidence at all to offer—anything beyond parrot talk? There's been an inquest, and a very thorough enquiry, and the Coroner's jury was satisfied it was plain accident. Can't you let it be?"

"If Coroner's jury was satisfied, why for did they send a detective down from Lunnon?" queried Hosgood. "I see mun, sitting on the bank staring at Little Thatch, iss, and talking to Alf, too. And do you know, sir, Mr. Vaughan never so much as lit his kitchen fire that Saturday, no, nor's lamp neither, 'cause t'was light when he got home. Colonel said there wasn't no light. Reckon Crowner's jury didn't think of all that. He's a tu'rble straight chap this Lunnon detective. Him's getting at things."

Mr. Holsworthy rubbed his white head and said, "You let him get at things, then, and answer any questions he sees fit to ask you, but don't go naming anybody without evidence. I've warned you, and don't let me hear any more accusations like I heard just now—and you, too, landlord—see to it that gossip doesn't spread from your house, or there'll be trouble for you too."

2

Mr. Holsworthy left the Blue Boar feeling troubled in his mind. Devon born, he was an educated man and on easy terms with his wealthier as well as his humbler neighbours. He thought the world of the Devon farm labourers and he understood them, and he knew the way in which Macdonald's appearance would cause them to gossip and surmise amongst themselves. Holsworthy had met both Gressingham and Radcliffe and disliked the pair of them heartily, but he believed that the suspicion in which they were held was due to the fact that they were "foreigners." A fellow-farmer had said to Holsworthy that day in all sincerity: "Miss Jameson, who's been helping with billeting, wanted my wife to take in a London family. I don't see it. Strikes me all Londoners are dirty. Look at the way some of 'em have treated the places they've been lent." Unhappily it was a fact that the habits and behaviour of some of the London evacuees had caused the name "Londoner" to be regarded askance in the countryside. Pondering deeply, Mr. Holsworthy got into his car and drove on to Exeter, where he had legitimate business to transact, and later he looked in at a recently formed Men's Club. This establishment had been organised by a few landowners and professional men who wanted to have somewhere quiet where they could eat, transact business and read their papers, and the unusual venture was a success. Holsworthy, looking in at the big sitting-room, found half-a-dozen men present, among them Howard Brendon, who was studying a sale list. Holsworthy went and sat beside him, saying:

"I'd be glad of a word with you, Brendon. I'm a bit bothered in my mind about some gossip around the Mallorys."

Brendon folded his catalogue neatly and put it in his pocket, and then turned and studied Holsworthy with his curiously light eyes, and waited for him to continue.

"You've heard there's a Scotland Yard man down working on this Little Thatch case?"

Brendon nodded. "Yes. As it happens, I met him. A very able fellow, I believe—one of the best type of police officials."

"Does his presence indicate that there's any fresh evidence—since the inquest?"

"Not to my knowledge. So far as I can gather, it means that a Naval officer—Vaughan's one-time commander—has been making a fuss in London, demanding a further enquiry. All tommy-rot to my mind, and waste of a good man's time."

"Very glad to hear you say so, Brendon, very glad!" exclaimed Holsworthy. "I followed the evidence carefully, and I've had a talk with our men down here, and I can't see there's the least reason to suspect murder. One of the main reasons that I deprecate this reopening of the case is the gossip it causes. I was in at the Blue Boar—our local—a short while ago, and the place was seething with gossip. I went into the bar and spoke my mind. The silly fellows were bandying names about—and that brings me to my point. Mr. Gressingham's a friend of yours, isn't he? I gather you introduced him to the locality, as it were."

"I don't quite see your point, but we might as well be accurate," replied Brendon. "Gressingham is my broker, and he's a very astute man in his own line. He wrote to me saying he wanted to buy property in this county, but it was not due to his acquaintance with me that he went to stay at Hinton Mallory. He went there, I believe, at the suggestion of young Mrs. St Cyres—a lady with whom I was not previously acquainted."

"Well, the plain fact is this: gossip around Mallory Fitzjohn is saying that Gressingham was out in his car on the night of the fire, and that he's denied the fact."

Brendon took out his cigarette case and lighted a cigarette with deliberation.

"Gossip is going to go a good deal further than that before we hear the last of this business," he said. "There's hardly a name that isn't being bandied about. You, I, Colonel St Cyres—we'll all be dragged in, as well as Gressingham and his friends. It's human nature. Hint at a mystery and the wildest tales become current. I admit Gressingham's a fool over this business. He's going round making the craziest suggestions instead of holding his tongue. The result is that half the members here come to me saying 'Gressingham's a friend of yours, isn't he? Is it true he had something to do with the Little Thatch business?' I tell you I'm sick of the whole thing. The Mallowton police and fire brigade made a very careful enquiry into the circumstances. Admittedly they couldn't produce an exact reason for the fire—the place was destroyed too thoroughly—but they were satisfied that accident accounted for it. Then this Naval fellow comes along and prevails on the authorities to reopen the enquiry. What happens? Every Tom, Dick and Harry starts making suggestions. Gressingham ought to have enough common sense not to join in—and I've told him so plainly."

Holsworthy nodded. "I agree with every word you say," he declared. "All the same, I'm a bit puzzled about Gressingham. He seems to have made himself disliked in the Mallorys."

"Natural enough, when you come to think of it," replied Brendon. "He's a City man. He doesn't understand country people, with their prejudices and narrow view points, their distrust of the unfamiliar. Gressingham brings town ways into the depths of a conservative countryside. The result is he's noticed, criticised and condemned. Of course every farm labourer is going round saying if there's been any dirty work it's the London stranger who's at the bottom of it."

Another man came and joined in the conversation—this was John Hartland, a well-known accountant. "D'you mind if I butt in, Brendon? I'm interested in what you're saying. As it happens, I've heard some of the gossip that's going round, though I don't know Mr. Gressingham, nor Mallory Fitzjohn either. The fact is country morals and town morals are different propositions. The country folk say 'He's got a wife, why doesn't she live with him?' and 'What's he doing making up to another man's wife?' If he were in London he could take young Mrs. St Cyres out to dinner *every* night and nobody would bother. In the country folk start talking, and once they start it's the devil to stop them."

"It is that," agreed Holsworthy, and changed the trend of the conversation a little. "What I can't see is this: why there's a palaver about Gressingham taking his car out that night. If he'd wanted to set fire to Little Thatch he wouldn't have wanted a car—quite the other way about. A car's too noticeable."

"Good God, man, if you're supposing Gressingham fired Little Thatch you're taking leave of your senses!" broke in Brendon. "The whole taradiddle is preposterous! The next thing you'll be saying is that *I* helped him with the job. Rumour begets rumour."

"That one won't wash," said Hartland. "I happen to know you were in Taunton that evening, and that you spent the night in Taunton. As it happened, I stayed at the same hotel; I saw you at dinner, and later as well."

Brendon looked at him with an expression of disgust. "It's come to a pretty pass if one can't spend a night where one chooses without accounting for one's actions," he said testily. "Well, here's my opinion of the Little Thatch business. The cottage caught fire by accident and Vaughan was overcome by the fumes. A ghastly thing to happen, but it's been known to happen before. All this suggestion of murder is balderdash, and I'm sick of the whole argument. The upshot of it all is that everybody gossips about everybody else and rakes up all the muck they can find. If I get first-hand evidence of accusations against Gressingham, I shall advise him to take proceedings. The motto of 'Mind your own business' is not only good manners, it's good counsel, too." And with that Mr. Brendon uttered a curt "good-evening" and left the room.

Hartland raised his eyebrows. "Seems we've said the wrong thing—but he's a peppery customer."

Holsworthy mopped his brow. "Said the wrong thing!" he exclaimed. "You put your foot in it properly, starting talking about Gressingham's wife."

The other's jaw dropped. "Good God! You don't mean that Gressingham's sweet on Brendon's wife! I thought…"

"No, no, no!" protested Holsworthy in horrified tones. "I never suggested such a thing, never! For heaven's sake don't let that rumour get to Brendon's ears—he'd be the first man to take you into court if you start gossip about his affairs. No. The thing you said that upset Brendon was 'He's got a wife. Why doesn't he live with her?' Brendon was married last year, as you probably know, but I gather that it wasn't a success. His wife has left him. She gave out that she was doing war-work—Red Cross or relief-work or something—and I've no doubt that's true, but Brendon didn't like your remarks. You can't be too careful when you make generalisations about matrimony."

"Well, I didn't know, and it was obvious I shouldn't have made that remark if I had known," said Hartland, "but Brendon doesn't really interest me. He's a dried-up stick of a cuss. What does interest me is Mr. Tommy Gressingham. I'm told he's a hot lot. Come to think of it—without wishing to involve myself in the law of slander—isn't there a possibility that Vaughan *did* see a little too much of Gressingham's goings on?"

"Now look here, that's just the sort of gossip which is mischievous," said Holsworthy. "What I say is this: if you have any evidence to offer in this case, take it to the police. If not, keep quiet. It's not fair to spread rumours which have no foundation. I don't know anything about Gressingham's relations with women, and I don't want to know, but I've a great respect for Colonel St Cyres. He'd be most distressed if he knew that his daughter-in-law's name was being bandied about. I don't like it, and I won't have it—not in my presence, anyway."

"All right: no offence meant, old man—but it's only human nature to wonder. If it hadn't been that the Yard had sent their biggest gun down here to make enquiries I should never have queried the Coroner's verdict."

"I agree with Brendon," replied Holsworthy. "I regret the case is being prolonged. I think the verdict was a fair one."

"So you may, Holsworthy," put in another voice, "but there's no smoke without fire—and the Yard doesn't butt in without a very good reason."

CHAPTER ELEVEN

I

LIFE AT MANOR THATCH HAD BEEN DIFFICULT THESE LAST days, and Anne, who generally refused to go away from home under any circumstances, was beginning to feel for the first time in her life that to get away for a while was the thing she wanted above all else. Since the fire at Little Thatch she seemed to be living under a constant strain, first in the effort to appear serene and cheerful, and then in the effort to keep her temper. Anne had not been in love with Nicholas Vaughan, but she had been very fond of him. Something in the steady way he worked—and enjoyed working—warmed her heart. She was aware that the work he did, both in garden and house, had the creative element in it. Vaughan had been making his own home, turning a house—which some would have described as a hovel—and a garden which had been almost derelict, into a beautiful and orderly place. Anne had envied him a little, for though she loved Manor Thatch, she was also aware that she herself would have enjoyed making a home, creating something that was characteristically her own, and which had not been completed before she was born.

She had never asked Vaughan any questions, neither had she discussed his private affairs with her father: she had not known if he intended to get married, but something about the way he was improving and decorating the house made her feel sure that he was not doing it for his own satisfaction alone. Reticent and self-contained as she was, Anne had enough of the romantic in her composition to derive pleasure from the thought of Vaughan working away so steadily to prepare a home for his bride. His death—a fact which Anne had never queried for one fleeting second—had been a shock to her: it was as though something had broken, something been lost and wasted, and it left her feeling desolate.

Anne had more reasons than one for concealing her thoughts: Colonel St Cyres had been deeply shocked and distressed by the tragedy at Little Thatch and he seemed to have aged years in a few days. He was generally a serene, steadfast man: no happenings in the war, not even the dark days of Dunkirk, had affected his quiet cheerfulness and confidence, but this lesser tragedy so nearly at his own doors had shattered his content and affected his nerves. All the more reason then that Anne should keep a steadfast front, and a sense of proportion. She hid her own feeling of desolation in the effort to console and cheer her father.

Apart from Colonel St Cyres' depression she had to face her sister-in-law's malicious gossip. June St Cyres had always resented the fact that Vaughan had been given the tenancy at Little Thatch, and she had nursed her grievance, never losing an opportunity to deride and belittle Vaughan in every way. She had also insinuated that Anne was in love with Vaughan and that the granting of the tenancy to him had been a put-up job. Anne had ignored all such innuendoes, but she found it much harder to ignore June's repetitions of Gressingham's opinions, and the suspicions which she cast on Vaughan's possible motive and behaviour. It was only by a determined effort of will that Anne avoided quarrelling with her—and also prevented her gossip reaching the ears of Colonel St Cyres.

2

Anne was busy in the garden when a message was brought out to her that a lady had called to see her. Regretfully leaving her job in the strawberry beds, Anne went inside expecting to see one of the members of the Women's Institute. Instead she found a stranger, a neatly turned out young woman in a well-cut suit, with a Henry Heath hat pulled on at just the right angle.

"Miss St Cyres?" The visitor's voice was a pleasant one, rather deep pitched—certainly not a Devonshire voice.

"How do you do? I am Anne St Cyres. I don't think we have met before…?"

"No. I am Elizabeth Vaughan."

Even then it was some seconds before Anne realised the identity of the unexpected visitor: the latter, seeing Anne's puzzled face, went on patiently,

"My brother was Nicholas Vaughan. I am told that you and your father knew him."

"I beg your pardon," cried Anne, her face flushed with vexation at her own obtuseness. "Of course we knew him. Do sit down, and forgive me for being so dense. We have been so distressed about it all, so very unhappy…" She broke off, pulling a chair forward for her guest, and Elizabeth Vaughan watched her in a detached, analytical sort of way as she seated herself composedly, saying:

"I am sorry you should have been distressed. It was a wretched thing to happen. I saw the remains of the cottage and it certainly does look pretty horrible. I should apologise for bothering you, because I know Nick was only your tenant, but it's so difficult to know who to go to for information. I have been abroad for some months, on an official job with the Rehabilitation Commission, and I couldn't get back earlier. Actually the news only reached me a few days ago."

Her voice was level and quite unemotional, and something about her very calm and her immaculate neatness made Anne feel dishevelled and clumsy. She replied:

"It must have been a terrible shock for you. I'm so sorry—it's difficult to tell you how sad we feel about it, too."

"That's very kind of you, Miss St Cyres. I'd better explain a little—I haven't seen Nick for years. We were never very much attached, and though I admit it was a shock to hear of him dying in such a way, I don't want to pretend—well, that it was heartbreaking for me personally. I'm sorry, and I think it was a miserable business, but I've seen so many horrors in the course of my job that I've had to develop a fairly thick skin. It's tiresome for you being harrowed by the thought of it all. I know it was very close to your home, and one feels things that happen near at hand like that—but I don't want you to feel you've got to worry about me, too. I came, as I said, for information."

"I'll do anything that I can, and so will my father," said Anne, "but first, can't I get you some tea? You must have had a long journey."

"No, thanks very much. I had lunch in Exeter. I'll smoke, if I may. Now, do you mind telling me—did you know my brother personally or was he just your tenant?"

"I knew him personally, in the sense that I sometimes went over to Little Thatch to see how he was getting on. You probably know your brother wasn't a sociable person: he didn't want to waste time paying calls or having meals out, and we didn't bother him with invitations to come over here—but my father and I both thought of him as a friend, and we liked him."

"I suppose he never told you why he came and settled in Devonshire?"

"I thought it was because Commander Wilton told him about Little Thatch—and he liked it."

"Yes, I see"; the calm voice was almost abrupt—the tones of one who did not want to waste time. "Wilton's a very good sailor, I believe," she went on, "but like many other sailor men he's a good bit of a fool. I gather that it's he who has started this crazy story about Nick being murdered. I hope you don't believe it?"

"No, I don't believe it," replied Anne. "I think it's a frightful suggestion. After all, why—why go out of your way to make mysteries? The whole thing was tragic—but fires *do* happen, and when they happen in old thatched houses the result is nearly always complete destruction."

"Quite—I'm glad to know you take the common sense point of view. I take it there isn't the least evidence about murderous enmity between Nick and his neighbours?"

"None whatever. People liked him and respected him—"

"They would," said the calm voice. "Nick was a reliable, steady-going fellow, very trustworthy and sensible, and most people liked him, unless he happened to dislike them, which didn't happen often, because he was quite good at suffering fools gladly—much better than I am. Now I want to explain quite clearly why I came to see you. I hate bothering people with my own affairs—"

"You're not bothering me. We'd do anything we could to help."

"Thank you very much. The point is this. Nick and I were left orphans at an early age, and we were brought up by an uncle and aunt in the north country. The aunt died a few years back, and our uncle died at midnight on the night of April 30th, the same night Nick died. In his will our uncle left his land to Nick, but if Nick predeceased him the estate was to go to a distant cousin. Do you see the difficulty? We don't know who died first, Nick or the uncle."

"Yes, I see, but it's going to be very difficult... No one could know."

"I suppose they couldn't. It's all a dreadful muddle. Uncle hid his will away among some old papers and it's only just come to light. I'm trying to straighten things up, because presumably I'm Nick's legal heir—his next of kin. Unless he was married...?"

The calm voice paused on a note of interrogation, and Anne replied: "I know nothing about his personal affairs, but I don't think he was married. You had better see my father. Mr. Vaughan said something to him about hoping to get married soon."

"That's good enough," replied Elizabeth Vaughan. "Nick was very truthful. He'd never have said that if he'd been married already. Did he say when he hoped to marry?"

"I don't think so—but I'll go and find father. He will be able to tell you."

When Anne returned with Colonel St Cyres a few minutes later, Elizabeth Vaughan was still sitting in just the same position, calm and self-contained. She stood up and bowed, replying to Colonel St Cyres' words of sympathy with a composure which almost shocked Anne—it was so deliberate and complete. As soon as they were seated again Elizabeth Vaughan went straight to the point, explaining what she wanted to know without wasting any time. Colonel St Cyres listened to her in silence, and said at length:

"I quite grasp the nature of your problem, Miss Vaughan, and I only regret that I cannot do much to help you. It is a very painful business and I am afraid it will be impossible to do more than to presume the hour of your brother's death. It must have happened some time between nine o'clock, when he was last seen, and three in the morning, when the state of the fire was such that no one could have been alive in the building."

"Surely it's possible to get nearer to the time than that," she said. "The cottage must have been all right when Nick went back there just after nine o'clock."

"Of course, of course," said St Cyres quickly. "The cottage was all right when I passed it at half-past nine—in fact later than that, because I passed it again when I returned from the post box just before ten."

"Well, the lawyers will have to settle that," she said, in her quick, determined way. "It seems to me that if the place wasn't burning at ten o'clock it must have taken more than two hours for it to have produced enough smoke to make a man unconscious. That's what happened, of course. People use this horrible phrase 'burnt to death,' but victims who die in fires are nearly always rendered insensible by smoke." She paused, and St Cyres murmured a pained acquiescence, and then he went on:

"It's the matter of inheritance which has to be decided, I gather. Is it landed property which is in question?"

"Yes. It's the farmhouse and land where Nick and I were brought up. We loved it, both of us. I hate to think of it going to the Hawkins branch of the family. They're town-folk, business men of sorts, and they don't care a hoot for Lannerdale. It oughtn't to have been left to them, but my uncle was determined to leave it to a man—he was too old-fashioned to like the idea of a woman land-owner, so he cut me out."

St Cyres nodded: Anne could see that this matter of inheritance interested him a lot, and he went on:

"Do you know if the property was left to your brother outright, without limiting clauses?"

"Yes, to Nick and to his heirs. Of course uncle thought he would marry and have a family, as he doubtless would have done had he lived. As it is, I am his heir. After Dunkirk, when he joined the Navy, Nick wrote to me and told me that he had made his will, leaving me everything, and I did the same thing, leaving all I'd got to him. We both inherited a little capital from our parents."

St Cyres nodded. "I understand. I only hope that the lawyers will take a sensible view and that the land will become yours, as you care about it so much."

"I love it," she said abruptly. "I shall fight for it, too. It's not going to those awful Hawkins if I can help it. Now about my other question. I asked your daughter if Nick were married."

"I should say emphatically, no," rejoined St Cyres. "Vaughan told me quite definitely, in confidence, that he hoped to get married shortly and to bring his wife to live at Little Thatch."

"He didn't mention her name?"

"No. Not in any way—but hadn't he mentioned the matter to you?"

"No. We had very little to do with one another after we left school. I went to Newnham—I got a scholarship—and thereafter our ways divided. We were quite good friends, but we didn't see eye to eye over life. It seemed quite natural and reasonable that we should make wills leaving our property to one another, pro tem—we'd got quite a strong family feeling, you see, but we didn't hanker after each other's company. Nick didn't like what he chose to call the 'academic' woman, and I think it's quite likely if he'd got married that he wouldn't have told me about it until it was a *fait accompli*—and vice versa. I didn't write to him and tell him about my doings, and I'd no idea he'd settled in Devon. I knew he'd been in hospital and was discharged and was well again. Nick was a very reticent person. He didn't let the uncle know he had got this place—and letters were sent by the lawyers to him to his ship, which, I believe, was in Iceland until recently. So now you see." She paused, adding, "I apologise for burdening you with all this family chit-chat, but you've spoken to me so kindly it seemed natural to try to explain things a bit."

"My dear Miss Vaughan, you are not burdening us. We held your brother in esteem—I may say affection—and we admired the way he worked and his sense of responsibility. I mourn his loss as I mourn a friend, and anything I can do to help you I will do most gladly."

"Thank you very much. Nick was an excellent person: he was, as you say, responsible and hard-working, and he really loved the land and farming. Although he was a good engineer and a keen sailor, I always knew he would end by working on the land. It was in his bones." She smiled, and in that sudden lightening of her face St Cyres saw Nicholas Vaughan again, grinning happily. "Nick derided me for an intellectual," she said. "He called me doctrinaire and theorist, but I could make a good farmer, too. I don't like messing about in the house—Nick was much more domestic than I am—but I love cows and dairy work and horses. I used to think that when Nick took over Lannerdale I'd buy a small farm adjoining. I never told him so, but I always looked forward to being somewhere near him... What a pity—"

Anne began to like her better: this Elizabeth Vaughan had quite a lot in common with her brother after all.

"A pity indeed," said St Cyres sadly, but Miss Vaughan put in:

"One thing I have learnt from all this welter of misery called war, and that is that it's no use lamenting what is past. I'm sorry about Nick, but he would probably have been killed in the Navy anyway, and he must have had some happy hours working in that garden."

Colonel St Cyres nodded. "You're right there. If ever I've seen a happy man it was your brother, working over there at Little Thatch. He was a fine lad—I admired him as well as liked him."

Elizabeth Vaughan paused a moment and then said: "I don't know if you can help, but isn't it possible to scotch this crazy idea of Wilton's about Nick being murdered? I'm sure it's just rubbish, and I do loathe melodrama and gossip and prolonging the agony."

St Cyres looked distressed again.

"I should be only too thankful to think the enquiry was at an end," he said. "It makes the whole unhappy story doubly wretched. I will do all I can to stop any gossip in this neighbourhood, but I have no power to stop the enquiry. However, I do think the Scotland Yard officer is a very able man, intelligent and sensible— the enquiry could not be in better hands."

"Scotland Yard! Good heavens—does that mean that there is any real evidence that things were wrong?"

"No, I don't think it does," replied St Cyres. "I think Commander Wilton prevailed on the Assistant Commissioner to send an officer down here to make certain that no mistake has been made, and Chief Inspector Macdonald is doing his job most conscientiously, and considerately, too. I think it might be a good idea if you were to see him. He will have had full reports of all the evidence available, and it's possible he could help you with regard to the time problem in your brother's death."

She hesitated, and for the first time looked uncertain and nonplussed. "Yes, I suppose I ought to see him," she said. "The sickening part of it all is that this business about inheriting Lannerdale will make the whole thing more involved and increase the suspicions about foul play. I can see that—but it's all such rubbish… However—can you advise me how I'm to get in touch with the Yard man?"

"I will ring through to the Superintendent at Mallowton," replied St Cyres. "He will arrange everything for you."

"And meantime I will go and get some tea," said Anne. "You must need it after all this talking and worrying."

"What kind people you are," exclaimed Elizabeth Vaughan, "and how much Nick must have liked you."

3

A little over an hour later Macdonald himself appeared at Manor Thatch, having suggested when Colonel St Cyres got through to him on the telephone that it would be simpler for Miss Vaughan if he came straight out to see her. Colonel St Cyres brought the C.I.D. man into the sunny sitting-room at the Manor and said:

"I will leave you to talk to Miss Vaughan here. If there is anything I can do you have only to call me."

Elizabeth Vaughan set about her explanation to Macdonald with the straightforward clarity which was characteristic of her, ending up by saying: "I should like to say that I have no sympathy with Commander Wilton's views: I think he is trying to make more trouble and create a melodrama from a wretched accident. I hope you have found that the straightforward explanation is the most probable one."

"The trouble is that I don't seem able to produce a straightforward explanation," replied Macdonald. "There were two suggestions put forward to account for the fire; one was that the electric

wiring was faulty, the other was that the kitchen chimney was at
fault. Neither of these is tenable. The wiring could not have been
to blame because there was no current—the storage batteries were
not charged. I have spent most of to-day finding an old builder
who once repaired the kitchen chimney, and he has assured me
that no beam impinged on the stone chimney. The latter was
almost a separate structure, built out clear of the cob walls in the
way characteristic of the period, so I am farther than ever from
finding a straightforward explanation."

Elizabeth Vaughan sat silent, a frown on her smooth forehead.
"So you believe the cottage was deliberately fired?" she asked.

"I am afraid that such a view must be considered. Why should
that cottage have caught fire? I think it probable that the kitchen
fire had not even been lighted on the Saturday of the fire, and from
what I have been told of your brother, he was not the type of man
to be careless with candle or lamp. He was said to have returned
home shortly after nine o'clock in the evening. At half-past nine,
when Colonel St Cyres walked through the garden, there was no
light in the windows. In short, the theory of accident has nothing
to uphold it."

Elizabeth Vaughan sat very still, and when she answered her
voice was tense.

"Do you suppose that my brother went to bed and to sleep
and that somebody set light to the cottage without waking him?"

"No. If his death were due to foul play, I think he must have
been killed first, and the cottage fired afterwards to conceal the
crime. I may be quite wrong, but such a possibility exists. Will you
answer a few questions about him?"

"Of course"

"Have you any idea why he came to live in Devon?"

"The only answer to that seems to be that Commander Wilton suggested this place and Nick liked it."

"Would you have expected him to settle in Devon?"

"Certainly not. I should have expected him to go back to Lannerdale. They would have been glad to have him there: Uncle Joe was an old man and needed help."

"Your brother was fond of Lannerdale?"

"He loved it. We both did."

"Then can you make any suggestion as to why he came and settled in Devon and at the same time told his family nothing of his doings? Was there any reason to keep him from Lannerdale?"

"None that I know of."

"Next, about his intended marriage. Have you any idea whom he meant to marry?"

"No idea at all. He never mentioned anything of the kind to me."

Macdonald sat back in his chair and went on: "Doesn't it seem reasonable to connect the two topics—his choice of abode and his choice of a wife? Isn't it probable that his wife-to-be was either a Devonshire woman, or else a woman who did not want to go and live up north in Lannerdale?"

"That's quite a reasonable supposition, but what has it got to do with his death?"

"I have been thinking about this problem from every angle, Miss Vaughan. Your brother seems to have been a very straightforward person. I can only find two points concerning him which aren't easy to answer; one is his choice of Devon as a place to live in, one is the identity of the woman he hoped to marry. If there is any mystery about his death, it may well be concerned with those points. Can you remember any woman he cared about up north?"

"I don't know. My brother was a very reticent person and did not discuss his affairs with anybody. I think when he was an undergraduate he was in love with a girl over at Kirkby Lonsdale—but I believe she got married to someone else. Since then I've never known Nick to show any interest in a woman."

"Can you remember her name?"

"No. I never knew her. Her first name was Molly, or Mary or Maggie—something commonplace. She wasn't a native of our parts: she used to stay with some people we knew in the holidays. I imagine she was a teacher. Oh, it's all ages ago—and what can it have to do with the fire at Little Thatch?"

"Possibly nothing, but will you try to find out her name and who she married?"

"Yes. If you want me to. How furious Nick would have been about all this! He simply loathed people who ran round asking questions."

"I'm sorry, but questions have got to be asked. Another point: did your brother always type his letters?"

"Of late years, yes. His handwriting was execrable. He took to typing when he first got things published. He wrote a bit, mostly journalistic stuff, but he produced one book—pretty good. He didn't tell me about it—that was just like him—but I got it out of the library and recognised what he was writing about. It was called *Simon the Dalesman*—it was all about Lannerdale."

"I read that book," said Macdonald. "I'd been on a job up north, near Lancaster, and I enjoyed reading about the country I'd just been in. Then your brother, Nicholas Vaughan, was the Henry Heythwaite who wrote *Simon the Dalesman*?"

"Yes. I only told you that because you asked about his typing. I expect when he settled at Little Thatch he meant to do some more writing."

"Next," went on Macdonald, "I think you had better tell me about the cousins who were to inherit Lannerdale if your brother predeceased his uncle."

"The Hawkins. Sidney Herbert Hawkins—our pet abomination. He was something to do with shipping. He lived at Barrow when we were young, then he moved to Liverpool, and of recent years he's lived in Southampton or Portsmouth, I believe. If you want to know about him you can write to uncle's lawyers—Prestwich & Bonner of Sledbergh. I can't imagine Sidney Herbert killing Nick in order to inherit Lannerdale. He despised the place."

Macdonald sat silent for a moment, then he said: "One of the reasons, among many others, that a case like this has to be fully investigated is this: to kill the gossip which always rages round any unsolved problem. Do you know that an enterprising journalist has wormed out the fact that Colonel St Cyres went to Little Thatch at half-past nine that Saturday evening, and has insinuated that St Cyres was responsible for the subsequent disaster because Nicholas Vaughan was making love to his daughter?"

"How loathsome! Why, the old man is a dear—the kindest, straightest person."

"So I believe," said Macdonald, "but stories like that make me determined to find out what *did* happen."

"Oh dear!" Elizabeth Vaughan sighed. "All this fuss and gossip about Nick who *hated* fuss and gossip—and he probably forgot to blow his candle out when he went and got some paraffin from the cupboard."

"I don't see him doing that—not if he was the man I imagine him to be," replied Macdonald.

CHAPTER TWELVE

I

"TOMMY, DO YOU KNOW THAT THERE'S A STORY GOING round that you were out in your car on the night Little Thatch was burnt?"

It was June St Cyres who spoke. She had walked down to Hinton Mallory for her evening cocktail, and Gressingham was filling their glasses.

"My dear, if you collect every story that's going round the countryside dealing with that subject you'll have enough material to fill several volumes, and to provide actions for libel and slander sufficient to keep the courts busy for a year."

Gressingham sounded as cheerful as ever as he carried over June's glass, saying "Try this one—and happy days."

June sipped her drink thoughtfully. "Yes. That's all right," she said. "All the same, Tommy, I should kill that yarn stone dead. It's all very well to sound so happy and confident, but you're not getting a good press among the natives, so to speak, and this long-chinned Scots inspector is still snooping around."

"Let him snoop, sweet child. That's O.K. by me. I was *not* out in my car on the night in question—and that's that. Who said I was anyway, and if so, why?"

"That filthy evacuee brat at Dickon's. He's got a swollen head because the police have asked him so many questions. He boasts he can recognise the sound of every car in the district as it passes Corner Cottage, and he says your car passed after dark that evening."

"Well, he's wrong," replied Gressingham. "What that lad wants is a thrashing, and, by gad, he'll get one if he goes on telling lies about me. Actually I shouldn't be in the least surprised if the young devil knows a lot more about the fire than he's admitted. Brats of that type have indulged in arson many a time before this."

June sipped her drink thoughtfully: "Aren't you a bit inconsistent, Tommy?"

"How so, angel? You're the last person who should say that."

"Oh, I don't mean that," she replied. "I mean about this beastly fire. You keep on producing fresh ideas. First you say that the tenant at the cottage wasn't Vaughan at all: then you say the corpse might be someone Vaughan himself bumped off."

"Quite true. I only say *might,* mark you. There isn't a ha-porth of proof anywhere."

June paused a moment, fiddling with her rings, then she went on: "Well, I wish you could prove that your car was *not* taken out that night. Everyone's asking what you were doing on the road after you've said you didn't go out after ten."

"They are, are they?" asked Gressingham, and for once he sounded nettled. June went on hastily:

"You've said yourself how country people gossip, and it's true. Since the Yard man came here everyone is talking harder than ever. Because you're a Londoner they're all beginning to say that you know more about it than you've admitted."

"And who are 'they,' June?"

"The farm labourers and the butcher and baker and oilman, and all the rest. I know, because even Pops is getting a bit fed-up about it. It was he who said it'd be a good idea if you could prove that your car was not taken out that night."

"Did he, by jove! Very thoughtful of him. Perhaps he'd like me to prove that he was not the last person known to have been at Little Thatch before the fire."

"Oh, don't be tiresome, Tommy. He's a crashing bore, I know that, but he'd never do anything he didn't think right. Tommy, can't you prove, bang out, that your car didn't pass Dickon's cottage between ten and eleven o'clock? Ridd's saying he saw it now."

Gressingham shrugged his heavy shoulders. "I can't stop these clodhoppers inventing things, June. You know I walked back to the Manor with you that Saturday, and I left you on the terrace about twenty past nine. I walked through the spinney to the post box and back here by the road. It must have been about ten o'clock when I got back."

"Did you look in your garage?"

"Of course not. Why should I?"

"Then how do you know the car was there?"

"It was there next morning, none the worse."

"That doesn't prove anything. How do you know somebody didn't borrow it?"

"What on earth for? I wish you'd tell me what you're really thinking about, June."

She pushed her glass away and sat with her elbows on the table and spoke slowly: "I believe the police suspect that somebody killed Vaughan in the cottage after he got back and then set light to the place. That must have been done after most people hereabouts had gone to bed. Say, if the man who did it came down here and borrowed your car in order to get somewhere else to prove an alibi and then returned the car later. It's not impossible. You've always said that anyone could open the padlock on the shed where you keep the car."

"Well, well! You've been thinking it all out in the best detective story style, angel. That means that it was done by somebody who knew all about my car."

"I know, but everyone knows you've got a car down here. Tommy, did you see Rummy Radcliffe when you got in that night?"

"No. He went up to bed early, like he does sometimes, the lazy devil. You remember he said to you he was going to turn in to read in bed."

"Oh, bother!" she cried. "Why did he want to go to bed early on that night for? It just means you can't prove anything."

"Steady on, sweet! I wasn't aware that I'd got to prove anything."

"I know, but it would be much more comfortable if you could, Tommy. It's all so beastly. You see, you *did* dislike Vaughan, and so did I. I loathed him. You remember that day he met us when we were down by the Mallow? He didn't say anything, but you could tell from his face what he thought, the puritanical beast! I didn't tell you, but that farm labourer—Joe Buck—was down in the river meadows that afternoon, and he saw you and me and Vaughan. He's quite likely to say that you and Vaughan quarrelled."

"Good God! I never realised you were worrying about it like this, angel. Is it any use telling you that I did *not* kill Vaughan and set fire to his cottage—because I assure you I did not!"

"Don't be an idiot! I know you didn't, but I wish we could prove that all this gossip is a lie. It simply gives me the horrors."

"My poor child!" Gressingham sounded really concerned for once. "Would you rather I went away for a bit? I can't have you bothered like this."

"No, no! Of course you can't go away, people would only gossip more. It might be a good idea if Meriel came here for a bit

though. If your wife were here people could see... it's all right
and we're all friends."

Gressingham shrugged his shoulders. "Sorry, sweet, but I'm
afraid Meriel might not oblige. She's rather taken to paddling her
own canoe—and I've just let her go her own way... You did know
that, angel. You can't have it all ways, you know. I don't want to
remind you about all the things we discussed—not now, when
things are a bit complicated by all this mess, but you did agree,
June. I just left Meriel to do as she liked—and she has her own life
to live, you know."

June St Cyres sat silent, and for once her face was frightened.
"What had we better do?" she asked, and Gressingham replied:

"Do nothing at all. Why should we? We're not involved in this
business, and there's no need to get in a state of nerves about it."

2

It was at this juncture in the conversation that a very unwelcome
interruption occurred. Mrs. Hesling showed Chief Inspector
Macdonald into the room, and Gressingham at least wished him at
the devil. June St Cyres' face was a study, and to anybody observant
of human physiognomy it was a study in fear—and Gressingham
knew it. Rising in his slow, rather clumsy way, Gressingham spoke
with his customary nonchalance.

"Good-afternoon, Chief Inspector. Have you met Mrs. St
Cyres—the Colonel's daughter-in-law. I was just going to walk
back to the Manor with her. Can you wait for just a few minutes?"

"Of course you needn't bother to walk back with me," protested June, but her voice was strained and unnatural. "I had better
get back because Michael will be wanting me. Give my love to

Meriel, Tom, and tell her to try to come down for a few days. She must be needing a rest after all that driving, and she always loves this place. Good-bye for now—and thank you for the drink."

She was out of the room before Gressingham had time to reply, and he turned to Macdonald with a gesture of irritation.

"This business at Little Thatch seems to be getting on everyone's nerves," he said. "Mrs. St Cyres is worrying herself because she's heard the yokels are saying that my car was seen on the road the night of the fire."

"Yes. It's partly on that account that I came to see you," replied Macdonald. "I take it you can give an assurance that your car was not on the road that night?"

Gressingham sat down deliberately and faced the other.

"I can give you my assurance that I did not take my car out that night, and to the best of my knowledge and belief my car was locked up in the garage—or shed, to be more accurate—all that night and the following day."

"When did you last take your car out?"

"The previous Thursday, when I came back here. I have only recently had a car down here: there is, as you know, no alternative transport for some miles, and the taxi-hire business is very unsatisfactory. I brought the car down here so that I could get into Exeter on necessary business if occasion demanded it."

"Quite—that does not come within my province, but I want to get at the root of this story about your car being on the road on the Saturday night. You say you had not had it out since the previous Thursday. Do you know how much petrol was in the tank then?"

"Yes. Four and a half gallons, approximately. I put in three when I brought it through Mallowton, and there were two gallons in the tank before I refilled. It took something under half a gallon to drive it here from Mallowton. The answer is the four and a half which remains."

"You say the car was in its place all the Saturday night—"

"Steady on, Inspector. What I said was that I believed it was in its place. I hadn't used it that day and I had no reason to go and look at it on the Saturday evening. The shed was padlocked and the key is in my possession. If the car was taken out it was done without my knowledge. No one heard it being taken out, and the petrol shows it couldn't have been run far, if at all."

"When did you go to examine it?"

"On the Monday after the fire. I didn't give it a thought until I heard a report that it had been seen on the Saturday night. Then I went and looked at the petrol gauge."

"Very good. Can we go and look at it?"

"By all means." Gressingham got up and led the way from the room and out by the back of the house, across the farmyard. Having closed the yard gate behind them he turned right towards a row of outbuildings, built on a slight slope above the lane.

"The last one is my lock-up," he said. "Here is the key if you like to look for yourself."

Macdonald took the key and went and unlocked the padlock—it was a commonplace spring padlock hooked through a ring in an iron staple. The double doors of the shed—an old stable—swung out easily, revealing the back of the gleaming car.

"You run it in yourself this way?" he asked. "That is, you don't back it in?"

"No, I don't back it in. No object. It's easy enough to get out. Try it yourself. Here's my ignition key."

Macdonald got into the driver's seat, turned the ignition, and studied the petrol gauge. He called to Gressingham: "There's more like five gallons than four and a half—come and look."

Gressingham did as he was asked, saying: "I said approximately, you know. There's about the same amount as when I left it."

He stood clear, and Macdonald started the engine, put in reverse gear, and backed the car neatly into the lane. He then leaned out of the window, saying: "What are the chances that anybody in the house could hear this engine started? It's as nearly silent as an engine can be."

This was true. The car was in beautiful condition and the purr of its engine was not much more than a low hum. Macdonald went on:

"Even though you had been awake, I doubt if you could have heard the engine from the house. We might try it late at night when everything else is quiet. Meantime, if I go back to the house, will you reverse the car and put it back in the lock-up? Give me three minutes before you start."

He got out and Gressingham took his place. Macdonald walked back to the front of the house—he knew that Gressingham's bedroom was above the sitting-room—and he listened by the open window. When Gressingham came back five minutes later Macdonald said: "I didn't hear a sound of it."

"No, I can quite believe that," replied the other. "In other words, the result is negative. It proves nothing either way. If the car had been taken out the petrol gauge would have shown it."

"The petrol gauge shows there is rather more petrol in the tank than you expected, Mr. Gressingham—and there was plenty of petrol at Little Thatch on the Saturday evening. Mr. Vaughan was allowed four gallons a month for his pump engine, and he collected it in cans."

Again Gressingham sat down, in his deliberate, ponderous way. "All right," he said. "There is a possibility that my car *was* taken out without my knowledge. By whom, and for what purpose?"

"I don't know, but the possibility had to be considered, among a mass of similar inconclusive evidence. One of the questions I have had to consider is this: where did Mr. Vaughan go on that Saturday evening, when his car was seen to pass and repass Corner Cottage?"

"Any answer to that one?"

"Not yet. We have only had one report which seems reliable. Mr. Vaughan turned towards Tiverton when he reached the main road." Macdonald was silent for a moment, then he went on: "You and Mr. Radcliffe told me of what you believed to be a code—the messages which arrived for Mr. Vaughan about delivering duck's eggs."

Gressingham's eye brightened. "Yes. Any result from that line of research?"

"Yes, some results. We have been examining the lists of incoming calls on Mrs. Hesling's telephone. We also interrogated the exchange operator—a very intelligent girl. There was, of course, a considerable increase in calls while you have been resident here. The London calls—incoming and outgoing—were all yours, I believe. Similarly the calls to and from Manor Thatch."

"Probably," said Gressingham. "June St Cyres generally calls me before she comes down here. She does not walk for the love of walking."

"Quite. Now Mrs. Hesling's calls—and her husband's—are easily recognisable: the trades people, the corn millers, the cattle market and cattle van people, also farmers and so forth. There is one set of incoming calls not accounted for. These were put through at infrequent intervals from the Tiverton exchange. Were these yours?"

"Definitely not. I have had no calls from Tiverton to my knowledge. Who was the caller?"

"We don't know. The calls came from a public call-box."

"Ah ha! The duck's eggs code."

"Maybe. Now we have no proof that these calls were other than they appeared to be—orders for eggs from a Tiverton client, *but* we have traced the dealer in Mallowton to whom Mr. Vaughan sold his eggs—and unless his ducks were abnormally prolific layers he could have had no surplus eggs to dispose of to private buyers."

Gressingham chuckled. "I hand it to you for thoroughness, Chief Inspector. You don't leave much to chance. Now just answer me this: have you been able to prove that the remains found in the cottage are indisputably Vaughan's remains?"

"No, not actually proved it yet, but the probability is very strong. If need be we shall get an exhumation order, and we have information which will put the matter beyond doubt. To return for a moment to the matter of Vaughan's movements on the Saturday evening. It seems reasonable to assume that he drove towards Tiverton. A call from Tiverton was put through to this house at five o'clock on the Saturday evening. The exchange knows the connection was made, and I want to know who answered the phone. Mrs. Hesling was shopping in Mallowton at the time: her husband and the other men about the place were milking. The servant girl was out over at Mrs. Ridd's—but that phone was answered. Can you tell me anything about it?"

"I didn't answer it myself, if that's what you mean. Five o'clock on Saturday... Radcliffe and I had tea in the garden—out yonder under the trees. Peggy, the maid, brought us our tea before she went out. I didn't hear the phone, but you don't hear it out in the garden."

There was silence between the two men, and at length Gressingham said: "Obviously you want to know who took that phone call. I did not. Radcliffe did not. It's possible that Vaughan himself came down here and waited for a prearranged call. He has done that occasionally when I haven't been here. He knew where the phone is, because he used it when he wanted to make a call."

"That's quite a possible suggestion," said Macdonald, "but do you think Vaughan would have gone into a room which was your sitting-room without ascertaining if you were about, or asking permission?"

"He wouldn't have done so if he knew I was here, but how should he have known? I had been in town for some weeks, and I came down here on the Thursday evening. I didn't see anything of him on the Friday or Saturday. It's quite possible that he walked down here about five o'clock on Saturday afternoon: he'd have gone into the kitchen and found nobody about. If he came expecting a phone call he would have answered the phone when he heard it ring. Nobody would have noticed—certainly Rummy and I wouldn't have noticed, we were asleep in our deck chairs to the best of my recollection. It was the first really warm day we'd had. Anyway, that's the most probable explanation, of how the phone got answered if no member of the household answered it."

Macdonald studied the other's face. Gressingham was as calm and unconcerned as though he were talking about the weather, not a tinge of apprehension on his stolid face. He returned stare for stare, and then spoke again.

"As I see it, Chief Inspector, there are two ways of viewing this business. The first is that taken by the Coroner's Court, and I still regard it as the most probable: the fire, and Vaughan's death in it, was due to accidental causes. The alternative view is foul play. If that is the explanation, I submit you have no proof, as yet, that Vaughan was the victim of foul play. He may have been the guilty party. That being so, the matter of this telephone call becomes plain. Vaughan would have been only too glad there was nobody about when he took that call. Then there's the matter of my car. Vaughan knew where it was kept. It would have been easy enough for him to borrow it. Such a small matter as an ignition key would have presented no difficulties to an expert engineer."

"Why should he have borrowed your car, and returned it? He had his own car."

"Certainly he had. He also knew that young Alf claimed to be an expert at recognising the sound of every car which passed Corner Cottage. If Vaughan was seeking to enlist the unsuspecting sympathy of the countryside for his own demise in a terrible fire, it was better for him not to advertise that he was wide awake driving his own car at midnight—when he ought to have been stupefied by accumulating smoke. In my view, the probability is that if my car were used at all, then Vaughan used it—to remove something from the scene of action, something too heavy or cumbersome to be carried. Having removed whatever it was, he returned my car and relocked the shed, having thoughtfully replaced the petrol used on his jaunt. Then, if anybody had noticed my car on the road, it was pretty certain that questions would be asked of me—questions which, as you have observed, I am quite incapable of answering, because I am totally ignorant of the whole matter."

Here Gressingham took a deep breath, adding, "And after that I reckon I deserve a drink—and I'm going to have one. While I do so, if I can't persuade you to join me, you will perhaps explain why my whole reconstruction is manifestly at fault and totally irrelevant."

"It isn't," replied Macdonald amiably. "I think it's a very logical effort. As I said once before, you are good at correlating evidence."

Mr. Gressingham had replenished his glass, and as he raised it he said: "Then I wish to God you'd tell me why you assume that I, who have a reasonably good record of lawful behaviour, should have batted that great tough over the head and left his corpse to incinerate in the cottage embers. Damn it all! I may be a fool, but if you believe that, then you're a bigger one."

His tone was quite cheerful and unaggressive, and he grinned as he put his glass down again. "What about it?" he asked cheerfully.

"The first essence of detection is scepticism," replied Macdonald. "A detective cannot afford to accept anybody or anything at its face value. Your persistent enquiry as to proof concerning the identity of the remains found in the fire is consistent with good detection—never take anything for granted. But just now you mentioned your own record for lawful behaviour. That is relevant, too, so you will agree it is reasonable to consider Vaughan's record. We have settled one point beyond doubt, by means of finger-prints on existing documents. The tenant of Little Thatch was the same Nicholas Vaughan who was Lieutenant Commander on H.M.S. *Absinthe*. Now consider that man's record and tell me if you think it consistent with murder and arson—because I find it difficult to swallow."

"All right—but that's assumption, not proof."

"Admitted. Now it was you and your friend who told me of one very interesting piece of evidence—the telephone messages for

Vaughan which probably came from a Tiverton call-box. I think that evidence may prove to be very important. Can you make any suggestion concerning Tiverton?"

Gressingham shifted his position a little. "I've already told you that I know nobody at Tiverton. Neither do I know the place, I don't think I've ever been through it. Why on earth expect me to know who put through calls from the place?"

"Without meaning any offence, Mr. Gressingham, I should say you have one quality in common with Kipling's famous mongoose, and that is curiosity. Curiosity can be very valuable to a detective. You have told me a number of interesting things, and you have, presumably, discovered those things by virtue of your own enquiring mind—a quality not to be despised. I suggest that you should carry your researches a little further."

"I might reply by a simple formula, also implying no offence," rejoined Gressingham; "do your own job. It's up to you."

"Certainly it is, but you may have a vested interest in the matter. It occurs to me that someone may have been providing evidence meant to reflect on you. If so, it's certainly to your interest to find out who it is."

"Do you know, I think you'd better enlarge on that. I like to know just where I stand."

"That's quite reasonable. First the matter of your car. It was undoubtedly taken out on Saturday evening, you say without your knowledge. Next, I believe you smoke Balkan Sobranie cigarettes. Two of these cigarette ends were found in the garden of Little Thatch, and someone has attested that the smoke from one of these cigarettes was hanging in the air in Little Thatch garden on Saturday evening. It has also been reported that you had reason to resent Mr. Vaughan's observation of your attitude towards Mrs.

St Cyres. On account of these points, I suggest that you should do all you can to clear the issue."

Gressingham sat silent, his shoulders hunched, his face less amiable, but his voice was as cool as ever as he replied:

"Well, that's straight. I agree with you that it looks as though somebody's been doing the dirty on me, and my guess is still the same—Nicholas Vaughan. I've said that all along, and I stick to it. You get your exhumation order. That's the only way of clearing this up. I've told you all I know, which is mighty little."

"But have you?" enquired Macdonald. "I may be wrong, but I have an idea you're holding out on something. You've a right to keep your own counsel, of course—but it may be a dangerous proceeding."

Again Gressingham stared. Then he said: "You're wrong. I'm not holding out on you. I think you've got hold of the wrong end of the stick. I've told you from the beginning Vaughan was a fellow who'd got something to hide. Do you know he typed all his correspondence—does that seem a natural thing for a simple farmer fellow to do?"

"How do you know he typed all his correspondence?"

"Because the farmers say so. It struck them as damned odd."

"They forget that Vaughan wasn't a simple farmer fellow. He was a highly educated engineer. In addition, he was a writer of repute."

"That's a new one on me. Never struck his name on a book yet."

"He didn't write under his own name. He used a pen-name—Henry Heythwaite."

"Good God!"

Gressingham was startled out of his immobility this time, and Macdonald went on: "Does that name enlighten you, Mr. Gressingham?"

"Well, I read that book—*Simon the Dalesman*—dashed interesting it was, too. I'd never have thought him capable of it."

"He wrote about his own country, on the Westmorland-Yorkshire borders. Do you know it at all?"

"No. Never been there. Well, well... I still tell you that that chap at Little Thatch had something to hide."

"There are very few men who have not got something to hide," rejoined Macdonald.

CHAPTER THIRTEEN

I

WHEN MACDONALD RETURNED TO MALLOWTON AFTER HIS conversation with Mr. Thomas Gressingham, he found Superintendent Bolton awaiting him with a troubled face.

"It looks as though we've unearthed a bit of hankey-pankey on Mr. Gressingham's part," said the Superintendent, "though if it's all of a piece with the Little Thatch business, I can't tell."

The new evidence ran thus: Macdonald had been impressed by young Alf's acuteness; he believed that the boy had been telling the truth when he averred that he had heard Mr. Gressingham's car pass Corner Cottage on the evening of the fire, though Superintendent Bolton had been disposed to attribute the statement to imagination on Alf's part. Macdonald had set routine enquiries on foot with the object of getting further information about the Daimler—he had instructed all patrolling constables to enquire of roadmen, farm labourers and cottagers if any such evidence could be found.

A roadman employed by the Rural Council of Creediford had that evening informed a constable that there were wheel tracks on a recently mended piece of road, which tracks corresponded with those mentioned by the police. Constable Thurgood had gone to investigate this report: he had found that a bad patch of road had been repaired in the rather sketchy manner of the times, and a coat of tar had been applied to the patch, the work having been completed on Saturday, April 30th. Some time before the tar had dried a car had been driven over it, and its wheel tracks showed clearly for some yards beyond the mended stretch of road. The road in question was a lonely by-road leading only to a farm, though it was possible to take a lane leading off to the right and to regain the main road without reversing. Constable Thurgood had examined the road-side with great thoroughness and had discovered tracks in a spinney where the undergrowth was beaten down. In the heart of the spinney, carefully concealed beneath the brambles, Thurgood had found two empty petrol cans and a heavy leather glove.

There was still an hour or two of daylight left when Macdonald heard these facts from Bolton, and in a very short space of time he and the Superintendent were in a car heading towards Creediford. Studying the Ordnance Survey map, Macdonald considered the distance and direction of Creediford from Mallory Fitzjohn. Driving from the Mallorys one reached a main road, and a left turn along it led towards Tiverton, and a fork on the right a mile farther on towards Creediford, the general direction being northwards from the Mallorys. The newly-repaired patch of road was just under six miles from Mallory Fitzjohn and four from Tiverton. When they drew up in the narrow road where repairs had been made Macdonald was in no doubt whatever that the tyre marks he saw were those left by Gressingham's Daimler.

The Chief Inspector had had a good look at the tyres on that car and had noted their magnificent condition; "as new" described them, the tread being quite unworn, a marked contrast to the condition of most tyres in these days of rubber shortage. The patch of repaired road was not more than a couple of yards in extent, but the tar on it had adhered to the tyres, and their marks were as clear as "finger-prints taken by a pro," to use Thurgood's expression. The tyre marks were clear for nearly a hundred yards before the tar faded out.

"That'll be the Daimler prints?" queried Bolton, and Macdonald nodded:

"Those were made by the Daimler all right. I saw it this evening, and there are still traces of tar in the pattern of the treads."

They walked on to the spinney at the side of the road, and walked through the fresh May undergrowth where windflowers and primroses still bloomed in the cool shadows. Macdonald turned to Constable Thurgood. "This seems a lonely place. Not much traffic along here at any time, I should say?"

"Nothing but farm traffic, sir, and not much of that save at haymaking and harvest. The farm below there—Swallowford's its name—has another approach to the main road. I asked them if anybody had been along this way on the evening of April 30th, and they said no. They're seldom out after dusk, and if they were there's nothing to bring them out here. It's the sort of place you mightn't meet anybody for weeks at a time, saving when the hay carts pass, or at harvest. I hoped I might get some information about the car that made these tracks—but no one saw it or could tell me anything about it. There are some children at Swallowford, but it so happened they were laid up—measles, they'd got. Now just you look here, sir."

Constable Thurgood indicated his find with pride in his eyes while Macdonald picked up the heavy leather glove and examined it. He then raised one of the petrol cans and turned it carefully over. Finally he said to Bolton:

"This is part and parcel of the Little Thatch case all right. That driving glove was Vaughan's, there's the companion to it in the door pocket of his own car. The petrol cans were his, too. He used a distinguishing mark like a cypher or monogram of his initials N.V. It looks like an awkwardly shaped W."

"Well, I'm damned," said Bolton, and his voice sounded despondent. "I never thought he would have been up to any tricks like this."

"How do you interpret the facts?" asked Macdonald.

"Plain enough at first sight," said Bolton. "It looks like Black Market dodges with petrol. Vaughan had an allowance of petrol for running his pump and lighting plant, and you found he hadn't even charged his batteries. I've heard of fancy prices being paid for petrol—as much as three or four pounds a gallon."

"And you think Vaughan cached his spare petrol here and Gressingham picked it up?" enquired Macdonald. "I admit that it looks like it, and it was intended to look like it, but it'll take a lot to convince me that Nicholas Vaughan was in the Black Market racket. However, we'll pick this stuff up and put it in the car, and then examine the road while the daylight holds."

They worked carefully along the road, and in the verge of the lane which led back to the main road they found further traces of the Daimler's balloon tyres, but no traces of Vaughan's ancient Morris. Macdonald pondered deeply. The spinney was a good place for a private meeting—Thurgood's evidence made that clear. If Vaughan had thus used the place, Macdonald guessed that he might have parked his car some way back along the road, where a recess in the hedge, once used for a heap of road metal, made a convenient parking spot. The fact that the spinney was about half-way between the Mallorys and Tiverton was suggestive.

Eventually, as the daylight faded out, Macdonald and Bolton returned to the police-car and set off on their return journey to Mallowton.

"What do you make of it, Chief?" enquired Bolton. "I always remember what you said to me in connection with Colonel St

Cyres—that you'd suspect anybody if you could smell a motive. I disagreed with you. I'd swear that St Cyres is straight, and I'd back him no matter what anybody suggested. Now you're backing Vaughan in the same way I backed St Cyres, although you can see a motive all right—profit and a big profit."

"Admitted," said Macdonald, "but I find it hard to believe that Vaughan was a fool. If he had been selling petrol to a man like Gressingham he'd have been a very big fool indeed. He'd never have been safe, because Gressingham is subtle enough to safeguard himself and leave Vaughan in the soup. Then there's this to it. Vaughan wouldn't have dumped petrol in that spinney and left it for an indefinite period. It might have been found by anybody, particularly by the farm children. Now that road was tarred some time on Saturday morning: the Daimler passed over the tar while it was still wet—but the Morris didn't. The only way the Morris could have reached the spinney was by the lane, and then it would have had to be reversed out, because there's no room to turn. We examined that lane pretty carefully, and the edges are damp and show tyre marks—but there's not a trace of the Morris. I don't believe you could back a car along that lane and not leave some marks of your passing."

"You could leave the car and carry the petrol cans."

"You could—but you'd look pretty fishy if anyone caught you doing it. I still don't think it's the sort of thing Vaughan would have done. If there's one characteristic which he showed in all his doings it was common sense."

"You still haven't told me what you make of it."

"I don't know," replied Macdonald. "It can be interpreted in half a dozen different ways. The first's your suggestion—that Vaughan was dumping petrol for Gressingham to pick up. The second is that Gressingham dumped those cans and the glove, intending them to be found, but that he didn't realise there was wet tar on the road, which gave away the fact that he'd passed, or his car had passed. Another reading is that someone borrowed Gressingham's car without his knowledge."

"What about this one?" enquired Bolton. "Someone went to Little Thatch to steal Vaughan's petrol in his absence. Vaughan came back and caught them at it; he was knocked over the head and the cottage left to burn. The thief decided to keep the petrol and get rid of the cans, so he dumped them out here."

"And used half the petrol in doing so—a fool of a thief, but thieves often are fools. I expect it's too much to hope for finger-prints on those cans, but we'll try."

They rode in silence for a while, each busy with his own thoughts, and then Bolton asked,

"What's your opinion of Gressingham, Chief?"

"I think he's a man with a lot of ability and natural shrewdness. He has got that type of gambling mind which makes a natural speculator, and that means he can take a hazard and keep cool until he sees which way the cat jumps. I should say at a guess that he has no moral values at all; he'd keep within the law because he'd find it inconvenient to be on the wrong side of the law. I have no doubt he'd buy off-the-ration petrol if he could do it safely, but he'd never do anything that was merely stupid. I have been get-ting a little private information about him, and I find his business associates agree with Howard Brendon about him—he's honest, so far as the ethics of the stock market demand honesty. He pays up on settling day."

"There's been a lot of gossip about him and young Mrs. St Cyres."

"That I don't doubt. The general opinion among his acquaintances is that he and his wife don't hit it, and that she is going off on
her own account. I should think it's quite probable that he hopes
that June St Cyres will take his wife's place in due course—but I
can't quite see how that fits in with the death of Nicholas Vaughan.
The Gressinghams of this world don't care a snap about reputation
in the old-fashioned sense of the word."

"Isn't it possible that Vaughan saw a bit too much? Perhaps
Gressingham didn't like to think of his lady-love being discredited."

Macdonald shook his head. "I don't think Gressingham would
care. The St Cyres would care—but that's a different story. In any
case I imagine Vaughan was the sort of chap to keep his own counsel. It was no business of his how June St Cyres and Gressingham
behaved. No. I'm still faced with the same two problems. Where
did Vaughan go on the last evening of his life, and who was the
woman he hoped to marry?"

2

After Macdonald had left him, Mr. Gressingham sat and pondered
for a while. Then he went out and had another look at his car.
Though he was not so quick as Macdonald, he was observant
enough, and soon spotted a fact which he had not previously
noted—there were marks of tar in the tread of the wheels. He
got into the driving seat again and studied the petrol gauge, and at
length went back into the house. Here he found his friend Radcliffe
stretched out in somnolent restfulness in the biggest armchair, his
feet reposing on a second chair.

"Wake up, Rummy. There's been some jiggery-pokery going
on, you'd better use your wits and do a spot of thinking."

Radcliffe opened his eyes wearily. "What's the trouble? I came here for a spot of rest and the place is overrun with police. Can't they make up their minds and done with it?"

Gressingham detailed Macdonald's observations, and Radcliffe sat up and listened: when the recital came to an end Radcliffe said: "So you're disposed to agree. Someone *did* take that car out. That it?"

"Looks like it. Bob gave the car a wash down to get the mud off. There was no tar on the wheels then. Look here, Rummy. If you took that car out that Saturday, say so. Nothing like understanding each other."

Radcliffe sat up. "I didn't take the car out, so get that clear. If I had I should have told you so. In any case, how the heck do you think I got the petrol to fill up again?"

Gressingham sat very still, and at length he said: "There was one place where petrol could have been pinched, and that place was Little Thatch. Vaughan would have had petrol in cans for his engine. That's what the Yard bloke was getting at, Rummy, and that's where you and I have got to watch our steps."

Radcliffe sat up, his round, foolish face looked annoyed.

"I don't quite get you, Thomas. If you've got any suggestions to make, make them quite clear. I told you I didn't take the car out. Got that?"

"Yes. I've got it. I also told the Chief Inspector that I didn't take it either. Unfortunately, there's nobody to corroborate what we said. You went to bed early. I've known you do that before, Rummy, and heard you come in a few hours later. If you like to go chasing skirts in the country it's no affair of mine. At least it hasn't been in the past. This time it's different."

Radcliffe sat up, and ponderously lowered his suède brogues

to the floor. "I've said my piece and said it quite clearly," he said, and his voice was several semi-tones higher than usual, "so I've no need to repeat it. I did *not* take the car out, *you* did not take the car out, but the car was taken out. That it?"

"That's it."

"Then who borrowed it? Damn it, Tommy, it oughtn't to be that difficult to decide. It's not everybody's car. No use suspecting the farm boys—they couldn't drive a Daimler. What about the ignition key?"

Gressingham pulled his key-ring out of his pocket. "My key is there, as you see; it's been on that ring, in my possession for years, *but,* as you happen to know, I keep a spare key in the locker of the car, just in case of accidents."

"Did you tell the Yard bloke that?"

"No, I didn't. I wanted to talk to you first—just in case."

"Thank you so much." Radcliffe's voice was acid now, but Gressingham went on quite placidly,

"As I see it, the number of people who could have taken that car out is limited. I am trying to look at it from a detective's point of view. There's our two selves, the old man at Manor Thatch, and Vaughan himself."

Radcliffe was silent, and Gressingham went on: "Anyway, Scotland Yard seems to have made up its mind on two points. A, My car was out on Saturday night. B, My car was somehow concerned in the doings up there—and I *don't like it.*"

"No use bleating at me about it," said Radcliffe, "and neither am I going to get the jitters over it. The fact is, Tommy, you've talked too much. Brendon was quite right when he said you'd better keep off the grass. You've been too ready to make suggestions and to cast suspicion on other people. Damned bad policy. Far better to keep quiet and let the police get on with their own job."

"Maybe; if other people had kept quiet, I should have followed suit. Do you know the Yard man told me that fag ends of my Balkan Sobranies had been found in the Little Thatch garden?"

"And you are wondering who has been pinching your cigarettes, eh? Not me, Tommy, I loathe Turkish tobacco."

"I never said it was you, Rummy, but I don't like the look of things. You mentioned Howard Brendon just now. I'm going to talk things over with him. He may be a dry old stick, but he knows his stuff as a lawyer. If folks are being slanderous at my expense, it's time they were told to stop it."

"Well, you've got to make your own decisions, and it's no business of mine to interfere," said Radcliffe, "but I agree with what Brendon said in the first place: Don't be in a hurry to talk too much. Keep off the grass."

"Admirable advice, I'm sure, but who was it who told Scotland Yard about Vaughan's telephone messages—his 'code,' as you were pleased to call it? I seem to recollect that you had a few words to say there."

"Certainly. That was evidence. Not inference."

"And damned awkward evidence it is, my lad. Those calls came from a Tiverton call-box, and one of them came through on the Saturday afternoon that Vaughan was killed in the fire. Macdonald has found out that the only people in this house at the hour that call was put through by exchange were you and me. I didn't answer that phone, I know that." Radcliffe sat silent, his round, heavy face furrowed with lines in a concentrated effort of recollection.

"I damn well know I didn't answer it," he said slowly.

Gressingham got to his feet. "I told Macdonald that you were asleep in the garden," he said. "All the same, if you have been getting calls from one of your girl friends at Tiverton, you'd better say so. Things are looking a bit unhealthy, if you ask me."

With his little mouth pursed up like the mouth of a codfish Radcliffe stared across at the other. At last he said: "Look here, Tommy. You and I have been very good friends for quite a time, and I don't let my friends down, but if you are going to make insinuations, or try to involve me in trouble in order to keep out of it yourself, you're asking for a headache. I'm an easygoing chap as a rule, but if I'm annoyed I'm a nasty devil to deal with."

"Your dinner's ready, Mr. Gressingham; I hope you'll find it to your liking."

It was Mrs. Hesling who spoke. She had opened the door without either man hearing it, and Radcliffe looked more put out than ever. Gressingham, however, replied quite cheerfully,

"Thanks, Mrs. Hesling, your dinners always *are* to my liking."

Mrs. Hesling went back to her great kitchen shaking her head.

"I'm worried, Joe," she said sadly. "I wish he'd never come here, nor his friends neither."

"'Tis too late in the day to think o' that now," replied Joe Hesling. "You would have it, mother. Wanted to make a bit of money on your own, and see how 'tis. Police in and out of the house and questions, questions enough to make a man's head ache. I'm fair 'mazed with it all. All I do say is this, there weren't no call for Little Thatch to burn as her did. Timothy Yeo lived there full twenty-five years and her didn't burn. And we've not heard the last o' mun yet. You mark my words. There's trouble to come and plenty."

"And him's quarrelling now," sighed Mrs. Hesling. "Iss, quarrelling—Him be a nasty devil to deal with, mun said."

"Ar... him could be, too, likely," said Mr. Hesling. "Tell you what, mother. You send mun packing. Sooner the better. Them's no call to do no quarrelling here. Send mun back where he do belong. We'm wanting no fires in our thatches. No, nor no quarrelling neither, money or no money."

3

Macdonald's post the next morning brought him several reports, but the letter which interested him most was from Miss Elizabeth Vaughan. With an energy which he judged to be characteristic of her, Miss Vaughan had caught the night train from Exeter to the north of England and had reached Lannerdale the following morning. Here she had set to work immediately to collect the information which Macdonald had asked for. She sent him chapter and verse concerning the Hawkins branch of the family whose claim to Lannerdale she intended to dispute. Sidney Hawkins and his son Richard now lived near Portsmouth, and Macdonald immediately sent a telephone message to the police of that district asking for discreet enquiries to be made as to their doings and whereabouts on April 30th. Elizabeth's next report dealt with the girl, the one and only girl, Macdonald noted, in whom Elizabeth Vaughan could suggest that her brother had been interested. "You asked me to let you know if I could get any news of her," wrote Elizabeth Vaughan, "and though it seems quite irrelevant to me, I have done what you asked. The girl's name was Molly White. She wasn't a teacher, as I thought, but a hospital nurse. She was back in this district as recently as January of last year, because she was posted to the Military Hospital at Longbeck Hall, about ten miles from Lannerdale. She came over to visit my uncle and aunt. I am told

that she left Longbeck last May and she was married to someone
in the south of England a month or so later. So far as I can gather,
she had not heard of or from my brother since before the war, so
I cannot imagine that her existence is of any interest to you. The
more I think about this business the more certain do I become that
accident is the real explanation. It seems quite crazy to think that
anyone should have attempted to murder my brother. Of all the
people I've ever known Nicholas was the least melodramatic and
the most able to look after himself. I can believe that his cottage
caught fire accidentally, but I cannot believe the other explanation."

Macdonald showed this letter to Bolton; the Superintendent
studied it carefully.

"Any chance she had a hand in the matter herself?" he enquired.
"She seems a cool card and very anxious to persuade you it was all
an accident. She's mighty keen on getting this Lannerdale place,
isn't she? and she claims her brother made a will in her favour."

"All quite true," agreed Macdonald. "Do you imagine she
borrowed Mr. Thomas Gressingham's car, and took two of her
brother's petrol tins and dumped them by the wayside some miles
away?"

Bolton rubbed his chin: "Maybe if she was stranded for petrol
she got it out to her own car that way," he said, and then brought
his fist down on the table with a bang. "Dash it all, Chief, the further we get with this story the crazier it becomes," he declared.
"Come to think of it, what evidence—solid honest-to-God evidence—have we which leads us to assume Vaughan was murdered?
Two empty petrol cans and a driving glove in a spinney. Isn't it
possible there's a simple explanation of everything?"

"I could give you a dozen simple explanations," said Macdonald
cheerfully, "but none of them would be really convincing.

Commander Wilton made one very good point when he reminded me that a sailor like Nicholas Vaughan does wake up pretty quickly if anything goes wrong. He'd be the last man in the world to sleep while his house is on fire. Then, remember this: Colonel St Cyres walked right past the front of the house, along the cobbles at half-past nine that evening. Wouldn't Vaughan have looked out to see who was on his property?"

"Well, if he looked out, he kept mum about it."

"Yes, and my guess is that Nicholas Vaughan was dead *before* Colonel St Cyres walked along the cobbles—but, admittedly, I haven't proved it yet."

Bolton picked up Elizabeth Vaughan's letter. "So it looks as though she'll inherit if that's the way of it, Chief... but you check up on her just to make sure."

"Yes. I seem to spend my life 'just making sure,'" rejoined Macdonald, "and it's time I got on with it."

CHAPTER FOURTEEN

I

MR. WILLIAM TOTHILL, SOLICITOR AND COMMISSIONER for Oaths, was an old-established and much respected legal practitioner in Mallowton. He and his father before him had drawn up leases and agreements, negotiated disputes, engrossed wills, advised on settlements and the management of property for nearly a century, working in the same dusty office, which looked out on to Mallowton High Street. Mr. Tothill was known as a very "safe" man. When irate clients demanded immediate legal action to redress their grievances, Mr. Tothill always advised settlement out of court. He was, as he explained, "anti-litigious." He held it a failure if he could not induce would-be litigants to compromise without going to the extreme of taking their cases to court.

Mr. Tothill was now seventy years of age—a dry, precise little man, not to be hurried in speech or action. It was to Mr. Tothill that Nicholas Vaughan had gone when he took the lease of Little Thatch, saying frankly that he had no knowledge of land tenures in Devonshire, and that he wished to have his agreement "vetted" by a local man of law.

Hoping for information, though hardly expecting it, Macdonald called on the lawyer. It was a new experience for Mr. Tothill to have a Scotland Yard man in his office: such a thing had not occurred before, either in his lifetime or his father's, and he told Macdonald so frankly. Concerning Nicholas Vaughan the lawyer spoke with approval and regard.

"Speaking from the short experience I had of him, I should say that Mr. Vaughan was a man unusually well endowed with common sense, practical and straightforward in his dealings. He knew that agreements about tenancies are not always the simple matters they appear to be, and he saw to it that each clause dealt fairly by both tenant and owner, and that no loophole was left for future misunderstandings."

"I take it that he gave you to understand that he meant to settle at Little Thatch for a considerable period?" queried Macdonald, and the solicitor nodded, peering at Macdonald over the top of his old-fashioned, gold-rimmed glasses.

"I gathered that he intended to stay there for ten years," replied Tothill. "That was the period to which his option applied. As you probably know, he was spending money and time on improving the amenities of the property, and I suggested to him that it was not always desirable to spend money on a property held on lease. He replied that the improvements he was making would probably be out-moded in ten years' time, and that he would have his money's worth out of them. With regard to improvements in the land, tillage and so forth, there was a clause in the lease to reimburse him at the close of his tenancy. As I have told you, I found him a shrewd, level-headed client, well versed in rural usages, and fully alive to his own interests and responsibilities as tenant. The agreement, to which he himself suggested some reasonable additions, was mutually satisfactory to both parties and was signed with a minimum of delay. Beyond supervising the agreement, I had no further dealings with Mr. Vaughan."

"Have you any idea if he had employed the services of any other solicitor at any period?"

"Mr. Vaughan stated quite explicitly that he had never needed legal advice, and had no solicitor in charge of his affairs. He owned no real estate, and his capital—a matter of a few thousand pounds—was well invested. I gather that Little Thatch was the first property he had taken on his own account, though, as I said, he was well informed on the subject of tenancies, particularly farms and small holdings."

"Did he never mention the subject of his Will?"

Mr. Tothill looked primmer than ever, his lips pursed up as though he deprecated such plain speaking.

"The matter of his Will was mentioned. He told me that he had made a Will and that he had drafted it himself, a mistake made by many otherwise business-like persons. He also said that he intended to make another Will shortly, and put the drafting in my hands. Unfortunately, he had not carried this intention into effect, neither had he given me any instructions about the matter. It is probable that his Will was destroyed in the fire at Little Thatch, since he had not deposited the document here nor at his Bank. The Manager of the Western Counties Bank enquired of me as to whether I held Mr. Vaughan's Will, or if I had any knowledge of his testamentary dispositions, and I regretted that I was unable to give any information. The result is that deceased died intestate and no indication of his wishes can be known to guide his heirs."

"Did he ever mention to you the fact that he intended to marry?"

"He did not; we had little or no personal intercourse."

Macdonald, realising that he could learn nothing further along these lines, changed his angle of approach with deliberate abruptness.

"Have you met a gentleman named Mr. Thomas Gressingham?" he enquired, and the lawyer stared at him for some seconds as though assessing the real meaning of this enquiry. Macdonald sat tight and waited, and at length Mr. Tothill replied,

"A gentleman of that name, who has been staying at Hinton Mallory, called on me to enquire if I had any knowledge of properties likely to come on the market in the near future. Speaking confidentially, Chief Inspector, and without witnesses, I am willing to tell you that the impression made on me by Mr. Gressingham was not favourable." Pressing his finger tips together, Mr. Tothill continued: "Mr. Gressingham seemed to have an idea that I should be willing to discuss my clients with him and give him a leader concerning possible sellers. He held the belief, it appeared to me, that everything and everybody had a price. My interview with him was brief, and he has not sought another one."

Macdonald allowed himself a chuckle. "I have no doubt you dealt faithfully with him, sir. Do you suppose that he visited all the legal men in the county in order to pursue his enquiries?"

"That I cannot tell," replied Mr. Tothill. "In my case he came with an introduction. Mr. Howard Brendon wrote to me asking me to assist Mr. Gressingham with any information I was able to give." Again Mr. Tothill paused and then went on: "Since you have mentioned Mr. Gressingham's name to me, Chief Inspector, I may take it that your interest in him is official?"

"Speaking confidentially, as you put it, sir, I admit that such is the case. I have nothing positive against Mr. Gressingham, but I admit he arouses my curiosity. I can't fit him into the picture, if you follow me?"

Mr. Tothill nodded judicially. "I follow you very well indeed. It is only natural that conjecture is rife over this matter. I have had occasion to rebuke several persons who carried conjecture too far. I think it only right to put you in possession of any facts known to

me. I first heard of Mr. Gressingham from Mr. Howard Brendon.
The latter, you may know, has a property in the Dulverton district. I think I may say without breaking confidence that Mr.
Brendon's property is coming into the market. He has been trying
to sell it privately for some months past—I gather he has bought
another property in the Midlands—and I think he hoped that Mr.
Gressingham would buy the Dulverton place. The latter, however,
did not care for it, and preferred to seek a property in the south of
the county. All this is open and legitimate business, and I should
have been happy to act for Mr. Gressingham over negotiating the
purchase of any property on the market. What I resented was
his implication that I was willing to discuss the financial status of
my clients with him, so that he might be in a position to jockey
them into selling property. Frankly, Chief Inspector, I found him
an unpleasant person, and one with whom I had no wish to have
any transactions."

"During your interview did Mr. Gressingham mention Little
Thatch?"

"Certainly he did. He said he wanted to buy it, together with
the farm where he is staying, but I told him that I had no knowledge of the properties save that they were not for sale."

Macdonald pondered for a moment, then he said: "I am surprised to learn that Mr. Brendon is selling his property. I had
thought of him as being firmly established in the district."

Mr. Tothill hesitated a moment and then said: "If you lived
in this locality you would soon hear a considerable amount of
discussion about him. A few years ago he had a dispute over a
Right of Way through his parkland. He closed a path, and his
gates were broken down. Unwisely, in my judgment, he took
his case into court, and he won the case. As so often happens, it

was a barren victory. If you live in the country you must live on reasonably good terms with your neighbours. Since winning his case I believe it correct to say that he has been ostracised by his neighbours. He is very wise to seek another home. This is gossip, Chief Inspector, but it is current gossip, such as you would hear in any market town around here."

"I believe that Mr. Brendon is a married man," observed Macdonald, and old Tothill stared at him with his shrewd, long-sighted old eyes.

"That is so," he observed, and then made a comment which puzzled Macdonald a little. "If you are connecting Mr. Gressingham with that matter, as I believe some ill-intentioned gossips have done, I think you are at fault. To the best of my knowledge, Mr. Brendon and Mr. Gressingham are business acquaintances, nothing else. Being a man who believes in speaking his mind, I told Mr. Brendon that I was not favourably impressed with his friend, and Mr. Brendon said that I should be ill-advised to make hasty judgments. Though Gressingham might on occasion lack discretion in his speech, he was a man of probity in his business dealings."

"I gather that you have a respect for Mr. Brendon's judgment, sir?"

"Certainly I have. I have had various dealings with him, and found his judgment was to be trusted."

"You might be interested in these facts," said Macdonald, and gave a terse account of the discovery of the petrol cans and the traces of Mr. Gressingham's Daimler.

Mr. Tothill listened intently, and then said: "I find this evidence a little bewildering. Do you deduce that Mr. Gressingham has been obtaining petrol illicitly and that the late Mr. Vaughan connived at the transaction? I find it difficult to credit. It seems quite out of character for Mr. Vaughan to have acted in such a manner. I could more easily believe that the petrol had been stolen—though I am aware that such an allegation would be slanderous."

"The idea of theft had occurred to me," said Macdonald. "In the first instance it might have been suggested as a rag—one of those pieces of foolishness which grown men have been known to commit when they have had a drink too many. If Nicholas Vaughan discovered that his petrol had been stolen, I can imagine him making a good deal of trouble for the thief."

Mr. Tothill nodded. "I see your trend, Chief Inspector. You believe that Nicholas Vaughan met his death through foul play, and you are seeking for a motive."

"That's it. I am pretty sure in my own mind that Nicholas Vaughan was murdered, and I am hunting for a motive. I have told you the connecting link which brings Mr. Gressingham into the picture, and I have been interested in hearing your opinion of him. You have also told me that Mr. Gressingham came to you with an introduction from Mr. Brendon. I wish you would give me your opinion on this point. I have it in mind to go to see Mr. Brendon and to put these latest facts before him, and to ask for his co-operation. Do you consider that in doing so I shall be defeating my own ends? Will Mr. Brendon be likely to act in a legal capacity for Mr. Gressingham?"

The lawyer chuckled, a dry sound but full of amusement.

"I see your point, Chief Inspector. If you want information likely to lead to the arrest of a miscreant, you would hardly expect to be provided with it by the latter's legal adviser. Mr. Howard Brendon is a solicitor, but he has not practised his profession for many years. He would not act for Mr. Gressingham—but he might advise him. If you want my opinion of Mr. Brendon, I can tell you that he has a name in the county for being a man of his word. He may be disliked by those who find him a hard man, but he is not mistrusted. Those who have had dealings with him can tell you that if he has given his word, he will abide by it, even to his own disadvantage: if he has said he will follow a certain course, he follows it."

"While I admire consistency, I deprecate mere obstinacy," observed Macdonald, and Mr. Tothill nodded, acknowledging the shrewdness of the oblique remark.

"You are right," he said. "I mentioned the matter of Mr. Brendon's lawsuit over the Right of Way. He would have been a wiser man if he had been willing to compromise, but because he claimed that he would close the path in question, because he claimed the full rights of the property owner, he went to the extreme of a lawsuit which alienated him from his neighbours. Now, in this matter of consulting with him over his friend Gressingham. If Mr. Brendon has undertaken to help Mr. Gressingham with advice—to back him, in other words—you will undertake a fruitless errand if you seek information from him which may inculpate his friend."

"Surely if Mr. Brendon be the law-abiding character you have indicated he would not hold a brief for a man who may have committed a crime?" asked Macdonald.

Old Tothill replied: "I have had a few words with Mr. Brendon on this matter and he stated his opinion very clearly. He believes that Nicholas Vaughan met his death by accident in a fire whose cause was accidental. Mr. Brendon regards the enquiry you are undertaking as an unjustifiable expenditure of public money to gratify the prejudice of a naval officer who cannot accept plain evidence. I tell you this to indicate that there is very little probability that he will be prepared to co-operate with you in the way you suggest."

Mr. Tothill paused again, and Macdonald waited patiently: the old solicitor's pauses seemed worth respecting, because in his dry, precise way he was capable of making interesting suggestions. The small rasping voice went on again at length.

"As you know, Chief Inspector, this case of yours is being debated in every house in the town—in every shop and bar, in the Council Chamber and the Chamber of Commerce, in every club and at every meeting. The public does not regard Mr. Gressingham with a kindly eye—in the minds of some he has been tried, sentenced and hanged already—but there is another individual who finds even less favour in public esteem, and that is Mr. Raymond Radcliffe. When it comes to misappropriating petrol..." Mr. Tothill fell silent, looking at Macdonald intently, with pursed-up lips, and the Chief Inspector allowed himself another chuckle.

"I rather favour the public judgment there," he said. "I might ask Mr. Brendon's opinion of the fellow. Meantime, many thanks for sparing me so much time, and for giving me some good advice, both explicit and implicit, Mr. Tothill."

2

At the same time that Macdonald was talking to Mr. Tothill, Thomas Gressingham came into his sitting-room at Hinton Mallory and found Raymond Radcliffe sitting at an old-fashioned writing bureau going through the papers which were stacked in the pigeon holes. Gressingham closed the door quietly behind him and advanced into the room with his hands in his pockets.

"What the devil do you think you are doing, Rummy?" he enquired. "That desk is mine, in the sense that I use it. Its contents are certainly mine."

"I know, old chap, I know," replied Radcliffe calmly. "Don't imagine I'm laying claim to anything, or that I take any interest in your papers. I don't. The fact is I've mislaid one or two letters of my own and I want to find them. The probability is that I left them about and Mrs. Hesling bunged them in here amongst yours."

"I keep that desk locked. It was locked when I went out," said Gressingham and Radcliffe nodded.

"Quite right, old chap, but, you see, the key of the bookcase above it fits the desk as well. Mrs. H. would know that and she probably just shoved any odd letters in. All these tidying up females are a menace—just can't leave things put."

Gressingham sat very still, and the expression on his face was not amiable. "It didn't occur to you to ask me if I'd seen any of your letters before I went out, Rummy? or to wait to ask me when I came in?"

Radcliffe stood up and lumbered over to the window, and then said: "I've been thinking a bit, old chap. You and I have been friends quite a while. Had some good times together, too, and done some nice bits of business. I'm an easy-going fellow, not prone to take offence or lose my wool—but I didn't like the tone you took when you were talking about that car, Tommy. You ought to have known that if I *had* taken the car out I should have told you about it. The fact is you're getting het-up about this Little Thatch business. It makes you irritable, and it's not like you to be irritable. I think you'd be better if you were alone for a bit, so I'm just packing my things up. No object in my staying here if you're feeling irritable. Tiresome for you—and tiresome for me. That's why I was looking for my letters. Don't want to leave any of my junk about."

Gressingham still stared, a frown creasing his heavy brows.

"Think you'll go while the going's good, do you?" he asked. "Let's wash out all that punk about getting irritated. You're clearing out before you're asked any awkward questions. It's a silly thing to do, Rummy. If the police want to ask you questions they'll find you all right. No use playing ostriches by doing a bunk up to town."

Radcliffe had pursed his small mouth up so that it resembled a fish's mouth, an absurd pouting cod-fish, and his eyes protruded a little bit more than usual, but his voice was well under control: "Just shows how this business is getting you down, Tommy. It's not like you to talk like that. If the police want any information from me, they're welcome to all I know. If it'll reassure you at all, I'll call in on the Superintendent on my way through Mallowton and tell him I'm going back to town, and give him a chance to ask any questions he likes. The whole thing's a damned tiresome business. I told you—and Howard Brendon told you—that you were making a mistake when you started all that storybook stuff about what might have happened to Vaughan. There's such a thing as talking too much as well as talking too little. I'm sorry this has happened: very sorry indeed, but the only thing I can do in the circumstances is to clear out and leave you to yourself. If you take my advice you'll pack up yourself and come back to town as soon as you can. This place is a washout now. No use to either of us—and, by the way, old chap, if you'd look through those letters of yours and see if you've got any of mine mixed up with your mail I should be grateful. Actually you'd be doing a sensible thing if you made a bonfire of the lot of them. It's a mistake to keep letters."

"Damn you! Mind your own business!" burst out Gressingham, and Radcliffe replied,

"That's just what I intend to do, old chap," as he ambled out of the room.

3

At the same time that Gressingham and Radcliffe were coming to loggerheads over the matter of the writing bureau, Macdonald was driving himself on the main road to Shermouth, and his objective was the Auxiliary Naval Hospital where Nicholas Vaughan had been treated in the first months after he had been wounded. Later he had been moved to the Convalescent Home at Torhampton, and Macdonald intended to go on to the latter establishment if need be. As he drove he considered all the enquiries he had set on foot, taxing his brains to discover if any consideration had been neglected. Miss Elizabeth Vaughan's movements and acquaintances were being followed up by a woman detective who was in one of the services. The Hawkins family—the alternative inheritors of Lannerdale—were also being subject to scrutiny. Mrs. Thomas Gressingham's activities as an auxiliary ambulance driver were being enquired into, likewise the excursions of Mr. Raymond Radcliffe. The latter had often been seen about in the evenings, and it was said—with what truth Macdonald was uncertain—that he pursued some of the Land Girls who were billeted in the locality.

As he drove, Macdonald pondered over the evidence he had collected during his four days in Devonshire, trying to weigh it up fairly and put it against the evidence which had led the jury to return a verdict of accidental death. Could it be said that he had disproved that verdict? He had to admit that it still remained a

matter of weighing probabilities. He had proved to his own satisfaction that the causes of fire suggested by the Coroner—defective
wiring or a beam bared in the kitchen chimney—had not been the
agents which led to the fire. For the rest, his theories were based on
evidence which few would consider conclusive. Macdonald believed
himself that Vaughan had been murdered before he reentered Little
Thatch, and his argument for this belief was one that would not
prove convincing to many. He argued that, given normal conditions, Vaughan having put his car away would have gone to shut up
the ducks before he entered the house. It was growing dusk, and it
seemed the natural thing to do to shut up the ducks before going
indoors—and they had not been shut up. Although country people
went early to bed, Macdonald did not believe that Vaughan would
have gone to bed before half-past nine, yet Colonel St Cyres said
there was no light showing in the house. It would certainly have
been too dark inside the cottage at that hour to read or to write,
and Macdonald had learned, by persistent enquiry, that Vaughan
did not habitually go to bed early. His windows could be seen across
the valley, and a farmer and cottagers from across the river Mallow
had said that the faint light from Vaughan's curtained windows was
always observable "late," late meaning after the hour that most
country folk went to bed. Superintendent Bolton and his men had
made very thorough enquiries as to whether any stranger had been
seen in the vicinity of the Mallorys on the evening of April 30th, and
could get no evidence of any one seen on roads or fields or bypaths.
Young Alf's evidence remained uncontradicted: between nine o'clock
and half-past ten two vehicles only had passed Corner Cottage on
the road to Mallory Fitzjohn—one was Vaughan's Morris, going
towards the Mallorys, one was Gressingham's Daimler travelling in
the other direction. If a car or pedestrian had approached from the

other side of the river the route would still have led past Corner
Cottage, because this was the only road leading to Little Thatch.
There was an alternative private road which led to Manor Thatch,
but anybody using this would have had to pass along the drive of
the Manor itself—a very improbable route.

As he drove Macdonald pondered over all these points, considering the report he would be sending in to the Commissioner's
Office. It could be boiled down to this statement:

"I believe that Vaughan was murdered and the cottage deliberately fired, but I have no direct evidence to uphold my opinion."

It was midday when the Chief Inspector arrived at Shermouth
Hospital, where he had made an appointment with the Matron,
and he was shown into an office as severely business-like as his
own office at Cannon Row. The Matron, a formidable lady of
commanding presence, sat at her desk, looking as impressive as a
judge in his robes. To Macdonald's mind no type of trained ability
produced a more notable personality than the hospital Matron, the
very apotheosis of controlled energy and organising power. He
felt that he had to proceed circumspectly in this august presence,
but he went straight to the point.

"I am the detective officer in charge of the enquiry into the
death of Lt. Com. Nicholas Vaughan, who was a patient in this
hospital from June to August, 1944."

"Yes, Chief Inspector. I remember the case you mention very
well. Lt. Com. Vaughan left here at the end of June and went on
to the hospital at Torhampton. The latter is in the nature of a
convalescent home, and he was discharged from there in October
last, having made an excellent recovery. I was very grieved to hear
of his death. We heard that he died in a fire, and I understood that
a verdict of accidental death was returned."

"Yes, madam. That verdict has not been disproved, but a further enquiry is being made to ensure that no evidence was overlooked. I am hoping that I shall be allowed to see the nurses who had charge of the case. Am I right in believing that a patient whose eyes have been seriously damaged is in charge of a special nurse during the crucial stages of his case?"

"Quite right, Chief Inspector. Lt. Commander Vaughan had two special nurses at first—a day nurse and a night nurse. It was essential that he should not touch his bandages or make any movement which might impair the treatment. The surgeons were particularly interested in his case—Mr. Lee Simpson, who is our greatest ophthalmic surgeon, performed something like a miracle of surgery in Vaughan's case, and he emphasised that nursing must do the rest. We did our best, and the result surpassed all our hopes. Now what is it you really want to know?"

The last words were spoken with a half smile, as though the mask of professional severity were doffed for a moment to allow the kindliness and humanity of the nurse's mind to shine out through her habitual severe dignity. Macdonald smiled back.

"I'm only too willing to tell you, madam, if you will allow me to do so in my unofficial capacity. As a human being I am convinced that Nicholas Vaughan's death was not an accident. As a detective officer I have very little evidence to offer to support my opinion. My only hope of getting that evidence is by talking to people who knew Vaughan's mind. He was an unusually reticent person. Would you not say that it is true that even the most reserved men do talk sometimes to their nurses, when physical weakness relaxes their habitual reserve?"

"Quite true, Chief Inspector. There is a child latent in us all, from our babyhood to our death, and helplessness often brings the child to the surface. The professional nurse is debarred—in most circumstances—from repeating what a patient may tell her, but I admit circumstances may alter cases. Again, what is it you want to know?"

"In all that I can find of Nicholas Vaughan there are only two points which puzzle me," said Macdonald. "He was a very straightforward, hard-working fellow, whose manner of life seemed consistent with all I can learn of him, but he was a north countryman, born and bred, who was devoted to the north. He came from that corner of England which lies to the west of the northern end of the Pennine Chain, just south of the Lake District. It is a countryside which grips the imagination, yet Nicholas Vaughan chose to settle in south Devon. I find that inconsistent and I want to know the reason for it. Further, Vaughan was meaning to get married—he had said so, but I can find no trace of the woman he intended to marry. Now both of those questions are intimate ones. It is possible that his nurses may be able to tell me the answer to them. My only justification for asking is that I believe Vaughan was murdered, and that it is some fact in his private life which may lead me to the murderer."

"You interest me, Chief Inspector: this is a new angle on detection. I am willing for you to see the nurses who did special duty for Nicholas Vaughan, and to instruct them to answer your questions if they can. Both are well known to me. They are neither of them young women, and both have fine records. The night nurse detailed for his case was Nurse Cranley—a grand old nurse who has specialised in surgical cases. The special day nurse was Nurse Whelpton. They are both still in this hospital and I will make arrangements for you to see them. Could you come back here about three o'clock? It would save us trouble if you could defer your interviewing until then."

"By all means," replied Macdonald. "I apologise for the necessity of bothering you at all. I know you are all working to the limit
without being interrupted by outsiders."

The Matron smiled. "Even in a hospital, among trained
nurses and sisters—people like myself—you will find that human
nature is as inquisitive as elsewhere. We want to know what
goes on, and you must remember that Nicholas Vaughan was a
favourite patient here. You won't have any difficulty in getting his
nurses to talk about him. Your difficulty will be to evade their
questions."

4

Nurse Cranley—she whom the Matron had described as a grand
old nurse—was a white-haired woman, and Macdonald guessed
that she must be over sixty. Her wide cheeks were still rosy, her
blue eyes bright, and she had a magnificent expanse of shining
white apron across her ample bosom. Seeing her kindly face and
comfortable presence, Macdonald thought, "If I'm ever ill I should
like a nurse like that."

He began: "I'm very sorry to bother you, Nurse. I know you're
on night duty and I have got you up early."

She laughed. "Bless you, I'm always on night duty. I like it,
and I often get up early, so don't bother about me. Tell me about
Nicholas Vaughan—we all called him Nick after a while. My eldest
son is called Nicholas, too. How was it he died, poor lad? We were
so proud of the way we got him better."

Macdonald explained, briefly and patiently, and then went on: "I
want to find out something about the real Nicholas Vaughan, and
to get to know him a bit. He talked so little, apparently: I haven't

had a chance of getting to know what he was like. He's still like a closed book to me: I have only read the title page."

She laughed a little. "You say he talked so little—but he wasn't like that when you knew him. He had a bad time at first. His eyes were bandaged and it was difficult to persuade him he wasn't always going to be blind. When he couldn't sleep I used to encourage him to talk. These boys are all alike—they talk about their homes and the things they did before the war. I got to know quite a lot about the place he came from—Lannerdale, wasn't it? How he loved that place. I'm a north country woman, too. I was born near Jedburgh, in the Border country, and many's the crack I had with Nick Vaughan about the north."

"Did he ever tell you what he meant to do when he'd recovered his health?"

"He meant to go back to Lannerdale, to his old Uncle Joe."

"That's just what I should have expected," said Macdonald, "but he changed his mind and settled in Devon. Did he ever talk to you about getting married?"

"No, but I told him he ought to marry. A farmer should never be a bachelor. He always said he didn't like the thought of getting married, he liked playing his own game by himself. He was a shy fellow, like so many of these big north country lads, but he'd have made a good husband."

"Do you imagine he got fond of any of the nurses here?"

Again she laughed. "No—not if it's marrying that's in your mind. He chattered away to me and to Nurse Whelpton because we 'specialed' for him for a long time. It's not usual for the patients here to have the same nurses over a period of weeks, but the surgeon was very anxious not to have the nurses changed—his was a tricky case. No, if it was marrying he had in mind, he must have

fallen in love after he left here. You'd better ask Nurse Whelpton—
I'm sure she'll tell you the same thing. Now tell me—do you really
believe he was murdered?"

Macdonald's answer was in the nature of "evasive action," and
as soon as he could he terminated the conversation and asked
for Nurse Whelpton. The latter corroborated Nurse Cranley's
evidence, inasmuch as Vaughan had talked to her, too, about
Lannerdale, and spoken about going to live there, to farm the
land where he had been brought up. Nurse Whelpton added one
opinion of her own, and Macdonald summed her up as a shrewd
woman.

"Nick Vaughan was an idealist—the type who would set a
woman on a pedestal. He gave me the impression that he had been
in love once, and that it hadn't come off, so he put all thought of
marrying out of his mind. I can't quote you chapter and verse, it's
simply an impression."

Before he left Macdonald asked a question which seemed to
have little bearing on his case.

"If a trained nurse gets married these days, under wartime
conditions, does she have to go on nursing?"

Nurse Whelpton laughed. "All women, married and unmarried,
between the ages of 19 and 50, are registered with the Ministry
of Labour, and liable to be 'directed,' subject to certain excep-
tions. All trained nurses have been registered separately, including
Hospital trained, Nursing College and Civil Nursing Reserve. If a
nurse gets married she might be allowed a period of leave—I don't
know much about it, we've been too busy in this hospital to think
about marrying, but she would soon find herself 'directed' again
if she didn't get a nursing job herself. Wives of men serving are
non-mobile, but they are still directed. We're all in it for duration,

save for mothers of young children. I should love to know who you've got in mind, Chief Inspector!"

Macdonald laughed this time. "I'm afraid I can't tell you, because I'm not sure myself. One last question: is a trained nurse allowed to choose another job—ambulance driving, or relief work, for example?"

"I shouldn't think so, although I've never tried. Nurses are in 'short supply,' to use the current jargon, and they're kept to their job. Quite right, too, otherwise their training would be wasted."

Macdonald agreed, thanked her very politely, and took his leave without having satisfied the very natural curiosity of two highly trained nursing specialists.

Immediately on leaving the hospital he put through a telephone call to Superintendent Bolton. The latter said: "I'm glad you've rung up, I was wondering where I could get hold of you. Mr. Thomas Gressingham has had a motoring smash. I'm just going out to look into it. He seems to have lost control of his car on Moorbery hill and crashed into a wall at the bottom of it."

"Is he alive?"

"They thought so, but only just alive. Terribly smashed up. Not likely to live, according to present information. Head wounds."

"You'd better carry on, Bolton, and give me a report when I get back. I want to finish off the job I'm on."

"Right. It looks to me as though Gressingham may have chosen his own way out."

"Maybe—but keep an open mind. I'll see you between five and six this evening."

CHAPTER FIFTEEN

I

IT WAS HALF-PAST FOUR WHEN SUPERINTENDENT BOLTON reached the spot where Gressingham's Daimler had crashed into a stone wall, and he found the once magnificent car a heap of wreckage. Its owner had been removed by ambulance, under the supervision of the local doctor, who had found that Gressingham's heart was still beating, though the nature of the head damage alone made it almost certain that his survival was impossible. He had been alone in the car, which had been seen to tear down the steep gradient, gaining speed as it descended. No one had actually seen the final crash, but the car had failed to take the turn towards the bottom of the hill and had hit the wall head-on, crumpling up with the force of its own velocity.

Moorbery hill was fifteen miles from the Mallorys, not on a main road, but on a by-road called "the old road" by the inhabitants. For centuries the only road or path between South Moorton and North Moorton had been the steep road which ascended over the ridge of moor and dropped again to the valley by a gradient which was one in four in that portion where Mr. Gressingham had come to grief. In 1920 a new road had been made along the river valley, so that very little traffic save farm carts and tractors used the old road. One of Bolton's first questions was "What the dickens was he doing on this road at all?"

The Inspector in charge was able to answer this query.

"He was going to see Moorton Place, sir. It's up for sale and Mr. Gressingham phoned this morning to say he was coming to look over it. He asked for directions, and they told him about the old road, and then said he would be wiser to take the longer route round by Withyford. It looks as though he thought he'd save time coming this way, and he lost control of his car."

Bolton looked at the heap of metal and grunted. So far as he knew, Gressingham was a reasonably careful driver, and certainly an experienced one. Daimlers, of all cars, were not likely to have inefficient brakes. It looked to him as though there must be some very good reason why a first-rate car should have got out of control, even on that dangerous road. He studied the surface of the road over which the car had travelled before it crashed. It was not a tarmac road, but an old macadam one, and rough at that. Being very dry, it showed few traces.

"What vehicles have been over this since the accident?" he asked, and the Inspector replied:

"First a farm tractor, then a farm cart: later the doctor's car and the ambulance. The driver didn't like bringing it down the hill, but what could we do? He couldn't back up—too steep and twisty."

Bolton bent to study the ground again, but had to admit himself defeated. He said to the Inspector: "Could you see any traces of braking when you got here? Any sane driver would have had his brakes on with all his might."

"There was nothing to see, sir. The tractor had been past before I got here. I looked for wheel traces, but I couldn't find any. I reckon his steering must have gone, so that he couldn't take the bend."

"Looks more as though his senses had gone," grunted Bolton. "He must have been travelling like an express train to get smashed up to that extent. That car's got to be left where it is until we've had a reliable mechanic out to look at it. If you start moving it we may not be able to get any evidence at all. I want to know if it was in gear, and if so, what gear. It ought to have been in one or two on a hill like this, and if it was in low gear it ought not to have attained a velocity that accounts for this." He looked in at the tangled wreckage: the gear handle had snapped off with the force of the impact.

"Can't think how the driver was alive at all," he said.

The Inspector replied, "He was shockingly smashed up, sir, but the doctor said he was still alive, so we had to get the ambulance up."

"Of course you did," agreed Bolton. "Now who was it who saw the car coming down the hill?"

"A man named Weatherby, sir—an old chap. He was singling turnips in a field halfway up the hill. He's still working there. Shall I go and fetch him?"

"No. I'll walk up, then I shall be able to get an idea of what he saw," said Bolton. He turned to the driver of his own car. "Go up to the top and wait. When you hear me whistle drive the car down—and be careful what you're doing." Bolton paused. He was a very conscientious man and he knew that his young police chauffeur was a better driver than himself. "Do you know this road?" he enquired.

"No, sir, only by repute. It's one of the worst hills in the county. Fit for engine trials."

"Do you think it's safe for driving?"

"Oh lord, yes, sir, provided your car's in condition and you're careful. Nothing to make a fuss about—just a steep hill."

"If that Daimler had been yours would you have hesitated to drive it down this hill?"

"No—except for thinking of the tyres—it's a pretty rough surface. That car was never suddenly braked on this road, sir. It'd show on those tyres if it had been. For whatever reason it was, the driver let it rip—as though he'd gone to sleep at the wheel, or had a fit or something."

The young chauffeur got into the police car and set it at the hill, accelerating the engine and then letting in the clutch smoothly at the critical split second, so that the car started moving up the steep gradient with as little fuss as if it had been on the level. Bolton watched with a feeling of exasperation that he could never start a car himself with the skilled nonchalance of these youngsters of to-day. It always seemed to him that the motoring age had evolved a specialised type of human to meet its needs.

Bolton trudged up the hill, his eyes scanning the ground for any evidence of wheel-marks with the brake locking them, while he considered the nature of the hill as far as he could see it. There was a quarter of a mile on the straight from the top downwards—quarter of a mile of good visibility, and then an obviously dangerous turn, also on a steep gradient, where the Daimler had come to grief and piled up against the stone wall of Moorbery Place. Towards the top of the hill, on Bolton's left, a gate led into a field of turnips, a field which sloped so steeply that it was difficult to understand how the ploughman had negotiated it. It was a four-acre field, Bolton guessed, and one old man was bent to the wearisome task of singling "tunnips."

"What a job!" thought Bolton, looking at the interminable rows of young green—it looked a lifetime's job to one not familiar with field work. The old man—as bent and gnarled as Reuben Dickon—seemed to be part of the field, something growing from the brown earth. As Bolton approached he straightened up as far as he was able and stood waiting patiently.

"Good day, Mr. Weatherby," shouted Bolton. He knew this type, and knew that kindliness and patience would get him farther than professional abruptness. "I'm a Police Superintendent. I'm told you saw a car coming down the hill before it was smashed up at the bottom."

"Iss, feggs, I saw mun. Shockin' thing, that be. I waved to mun, to warn him like, but he took no notice."

"Where you working when you saw the car?" asked Bolton.

The ancient pointed farther up the slope, some yards farther away from the road. There was a stick in the ground, with a bundle tied on its crook.

"'Twas just there," he said. "I was goin' to have a bite and I'd stopped workin' a minute. I seed mun, he'd come over brow o' t'hill and he was agoin' faster and faster, 's if the de'il were drivin' mun. I knew how it'd be. Iss. That carner's a praper teaser. 'Im couldn't turn carner drivin' like that."

Bolton walked up to the stick. He found he could see over the hedge, and he took out his whistle and blew a short blast. In a few seconds he saw the police car appearing: there was a copse on the ridge of the hill, so that he could not see the road at the top, but he got a clear view of the car as it crept cautiously down, and he could hear the engine in low gear. The hedge hid it from sight before the turn where Gressingham had crashed. Not much to be learned from here, although old Weatherby must have been able to see inside the car.

Bolton went back to the old man. "Could you see the man driving the car?" he asked.

The other scratched his head. "Iss, I saw mun—just so's to see there was a driver, though I couldn't see what sort he was. Car was goin' turble fast, and me eyes aren't what they was. I seed him though."

"Did you see anybody else except the driver?"

"No. Nobbut him at t'wheel."

"Did you hear the car coming?"

Again the old man shook his head. "I'm hard o' hearing. I never heard nowt. I was standin' up here and I chanced to see car ower yon bank, faster and faster mun went. I knew how it'd be. I went down along and saw mun, and then I went to the Hall and towd 'em there'd been a turble smash. Couldn't ha' done no more, could I, now?"

"No. You couldn't have done anything more," agreed Bolton. "When you got on the road, did you look round to see if there was anybody else about?"

"Nay, there was no one. 'Tis a lonely road, this. Times I'll work all t'morning and not see a soul. Folks at the Hall, they don't use this road. Mr. Venning, him brings tractor this way betimes, and the farm carts use t'old road, but most keeps off it. 'Tis a hill, that be."

Bolton agreed, and leaving the old man to his interminable job, the Superintendent went back to the road and trudged up to the top of the hill. On the summit was a small spinney, stunted pines growing in the sour moorland tract on either side of the road, but looking southwards there was a magnificent view across to the tors of Dartmoor. The road surface told nothing at all. Walking a hundred yards farther on Bolton found the road dipped again. He calculated that anybody driving up the farther slope would see nothing but the road mounting to its final ridge until they were actually at the top, and then the road dropped in a violent gradient, dead straight, to the turn near the bottom where it was edged by the stone wall. Pondering deeply, Bolton walked down the hill again and rejoined his driver. Getting in the car he said:

"I want to go up to the top and reverse somewhere on the downward slope if it's possible. If not, go to the bottom and reverse there."

"That's just what I've been wanting to do myself, sir," replied the chauffeur. "Then we shall see just what the driver of the Daimler saw."

Again the police car mounted the hill and reached the summit, but it was nearly a mile farther on before the driver thought it expedient to reverse, using a gateway to give him space to turn. Going up, it was as Bolton had expected—he could see nothing but the mounting hill in front of him until they gained the ridge, where they pulled up. The driver—a young policeman named Rainsford—spoke.

"It's like this, sir. Any driver coming up this hill would be on the alert as he approached the ridge. It's nothing like so steep on the far side, but it's a long hill. You couldn't rush it in top gear, like you can a short hill, you'd have plenty of time to wonder what was coming, and the road drops so steeply this side it's like driving at a cliff-edge. Anybody'd be careful to slow up, or even stop, at the top. No one in their senses would tear on down that gradient. I should say it's so obviously dangerous that it's not dangerous at all, if you see what I mean. You'd know you'd just got to go in low gear and take it slowly with that turn at the bottom."

Bolton nodded. "Yes. I see what you mean," he said. "What'd be your guess as to what happened? Defective brakes?"

"No, sir—not on that Daimler. Besides, if the brakes had been faulty the driver would have known it. You can't drive in country like this without knowing if your brakes are holding. Then there's this to it: if you came over that ridge you'd know at once if the brakes didn't function, and you'd have time to steer the car into the bank to check it before it had gained speed. No. I'd guess it was something like this. The driver pulled up at the top to look at the view; it's a wonderful view from here. Maybe he fell asleep, and didn't realise he hadn't pulled his hand-brake back properly and the car slid forward, very slowly at first, and then gained so much momentum he couldn't stop it when he woke up. If a man's muzzy with sleep he can't act quickly enough to stop an accident."

Bolton studied the road. "Might have happened that way, but I don't think so," he said. "There's twenty feet of level ground here. If he'd pulled up he'd have stopped on the level, as you've done—and the car wouldn't have moved."

Rainsford let in the clutch, moved the car forward a yard and then pulled up again. After a few seconds he released the hand-brake and waited. Bolton waited, too, and after a few seconds he realised the car *was* moving—the apparently level road did slope a little.

Rainsford pulled the hand-brake on hard. "You see, sir, it's difficult to tell. A car will move on the very least gradient. That's why you're always taught to leave the hand-brake on. It could have happened that way. I believe it did: the driver woke up, found he was moving at a hell of a lick, and being sleepy all he managed to do was to keep the car in the middle of the road. He may have tried to brake and his foot was numb—foozled it or something."

"What about his hand-brake?"

"Maybe he dare not let go of the wheel and drive one-handed with that turn rushing at him."

Bolton studied the other's cool, intelligent face. "That explanation satisfy you?"

"Not altogether, sir, but it's a possible one. It's difficult to make any other. If you guess at foul play, you can suggest he was shot at the wheel just as he started driving down the hill, but I don't see how the car kept straight. He'd almost certainly have jerked the wheel as he slumped over it, and the car would have piled up on the bank. Also, he'd have been in low gear, and I doubt if he'd have come quite such a smash. That car was either in neutral or else in top gear, judging by the pace it was going when it hit the wall."

Bolton was meditating aloud. "He was coming to see that house, so I'm told… It's probable he'd have pulled up at the top here to look at the view… quite a natural thing to do. The car wouldn't have been in gear then… he'd have pulled the hand-brake on… second nature to do that…"

"Yes, sir. If he'd started again he'd have put her in low gear and then released the hand-brake slowly as he let the clutch in. I think my suggestion meets the facts better. He pulled up on the level, as he thought, and didn't get his hand-brake on properly. Then he went to sleep and the hand-brake gave. The car was in neutral and he wasn't awake enough to stop it once it gained momentum."

"A nasty accident, eh?" queried Bolton. "If it wasn't an accident, how could it have happened? You're right about the car keeping the road until it reached the turn."

Rainsford considered afresh. "I'd say it was impossible for him to have been killed while the car was travelling—it'd never have kept straight. There's this possibility. He was killed while the car was pulled up on the level and his hands were off the wheel. The car was moved forward and left with its nose pointing dead straight down the middle of the road. Then the murderer got out, stood on the running board, released the hand-brake, and jumped off. That's a possibility, but it'd have taken a cool nerve to do it."

"That hill's dead straight," pondered Bolton. "If you headed the car straight there's nothing to deflect it… Well, now we shall have to find out if anyone else was seen mounting the hill, or if there was any other car about… No man would choose that way of committing suicide."

"No. That's one explanation I wouldn't consider for an instant," replied Rainsford.

Bolton went on: "Try to imagine yourself waking up in a car that was tearing to perdition down this hill. Wouldn't you have grabbed the hand-brake and pulled like hell, even if it meant a spill? Wouldn't you have gone for the brake instinctively?"

Rainsford looked at the straight hill and the turn at the bottom. "I don't know, sir. Maybe I'd have held on to the wheel and tried to take that corner… you couldn't turn the car with one hand… I just don't know."

And Bolton didn't know either.

2

That evening, before Macdonald returned, Superintendent Bolton sat and wrote his report. In the course of many years of police work he had learnt to write an admirable report, terse and factual, and he no longer found writing a toil as he had done when he was younger. He told his wife that putting facts down on paper often helped him to realise the significance of the evidence he had collected. On this occasion, however, Bolton found himself worried, and his worry was due to the fact that he could not determine if the matter of Gressingham's car smash were a case which must be judged as a thing apart, or if it was part and parcel of the Little Thatch case.

While Bolton had been busy investigating on Moorbery hill, Mr. Hesling had been talking to the Inspector, who went to Hinton

Mallory to make enquiries about Mr. Gressingham's next of kin,
that information might be sent concerning the accident. Hesling
had told the Inspector that Gressingham and Radcliffe had had a
furious quarrel the previous evening, and though Gressingham
had attempted to make out that things were normal between
himself and his friend, it was obvious to the Heslings that Radcliffe
had taken his departure in a state of sullen rage. The news of
Gressingham's smash—and his own dying condition—came
as a shock to the Heslings, and they immediately connected it
with Radcliffe. The Heslings were only able to give a guesswork
description of the cause of the quarrel between the two men.
Mrs. Hesling maintained that the dispute was concerned with
Gressingham's car, Gressingham having accused Radcliffe of taking
the car out on the night of April 30th. Mrs. Hesling, however,
believed that the trouble was concerned with Radcliffe's pursuit
of a certain Land Girl of whom he had been enamoured. Mr.
Hesling was able to give information on this score: it seemed
plain enough that Radcliffe had on some occasions gone out late
in the evening to meet a girl in the fields between Hinton Mallory
and Little Thatch, and Hesling believed that he had done so on
the night of April 30th. When questioned more closely on this
point he admitted that he had no evidence to offer—it was just
guesswork. He had certainly not connected Radcliffe's "going
after the girls" with the fire at Little Thatch, but what he had
overheard of the final quarrel between the two men led him to
believe that Gressingham suspected that Radcliffe knew more
than he had admitted. The Inspector had immediately enquired
when and how Radcliffe had left Hinton Mallory and was told
that Gressingham had taken him to the station in his Daimler.
Radcliffe had rung up for a taxi, but had been unable to get one

at short notice, and Gressingham, who was endeavouring to keep up appearances, had said he would take him. The two men had left in the Daimler, with Radcliffe's suitcase, at ten o'clock that morning. The Inspector had enquired if Gressingham had said where he was going, and to which station he intended to drive Radcliffe—Exeter, Mallowton, or Creediford. On this matter Hesling could give no information, though Mrs. Hesling had said that Gressingham had told her he would not be in until his evening meal. He had had a long conversation over the telephone early that morning, and Mrs. Hesling had overheard enough to gather that he was making an appointment to meet somebody, and was also asking for directions as to route.

The next point on Bolton's report dealt with sending information to Gressingham's London address. He had a suite of rooms in Mount Street, to which the police had telephoned, and his personal servant had said that he had no knowledge of Mrs. Gressingham's whereabouts, but he gave the address of Gressingham's partner and his lawyer. Bolton's next point concerned the Land Girl who had been the focus of Radcliffe's attention. Hesling did not know who she was, but had assumed the girl was one of a trio who had been billeted about three miles away from the Mallorys. When the Inspector enquired at this farm he found that two of the three girls had left the farm a week ago, after quarrelling with their landlady—a stout Devonshire dame, who said roundly that they were a good for nothing pair and not fit to be in any decent house. When the Inspector described Radcliffe the landlady admitted he had been one of those who "came after" the two girls—Doris and Flossie. "I know his sort, turning a girl's head, giving her expensive cigarettes and chocolates and taking her out after dark. I don't hold with it and I told them so," declared the irate dame.

"Had either Doris or Flossie been out late on the night of the Little Thatch fire?" enquired the Inspector, and the landlady gave him what he described as an "old-fashioned look."

"I don't know," she declared. "I never could keep even with them. They'd get out of their bedroom window after they'd said they were going to bed—oh, proper naughty they were."

Bolton concluded his neat precis of all this information with one startling fact. He asked Exchange for the telephone number which had been connected with Hinton Mallory for Gressingham's long conversation that morning: it was the number of the call-box in Tiverton from which the so-called "code messages" had been sent to Nicholas Vaughan. Bolton, by the time he had completed his report, had only one wish in mind—that Macdonald would return shortly and discuss all these events with him.

CHAPTER SIXTEEN

I

MACDONALD HIMSELF HAD BEEN HAVING A BUSY DAY. After leaving Shermouth he had driven to Torhampton, where he had again interviewed a hospital matron. This time he had acquired information which had a much more direct bearing on his case—information which he had expected, after long consideration of all the facts known to him, plus his own estimate of Nicholas Vaughan. During Vaughan's convalescence there had been a Nurse White in the hospital, and the Matron admitted, though unwillingly, that she had known that Vaughan became devoted to his nurse to an extent not approved of by the Matron or Sisters. On this account Nurse White had been transferred to another hospital in Devon, in the neighbourhood of Tiverton.

Macdonald had sat silent for a minute or two, studying the stern, troubled face of the Matron. At length he had said:

"I don't want to press you to give me information which I know you would rather withhold. Later, it may be necessary for you to give information in a Court of Law—but I hope it won't be necessary. Will you answer this question: is it not true that Nurse White is a married woman who had resumed her maiden name for her professional work?"

"Yes," replied the Matron. She then added: "While I make no inquisition into the private lives of my nurses, especially under present-day conditions, it is essential that I should know a little about those who are working here. Nurse White is a most skilled and conscientious nurse, and I had complete trust in her ability and trustworthiness on duty. I was very sorry to lose her. I knew that she had had a disastrous marriage, and I gathered that her decision to leave her husband had very strong grounds to uphold it. He was a sadist—a pathological type well known to the psychologists. I should like to add that I think it highly improbable that Nurse White has done anything for which she could be condemned by any person of human sympathies. If your enquiries mean, as I fear, that further trouble lies in store for her, I can only say that I deeply regret it. The work she did here proved her to be a woman capable of devotion and self-sacrifice—two essential qualities in our calling."

Macdonald bowed: a quietly courteous gesture which was an acknowledgment of the respect for the lady who was talking to him.

"Thank you for what you have said," he replied. "Your calling is one for which I have the deepest respect, and I can assure you that I shall endeavour to avoid causing distress to any nurse. I have seen something of the devotion and self-sacrifice of the hospital staffs in the London blitz, and, believe me, I shall never forget it. Thank you for having answered my questions."

He got up and took his leave. The Matron sat on for a few moments, staring straight in front of her. She, like Macdonald, had often to study the complex pattern of cause and effect. She had not told him so, but the Matron had often dreaded such an interview in the past few weeks, had often wondered how she would answer the questions which had just been put to her. Because truth was inherent in her she had answered truthfully, but as she sat her lips formulated soundless words: "Poor child... poor child."

2

It was evening before Macdonald came into the presence of the woman whose identity he had believed all through his enquiry to be the key to the riddle of Nicholas Vaughan's death. As he rose to his feet when she came into the room he found himself facing a tall, pale girl, clad in the immaculate white and blue of hospital uniform. She was very fair, with smooth, pale hair brushed back severely under her starched cap. Her face had the even pallor, not of sickness but of health—firm cheeks, firm lips, rounded chin, and clear grey eyes: a Norse type, with something statuesque in her stillness and dignity. She faced Macdonald steadily, meeting his gaze with her own.

"I am Nurse White. Matron says you wish to speak to me."

"Yes. Will you sit down. I am the officer in charge of the enquiry concerning the death of Nicholas Vaughan of Little Thatch."

She sat down in the chair he drew forward and sat erect, her hands lightly clasped on her lap, and waited for him to continue, very still and self-controlled.

"You knew Nicholas Vaughan?" he asked.

"Yes. I have known him for many years. I nursed him at Torhampton Hospital."

"The Matron there spoke to me of your work—and praised it highly. I don't want to ask you more questions than I must, Nurse. The situation is a difficult one, but I must tell you this. I have reason to believe that Nicholas Vaughan was murdered, and it is necessary for me to find out what he was doing on the last evening of his life. First, will you tell me what you yourself were doing on the evening of April 30th last?"

"I was on night duty here. I came on duty at eight o'clock in the evening, after I had had breakfast—as night nurses call it—at seven. I was in this building from five o'clock onwards, if that is what you want to know."

Her voice was low and steady, and Macdonald guessed it was her nurse's training which enabled her to maintain such a stead-fast front.

"Thank you. My next question is this: have you on some occasions telephoned a message to Nicholas Vaughan, using the telephone in Bridgeway, Tiverton, and calling the number of the phone at Hinton Mallory?"

"Yes. I frequently used that call-box and sent a message by Mrs. Hesling at Hinton Mallory."

"So far as you know, could anybody else have known that you did so—that is, that you communicated with Nicholas Vaughan in that way, using a specific form of words?"

She sat statue still, her face white, but her hands still relaxed, her grey eyes dilated but steady.

"I don't know, Inspector. The only way anyone could have known was if they took my message at the Hinton Mallory tele-phone and recognised my voice. I can only say—I do not know."

"Very good. Next, did you occasionally meet Nicholas Vaughan in a spinney on a by-road between Tiverton and Creediford?"

"Yes."

"How did you reach that spot?"

"On my bicycle."

"Did it ever occur to you that you were followed or observed?"

"No. Otherwise I should not have continued to meet him there." Her self-control gave a little, inasmuch as her hands sud-denly clenched and she spoke quickly without waiting to be questioned. "I read of Nicholas Vaughan's death in the paper. I don't want to tell you what I felt about it... then, I read about the inquest. It seemed certain that his death was due to accident. I believed that to be true. There was nothing I could do..."

"I know," replied Macdonald quietly. "I don't want to distress you by going over matters which are not relevant, and you know enough about the law to know that there are questions on which your evidence may not be invoked. I want to ask a minimum of legitimate questions. If Mr. Vaughan ever asked for you on the telephone here, did he use the name under which he wrote— Henry Heythwaite?"

"Yes."

"Do you think it possible that anybody in this place could have listened in to your phone calls, or spied on you—to put it bluntly?"

Again she sat with that curious stillness, tense and erect.

"I don't know. It may have happened... In all institutional life there are jealousies and frustrations... and gossip. It may have been so."

"Do you know a Mrs. Gressingham? Have you ever met anyone of that name?"

"No, but there is a member of the office staff here who talks about a Mrs. Gressingham—an auxiliary ambulance driver."

"Did you know that Mrs. Gressingham's husband retains rooms at Hinton Mallory?"

That question shook her: the firm lips quivered and her shoulders jerked in surprise. "No, indeed, I did not know... I had no idea."

"Did Mr. Vaughan ever mention Gressingham to you?"

"No, never. The only people he spoke of were the St Cyres. I have met Mr. Gressingham... but I never thought of him going to Mallory Fitzjohn."

"Was the name of Henry Heythwaite ever mentioned in conversation when you talked to Gressingham?"

She sat frowning, intent, rigid, her hands gripped together. "I believe so... once. I avoided saying anything... but—"

She hesitated, and Macdonald said, "That was all I wanted to know—that that name was mentioned."

She put her hands up to her eyes—a gesture of intolerable distress, and then resumed her pose of quiet attention, the trained stillness which Macdonald could not but admire.

"There is something else I ought to tell you, Inspector. I wonder if you can understand... I'm so tired of my own wretched problems that it's only when I'm working I find life bearable. If you work very hard you have no time to think of yourself... I married on impulse, foolishly, thinking, as many women do, it would be good to have a home and a reliable husband. Soon after I was married I had cause to suspect that my husband had been married previously and was a bigamist."

Macdonald's question came quickly. "Did Vaughan know that?"

"Yes. He knew what I suspected, and he was trying to find out." She watched Macdonald's face and cried out, "It wasn't that! It couldn't have been. *He* couldn't have been there that evening. I found out where he was."

Macdonald had risen to his feet. "You must leave all that to me," he answered quietly. "Just now you spoke about your work. You are on night duty, aren't you? Go back to the Wards and do your work, and think only about your work. I hope you will have a very busy night—too busy to think about yourself. Believe me, I am sorry for all these distresses and sorry I have had to worry you afresh."

She looked back at him, her grey eyes dark and desolate, but yet with that trained calm which never quite forsook her.

"Was it all my fault?" She asked the question of herself rather than of Macdonald, and he replied:

"The Matron at Torhampton told me you were a good nurse, capable of devotion and self-sacrifice. Put that in the balance. I do."

She gazed at him wide-eyed, her face drawn and strained, but then replied: "That was a kind thing to say. I am grateful for it."

"I think there's one other thing I should like to say—as a human being and not as a police official. While Nicholas Vaughan was at Little Thatch, he was very happy. He died, I am certain, without knowing anything of suffering or trouble. Think of that, too." And with that he left her.

3

It was nine o'clock before Macdonald saw Bolton. The C.I.D. man had had a lot of telephoning to do and many matters to arrange before he sat down with Bolton's typed sheets in front of him. Macdonald read the sheets with only one half of his mind: the other was listening for a telephone call. Bolton was worried because he could not get on to Raymond Radcliffe's trail. The absurdly fat man seemed to have disappeared without anyone noticing him.

"I've tried the Exeter stations and the bus station, the taxi hire offices and garages, and none of them report seeing him," said Bolton.

"It's quite likely he got on the train at a small station on some branch line," said Macdonald. "These days there are very few porters about on the small stations and none at the halts. We shall find him all right—Radcliffe hasn't the physique to stage a disappearing trick."

"Do you think Rainsford's idea is feasible?" enquired Bolton, "that Gressingham was killed and the car started by the murderer heading straight down that hill?—or did Gressingham go to sleep at the wheel?"

"Either is possible. If it hadn't been for previous events accident might well have been accepted as the explanation," said Macdonald—and then the phone bell rang.

"For you," said Bolton, handing over the receiver.

Macdonald gave his name and listened for some time. Then he said, "All right. I'll come over at once. Thank you for notifying me."

He hung up the receiver and turned to Bolton. "That was Mr. Howard Brendon. He says Radcliffe is at his house and he's feeling uneasy. Will you come over with me?"

Bolton got up. "I'll come. This is the last lap, Chief?"

"I think so—and it may be rough going. When a man has committed one murder he has nothing much to lose. I shall be glad to have you, Super, and we'll take a couple of your men—but this is my show, and I do it my own way."

"Right, but look out for yourself."

"I will. It's no part of my duty to get murdered. From the point of view of detection that's merely making a mess of it," replied Macdonald.

4

Howard Brendon himself admitted Macdonald to his house at Dulverton, apologising for the absence of any servants, and adding that he was shortly shutting the house up. He then lowered his voice, saying, "I'd like to have a word with you alone before you see Radcliffe. There are one or two points I should like to make."

"Of course," Macdonald replied, as he pulled his driving gloves off and undid his top coat. "Can I leave this here? It's turned very warm," he observed, and as he spoke a telephone bell shrilled in a room opening out of the hall.

"Yes, leave it on the chest. I'll just answer that damned telephone," replied Brendon. A moment later he was back in the hall. "Wrong number. Come along in."

Macdonald followed him into a finely panelled room. It was gloomy, despite the electric lamps, for the dark panelling seemed to swallow up the light. The two men advanced towards the fireplace, where there were two armchairs, and Brendon suddenly said: "Do you hear anything? That chap's behaving queerly."

Macdonald stood and listened, his eyes on the other's. Brendon had curiously light eyes, and the pupils were contracted to pin points. Still holding the other's gaze, Macdonald replied in a deliberately equable tone of voice:

"No, I can't hear anything. Why was it that you borrowed Gressingham's car that night? I often wondered."

There was dead silence, in which the two faced one another, perfectly still. Brendon stood firmly, his chin up, his hands in his pockets, and he looked perfectly normal except for his eyes. Macdonald guessed that he was on the verge of mental instability, and he had risked his question to surprise the other into replying. The answer was startling in its simplicity.

"I ran out of petrol. It was awkward. I had to get back…" He ran his hands over his head, in the gesture of a tired man, and suddenly jerked his head up.

"What the devil are you talking about? You want to see Radcliffe."

"I'm much more interested in talking to you," replied Macdonald, still in that even voice. Brendon's face twitched and his expression altered, as a sleep walker's might when he became aware of his surroundings.

"You're interested in me? That's funny... We're alone here, you know. I saw to that."

"Very wise of you. We don't want to be interrupted, do we?"

Again that silence and stillness, broken now by Brendon's quickened breathing.

"I'm tired," he said. "I've had a lot to think about. I'm going away from here. Sick of the place. You'll stay here, of course. You realise that. You and Radcliffe. I've thought all that out, too."

"I see. I wondered how you would arrange things," said Macdonald. "It's an ingenious idea: your ideas *are* ingenious, and you have a great sense of detail. I suppose that you have arranged to stay at that hotel in Taunton, as you did before? The outside lock-ups for cars are just what you need for your plans."

Brendon stared back, and Macdonald could see the small muscles twitching round his eyes and the pulses of his temples throbbing. He answered at last, his curt voice rather hoarse: "Yes, just what I wanted. You're intelligent. I realised that the moment I set eyes on you, but you've the usual defect of the Scots—you're too sure of yourself. It's conceit that has finished you. You came here alone, thinking you could be master of the situation, and I've got you covered. You're quite helpless. I've noticed the way you prefer to work alone. I've been watching you quite a lot—just as I watched Vaughan. Creature of habit, you know. Men tend to grow like that."

"Yes," agreed Macdonald. "That's quite true. I realise the situation all right, but I'd like you to know this. I've got my duty to do, no matter what my position may be, and it's my duty to caution you that anything you say can be used in evidence against you."

Brendon laughed. "You haven't much sense of humour, have you? Keep your hands on that chair. I'm not risking anything. Whoever gives evidence, it won't be you. This house is well and truly secured. There are shutters at all the windows and the doors are good ones. They'll burn eventually—but not for a long time. I've got it all arranged."

"Then before you stage the final act, wouldn't you like to hear a reconstruction of the story? This is a unique situation, isn't it?"

Again came that short, rasping laugh and the queer twitch of the eyes. "I'd say it is. I'll give you five minutes. I shall enjoy hearing you talk. I promise I won't repeat any confidences."

"That's for you to decide. When I've finished you can tell me where I went wrong. I think the crucial point was the matter of Gressingham's car. Somebody used it that night, and somebody obtained about a gallon of petrol from Little Thatch—counting what was left, after refuelling the Daimler. Now it seemed unreasonable to suppose that Gressingham took his car out. If he did the job at Little Thatch he had no need of a car. Even supposing he had killed Vaughan in that spinney where the petrol cans were dumped, there was Vaughan's Morris to bring him back to Mallory Fitzjohn. The man who took the Daimler out did it in order to take a little petrol to refuel his own car, which had run short. He couldn't go to a garage to refuel, could he? It was essential for him not to be seen about. Theoretically he was in his room at a hotel in Taunton—and he had got to get back there so that he could be seen in the lounge as soon as possible—say about eleven o'clock. I worked it out like this: Vaughan reached the spinney at 6.15, in response to the telephone message. He was killed in the spinney.

He had backed his own car into a recess in the road where road metal had been dumped. The killer drove back to Taunton and had dinner at his hotel—it was only a twenty-mile drive. He went into the lounge from seven-thirty to eight-thirty, and then said he was going to work in his room. He slipped out of the hotel, got out the car he had hired for the purpose, and drove to the spinney again, putting on Vaughan's coat and hat. He then drove back to the Mallorys in Vaughan's Morris. It was twilight, and he risked sounding the horn and waving in Vaughan's habitual manner at Corner Cottage. The rest he managed skilfully—but he had a lot of luck when he dragged a sack unseen into the cottage."

Brendon's face twitched more than ever. "That was the difficult part," he said. "I can use my brains—but it took a lot of muscle to move that sack..."

Macdonald went on in his even voice: "Having completed all that it was necessary to do at Little Thatch, the killer went down to Hinton Mallory. It was getting dark now, and he risked walking in Vaughan's old coat and his ancient hat. He got the Daimler out without being observed, drove up the hill and picked up the petrol he had dumped, and drove back to the spinney. He put some petrol in his own tank, and drove back to Taunton. I know that because he was seen in the hotel there at half-past eleven. I think he must have left Gressingham's Daimler parked by the spinney where the petrol cans were concealed. Very few people pass that way, and none of the folk at the farm near by went out that evening after dusk. This plan necessitated another drive: leaving the Taunton hotel in the small hours he drove back to the spinney and returned the Daimler to the shed at Hinton Mallory, with added fuel in its tanks. Then, a walk back to the spinney and a final drive in to Taunton, and the matter of getting back into the hotel again by the bedroom window—not too difficult for a determined man. It was very well thought out."

Brendon was breathing heavily, but his pale face was more under control, the twitch around his eyes less noticeable. "You interest me," he said, and his dry voice was almost his normal curt tone. "You have a hypothetical case, but you have no evidence. It's all assumption. I should be interested to hear the case put forward by Counsel for the Prosecution, and to hear it riddled by defending counsel—as it would be—but it won't come to that. I've thought it all out."

"Your mistake was in using Gressingham's Daimler, and thereby bringing Gressingham into it," said Macdonald. "He began to think, and, unlike you, I never despised his ability. I always thought he was shrewd and observant—and you found that to be true in the end. Gressingham guessed, and you had to finish him, too, to safeguard yourself. You might have got away with the Little Thatch fire, but not with the second business. The case is complete against you—including motive and method."

"So you boast. Do you think I have planned thus far and not thought ahead? I know what I'm going to do, and I know what I'm going to do with you, too. You've come here to see Radcliffe, and you'll see him—and that will be the end… another fire. I tell you I've dreamed of fire, dreamed of it… flames rising higher and higher, flames burning up all that went against me. Nicholas Vaughan thought he could beat me, thought he could win… I tell you I killed him as easily as I could kill a rabbit, as easily as I can kill you…"

The curt voice rose, getting sharper and shriller with each word. Brendon stood there, a pistol in his hand, the light of madness in his eyes, and suddenly there was a sound from the other side of the room as the old door creaked on its hinges as it opened. In the door space stood Bolton and two of his men, and when he saw them Brendon squealed as a rabbit squeals in a trap. He lifted his pistol to his head, and the shot reverberated through the room before the heavier thud of his own falling body.

5

Bolton mopped his forehead and sat down heavily on a chair. "That was an ugly sight, Chief, but you took an almighty risk."

"No, not much of a risk. When I got his phone message I realised his mind must be going. If he thought he could trick me into coming here alone it meant that his normal mental capacity was failing. When I saw him I knew at once he was mad—and a madman is not dangerous when you're prepared for him. When the phone here went as we arranged when I came in, he gave me the chance I wanted to open the front door for you to come in. He never noticed that. Now we'd better look for Radcliffe. He's here somewhere, and I've a feeling he's still alive."

Radcliffe was found in the dining-room. He was lying back in one of the big leather armchairs, snoring as a drugged man snores.

"He was luckier than his friend Gressingham," said Macdonald. "I can't say I've ever liked the look of Mr. Radcliffe, but I think he may be useful for once in his life, answering a few questions."

CHAPTER SEVENTEEN

I

IT WAS TO COLONEL ST CYRES AND HIS DAUGHTER THAT Macdonald gave an exposition concerning the Little Thatch case. Sitting in the sunlight on the terrace at Manor Thatch, the Chief Inspector talked to the troubled pair, his voice gentle, for he realised that both of his hearers would feel sad for a long time when they thought of their last tenant.

"When Commander Wilton urged his point of view about Vaughan's death I felt that he had one or two strong arguments," said Macdonald. "First, in saying that Vaughan was a skilled engineer and a very careful workman: secondly, in urging that a sailor was the last person who would remain asleep while a fire took hold of his dwelling. Examination of the investigation by the local police force showed a very careful piece of work in which there were two gaps which needed to be filled—in my opinion. One was 'Where did Vaughan go to on the last evening of his life?' Two, 'Who was the woman Vaughan hoped to marry?' The first seemed important to me, because if Vaughan had been to see one of his farmer friends, or had been doing any of the business transacted in the usual run of agricultural life, I was certain that the farmer or merchant he visited would have come forward and said 'I saw him that evening.' The fact that nobody *did* admit having seen him proved, to my mind, that there was probably a secret in a life which had appeared to be open. Then, concerning the woman he hoped to marry: she did not appear. She made no enquiries, and yet I believed that he was preparing a home for his future wife.

This again prompted me to believe there was a secret—and in detection, a secret is like a pointer, urging a detective to find out."

Anne St Cyres frowned unhappily. "All that is rather dreadful. Mr. Vaughan seemed such an open person, for all that he was so reserved. I hate the need for prying."

"I hate it, too, in one sense," said Macdonald, "but I should have hated more for Vaughan's murderer to be undetected. A murderer at large is a potential menace. However, to leave that and get on with my problem. I had another argument to go on—a private and personal one with which you would not have agreed. I asked myself 'Why did Vaughan choose to live in Devon?' I think all men who have lived and worked in the country grow to love the locality in which they were reared. The countryman tends to take roots. I have seen something of the dalesmen in that part of England where Vaughan was brought up, and their devotion to their locality is profound, though it is seldom put into words." Macdonald turned to Anne: "Amn't I right in saying that it would take a very strong motive to make you forsake the West country and go to live in the North? When you saw the colourless limestone and the greyness of the fells, wouldn't you be sick at heart for your rose-red soil and the deep flowered lanes of Devon?"

"Of course: it would be like transplanting a deeply rooted tree—but I can imagine agreeing to it in some circumstances."

"Of course you would. So did Vaughan. He settled here, and I guessed the motive which made him do so was concerned with the woman he meant to marry. Either she was Devonshire born, or else she was a woman who had some reason for avoiding Lannerdale and the country around there. That was my guess, and you will see how near it came to the actual facts."

Colonel St Cyres pulled his pipe out and began to fill it. "I have thought a lot about this same problem," he said. "I remember when Vaughan first said he would take the cottage I suggested it was only fair to his future wife that she should see it first. Later, when he got to know Anne, I wondered why his wife-to-be wasn't brought into the picture—but it wasn't my business to probe into another man's affairs. I put it out of my mind."

"Well, there was my starting point," said Macdonald. "Just an idea, one of these 'I wonder ifs' that come into a detective's mind at the outset of a case. The immediate practical job was to determine the likelihood of the theory of accident, and the more I examined it the less I was convinced of its cogency. Wilton's case seemed to be strengthened and the accidental explanation shrank into insignificance. That being so, what grounds could I find on which to base a case? It was young Alf who started me in the right direction. I believed him when he said he had heard Gressingham's car pass Corner Cottage."

Colonel St Cyres puffed hard at his pipe. "I never liked the chap," he said unhappily. "I knew I was incapable of being fair to him, just because I didn't like him. Then there was that business of smelling his cigarette smoke that night…"

"We'll get that cigarette smoke cleared away at the outset, sir," said Macdonald. "It always seemed to me in the highest degree improbable that if Gressingham were concerned in the case he would have been so foolish as to smoke in the garden of Little Thatch that night. There was a possibility that the person who smoked Balkan Sobranie cigarettes had done so in order to throw suspicion on Gressingham, but as it turned out the cigarette smoke had a quite different explanation. Radcliffe gave a box of Balkan Sobranies to the land girl he had been amusing himself with, and this girl came out to Mallory Fitzjohn that evening and sat below the hedge of the Little Thatch garden, wondering if Radcliffe would come out to meet her there, as he had often done. She threw the stubs of her cigarettes back over the hedge, where I found them—but Radcliffe did not come to meet her, and the cigarettes had no bearing on the case—except to point to the unfortunate Gressingham."

"Didn't you inevitably suspect Gressingham to begin with?" enquired St Cyres.

"Yes—but I suspected everybody. It was my business to do so. When I first met him I was interested in his reaction to the case. Had he been guilty I should have expected him to avoid any discussion of the case, and to express a strong belief that the jury had been right and accident accounted for everything. Gressingham never struck me as any sort of a fool: I thought he was shrewd, observant, and far-seeing. Had he been guilty he would have realised the risk he took in prolonged discussion of the case—it is so very easy to slip up and show that you know just a little more than an innocent person has any business to know. However, far from avoiding discussion, he fairly spread himself and talked over the matter in all its bearings. He was genuinely interested: he admitted to disliking Vaughan—none of the 'poor chap... shocking accident' attitude about him at all. Gressingham was full of enthusiasm for an investigation which, if he were guilty, was fraught with danger to himself. No. If Gressingham *had* been guilty he would most likely have produced some convincing evidence which would have reinforced the accident theory."

Anne sighed. "I should never be any good at detection. It's like chess, you have to suspect what every move leads to."

"That's quite true," agreed Macdonald. "Now I think it was pure chance which determined that Howard Brendon should have been present when I first saw Gressingham, and I was immediately interested in him. He stayed deliberately while I talked to Gressingham, rather in the manner of a solicitor holding a watching brief—but Gressingham didn't care a snap for the caution advised by Brendon. Gressingham talked and talked, and Brendon was quite unable to hide his own exasperation at the fool who tried to open the doors of the enquiry wider and wider. Brendon was white-faced, tight-lipped, and his eyes were as wary as the eyes of a wild animal expecting attack. It was his eyes that interested me, very light eyes, but very cruel ones. Then there was this point: Gressingham irritated Brendon to the point of fury: it was unmistakable—and also understandable. Brendon was by nature secretive, impatient, not given to suffering fools gladly. He despised the other, and disliked him, yet I learnt a little later that Brendon had been coming over to Hinton Mallory frequently to play bridge with two men whom he despised. I think Brendon himself realised that he had made a mistake in showing his irritation so plainly, for he waited for me on the pretext of adjusting his car, in order to say a few polite things about the man he had shown he despised. I was very much interested in all those three men—Gressingham, Radcliffe and Brendon."

2

Macdonald paused for a moment and turned to Anne, who sat with bent head, slightly turned away from him.

"You are hating all this," he said gently. "Wouldn't you rather go away and not listen?"

She shook her head. "No. I want to listen, and I'm grateful to you for talking to us. I want to understand, so that I need never wake up and wonder again how it all happened."

"You are very wise in that," said Macdonald quietly. "To understand is the best way of setting your mind at rest." He turned to St Cyres again. "Here then was my case. I felt sure that murder had been committed: I had the three men at Hinton Mallory to consider: in addition was the farm-labourer Benworthy, the would-be tenant of Little Thatch; yourself, sir, because you touched the case so nearly, the Heslings at Hinton Mallory—and, using Gressingham's inverted argument, Vaughan himself. The next thing was to find a motive. One point of real interest emerged from my interview with Gressingham and Radcliffe, and that was the matter of the telephone calls which came from Tiverton. Here was a suggestion of great importance. It seemed probable that Vaughan would act on these messages—go to an appointed place at a given time, and if that place were a secluded place, he could well have been killed there."

"But what made you believe he was killed in some other place than the cottage?" demanded St Cyres.

"This. From all I could learn, Vaughan never invited anybody—barring Miss St Cyres—inside that cottage. He certainly did not invite Gressingham into it. It was as though his habitual reticence expressed itself in a desire to keep the cottage to himself. I couldn't see him saying 'Come in and have a chat' to any of the trio at Hinton Mallory, and certainly not to Benworthy, the farm-labourer. Farming custom seldom involves going inside another man's house: the business is more often transacted in the garden. Then there was this: if anybody called on Vaughan, they would have run the risk of being seen in the locality. If they wanted to reach Little Thatch unseen, the idea of driving there in Vaughan's car, wearing his coat, with his old hat crammed down to conceal the driver's face, was a good one. It was growing dusk and the risk was very small. That idea came off all right. Alf said he *saw* Vaughan. What he saw was Vaughan's car, his coat and hat, and the hand he waved. I believed all along that Vaughan was in the car— but that he was dead long before the car reached Little Thatch."

"Yes. I follow all you say there," said St Cyres. "It's all well-reasoned—particularly the fact that Vaughan did not ask people into his house. I think he had a feeling that he didn't want every-body to talk about the work he was doing there. Anybody who saw it would have realised at once that it wasn't for himself alone that he was taking such pains with it."

"Well, that was my reasoning," said Macdonald. "I assumed—for the time being—that Vaughan had gone to keep an appoint-ment, but that appointment had been made over the telephone by someone who had a motive to kill him. There was a likelihood, to put it no more strongly, that the secret of this method of making the appointment had been learnt by someone who took a tele-phone message for Vaughan at Hinton Mallory itself, and that 'someone' recognised the woman's voice which spoke over the phone, and having recognised it, took steps to watch the woman in question and thereby learned the place of the appointment. All this was hypothetical, but it gave me grounds for further enquiry."

Anne asked a question here: "Who told you about the phone messages? Was it Mr. Gressingham?"

"No. That's quite a point," said Macdonald. "It was Radcliffe. If Gressingham himself had told me about it I should have counted him out earlier. It's obvious that if the murderer had used the phone message idea to decoy Vaughan to his death I should not have been told about it by him. Now here was the position—on hypothesis. Vaughan was meeting a woman with whom he used the 'duck's egg' code to give the time of an appointment at a given place. It might be argued from this that the woman he met had need to meet him more or less secretly, and from this again came the possibility that the woman was either married or engaged to some other man, and the jealousy motive—which is a very potent one—gave rise to murder. Now having got thus far, the original question arose, who was the woman whom Vaughan hoped to marry? You both know that I saw Miss Vaughan and she told me that she knew of only one woman in whom her brother had been interested. Later she told me that this woman was a trained nurse. It seemed fairly obvious to do a little research at the hospitals where Vaughan had been nursed, and it did not take me very long to find the woman in question, but before I tell you about that I should like to put in a word or two about Howard Brendon."

"Yes," said St Cyres. "I shall be interested to hear how you got information about him. You must have been very cautious, because no one seems to have had any idea you were making enquiries about him."

"I felt need to be cautious. Brendon always struck me as the one potentially dangerous person in the case. I frequented the bars of Mallowton and the district in the evenings, and I listened. I went and talked to old Mr. Tothill. I heard enough to assume several things: first, that Brendon was trying to sell his Dulverton property privately and that he had bought another property in the Midlands. Next, that though he had only been married a short time it was believed that his wife had left him. Finally, that he was disliked by his neighbours to an extent which is unusual unless a man has some really bad traits in his character. It seemed worth while making a few enquiries about what Mr. Brendon was doing on the night of April 30th. I learnt that he had stayed in an hotel in Taunton, where he had been seen by different people at the hours of four o'clock, half-past seven, and finally between half-past eleven and midnight."

3

Macdonald paused here a moment and gazed across the sunlit valley before he resumed: "Obviously the man I wanted had had to be free at certain hours on April 30th. He had had to be at Tiverton to phone the message purporting to come from Nurse White which Vaughan himself took on the phone at Hinton Mallory—and at the back of my mind all the time was the problem of Gressingham's car, its errand on the night of the fire, and those petrol cans of Vaughan's. Who could have needed the car and the petrol? Certainly nobody at the Mallorys—not in connection with the Little Thatch case. But if the murderer came from a distance he *might* have been desperately pressed for some extra petrol. I began to try to fit Brendon into the scheme of things: Could he have been at Tiverton at five o'clock to phone? Yes, since he was not seen in his hotel between four and half-past seven. If he had committed the murder he must have had to drive best part of a hundred and fifty miles to achieve his various appearances at Taunton—but the thing was possible, as anyone can see who looks at any map of the county. The distance from Taunton to the spinney is only just over twenty miles, but it's a very hilly road and is expensive on petrol: the return journey of forty-three miles would have taken two gallons in Brendon's car. I tried the following assumption for purposes of argument: that, Brendon, who had booked a room

in a Taunton hotel at four o'clock, could have got to Tiverton in
time to phone at five, and then could have driven to a spot near
the spinney, arriving before Vaughan got there at 6.15. He could
have killed Vaughan with a loaded stick as the latter got out of
his car, which I assumed that he parked at the roadside a little farther back—before the tar strip. Vaughan's body was then hidden
under a rug in the back of his own car, and Brendon returned to
Taunton in his Sunbeam, arriving in time for dinner at his hotel.
That is forty-three miles of driving, and two gallons of petrol
used. Brendon left his hotel again unseen after dinner, drove back
to the spot near the spinney where he left his own car, got into
Vaughan's Morris, having donned Vaughan's hat and coat, and
drove to Little Thatch, hooting and waving at Corner Cottage en
route. He got Vaughan's body into the cottage, and prepared the
fire by means of a slow match and paraffin. Next, he had to get
back to his hotel in time to be seen in the lounge before everybody
was in bed, so he went down to Hinton Mallory and borrowed
Gressingham's Daimler to cover the six miles from Little Thatch
to the spinney, and he took two gallons of petrol from Vaughan's
store, to refuel the Daimler and to help him out if his own tank
were running low. This involved having to return yet a third time
to the spinney—shortly after midnight—to return Gressingham's
Daimler to Hinton Mallory. It sounds complicated in the telling,
but the whole performance was possible on account of the loneli-
ness of the roads. At any rate, I assumed that it *could* have been
done, especially if Brendon knew that he could get in and out of
his hotel unseen, and collect his own car from its lock-up without
being noticed."

St Cyres shook his head helplessly. "What beats me is this,"
he said. "Why didn't he leave poor Vaughan's body in the Morris

where he killed him? He hadn't been seen: there was *nothing* to connect him with the murder."

"The whole point was that he tried to guard against the word 'murder' ever arising," said Macdonald. "He was convinced he was clever enough to stage an accident—and he very nearly got away with it. Unfortunately for him, he over-acted his part. Since it was obvious that Vaughan's death was to be labelled 'accident' I was particularly on the lookout for someone who emphasised that aspect of the matter: that's why I was interested to note that Gressingham did nothing of the kind."

Anne St Cyres lifted her head and asked a question here. "Do you think Mr. Gressingham suspected who had done it?"

"Yes. I think eventually he did—and, unhappily for himself, he did not tell his suspicions to me. Gressingham was very astute and he had a lot of information to ponder over. He knew that Brendon had taken to coming over to Hinton Mallory frequently *after* he had heard something about the tenant at Little Thatch. He knew about Brendon's marriage and its break-up. He knew that Brendon had answered the phone at Hinton Mallory on at least one occasion—Radcliffe knew that, too. He knew that the name 'Henry Heythwaite' had been mentioned at Brendon's home. He knew that Brendon could drive his Daimler. I think Gressingham thought it all out for himself—and then made the mistake of trying to do a little extra detecting on his own account by ringing up Brendon and suggesting a meeting. That was fatal for him. Brendon guessed, too, and arranged to meet Gressingham at a spot where a car accident could be staged only too easily—as happened. Brendon killed Gressingham, put the car in neutral and released the hand-brake—"

Anne shuddered. "Brendon must have been mad," she said, and Macdonald nodded.

"Yes, I think he was. He was of the megalomaniac type. I never saw a more ruthless face. He was a man who was utterly self-centred and self-satisfied. When things went against him his ingenuity and determination seemed to curdle his brain. He had worked out some fantastic scheme to get rid of me in a manner which involved my body and Radcliffe's being found together. To that end he got Radcliffe to come to his house and drugged him—to be ready for the final dénouement. Undoubtedly Brendon was mad then—but I always thought him capable of violence. Any psychologist could have told that he was abnormal by his eyes."

4

"Let us have the whole story in perspective," said Macdonald at length. "Nicholas Vaughan fell in love with a girl named Molly White up at Lannerdale, but was too slow to tell her so. This girl, having come to the conclusion that she would never have a chance of marrying Vaughan, married Howard Brendon—for security and a home. She soon found out that her husband was a sadist, a cruel, unprincipled man. She also had reason to suspect that he was a bigamist. She left him and went back to hospital work. Here she met Vaughan again as a patient, and they fell in love. She told Vaughan the truth about her husband, and he said: 'Whether he is a bigamist or not, you're never going back to him. You are going to marry *me* when we have got things straightened out.' Vaughan took Little Thatch for two reasons: one was that Brendon was selling his Dulverton home and going to a place in the Midlands: two, was that he could not take Molly White home to Lannerdale for a few years, because people up there knew that she had recently married another man. So Nicholas Vaughan took

Little Thatch, and Nurse White went to the hospital near Tiverton. From this place she used to phone the code message to Vaughan telling him the hour she could meet him at the spinney. Unhappily, Brendon heard her voice over the phone sending a message—about duck's eggs—to Nicholas Vaughan. He began to think—for he was a desperately jealous man—and he also knew that he was in a dangerous position if his wife suspected his own past doings. Brendon undoubtedly spied on his wife, and at length learnt the place of her meeting with Vaughan. When any one person goes frequently to a given spot, like the spinney, it's not very difficult to trace them, if you have a car and plenty of patience. Brendon decided that an accident should end Vaughan's life—and I have no doubt if the 'accident' verdict had been accepted another accident would have happened to Nurse White."

"You put a stop to that," said St Cyres gruffly, for Anne was incapable of saying anything at all.

"Yes. The story has been pretty horrible, but think out the few good points which can be said to emerge," said Macdonald. "I hold it as a good point that Brendon eliminated himself. He was a menace to the community. For Vaughan—I can only say what I have said before: he was very happy during the last months of his life, and he would have died without knowing it. Brendon wasn't the man who would have fumbled his blow. And for Molly White—she at least had the joy of Vaughan's devotion to make up to her a little for her disastrous marriage." He broke off and spoke to Anne: "I am so sorry about the distress you have suffered over all this… and about Little Thatch. I know you loved it."

Anne wiped her eyes vigorously. "I still do," she said. "I'm not going to leave it like that. I'm going to rebuild and re-thatch it, and keep that garden cultivated—as Nicholas Vaughan would have done… and one day I'll ask Nurse White to come and stay there and see if she'd like to have the home that was being got ready for her. It ought to be hers…"

Colonel St Cyres put in one final question: "I wonder what will happen to that place… Lannerdale, wasn't it? Somehow I sympathised with Miss Vaughan: she did care about that place, and I'm afraid it will have gone to those shipbuilding cousins who didn't care about the land."

"'The awful Hawkinses,'" said Macdonald, and he smiled as he spoke. "They weren't so awful after all: they renounced all claim to Lannerdale and said that Elizabeth Vaughan could have it and welcome. Farming isn't everybody's notion of bliss."

"Quite true," said St Cyres, "but if you are born in the country and learn to love the land—well, you're as happy as young Vaughan was, digging away in that garden."

Macdonald got up and held out his hand to the old man and then to Anne: "You stick to your idea and rebuild Little Thatch," he said as he shook hands. "One day I'll come here again, and I shall hope to see that cottage looking as it did when Vaughan asked you to tea there at Easter."

Anne gripped his hand and smiled back at him, though her eyes were still misty: "I'll write and ask you to come and see it," she said. "I'm going to get busy on the garden straight away. It's the best way of making me forget all the waste…"

"Yes, and Vaughan would have said so, too," agreed Macdonald.